The Beltane Witch

Siobhan Muir

ISBN: 0692421009
ISBN-13: 978-0692421000

DEDICATION

Dedicated to all the single moms out there. You're stronger than you know and my hat's off to you.

ACKNOWLEDGMENTS

Thanks go to Nichole Severn for reminding me that bad guys don't go away that easily and yes, you do have to finish their stories, too. Shannan Albright caught my pet words and social faux pas. As always thanks to Lanya Ross for reading for logic and giving me a good peer review. Thanks also to Emily Yenawine for catching my mangled sentences and overactive paragraphs.

CHAPTER ONE

Sabrina Foxglove stepped out the side door of Mazie's Five and Dime and took a deep breath of cold spring air. Cloudburst, Colorado, hadn't gotten the memo on mild temperatures for the season. Still, hinted scents of new growth in the cool breezes and the crocuses in her garden warned of warmer weather.

The weather is turning and it's Beltane in a week. Yay, May Day.

Sabrina had long chosen Beltane, the Goddess's celebration of fertility and rebirth, as her favorite holiday next to Yule. She loved the dancing, the small campfire—she couldn't have a bonfire in her backyard. Forest fires in the National Forest were frowned upon—and the brightly colored ribbons around her own miniature May Pole. She and her daughters always dressed up, baked goodies to share with her neighbors and sang the special prayer songs as the night moved to Midnight.

This year, Tansy's school would hold a May Day celebration and she'd promised to bake brownies for the class.

Sabrina heard extra footsteps as she walked down the alley toward the back parking lot after locking the door to

Mazie's. The sounds of those feet sent a frisson of fear and anxiety down her back. She didn't want to look back, but it'd be better to see her attackers, just in case she had to identify them later.

When she reached the single bulb illuminating a small portion of the parking lot, she turned with her keys pushing between her fingers like claws and raised her chin. What met her eyes made her blood run cold.

Five men filed out of the alley led by Marty Robinson, one of the most outspoken about her marriage status. Or lack thereof despite motherhood. He'd given her trouble in the past when she'd politely refused his invitation to attend one of the church gatherings, but she never thought he'd do anything rash. *Apparently he's changed his approach.*

"Did you need something at Mazie's, guys? Sorry, we're closed." She hoped her voice sounded nonchalant and wished she stood closer to her minivan.

"It's not safe to be walking alone at night, Sabrina." Marty's buckteeth always made him whistle when he spoke, lending to his overall unpleasantness. At least he didn't have a lisp, and if he kept his mouth shut, he could be considered somewhat attractive.

"Thanks for the reminder. And thanks for accompanying me to my car. I'll just be getting in and going home now."

"If you had a husband, you'd be safer," one of the others snapped, his voice full of frustration. *What is his problem?*

"Thanks for the concern, but—"

"A husband could protect you from just these kinds of situations," Marty said.

She raised her eyebrows and tightened her fist on her keys. "This is a situation? Is there some problem?"

"Being single is a sin against God," Mr. Frustrated shifted his weight and his hands fisted at his side.

"I didn't think marital status was one of God's main

concerns."

"Mothers shouldn't be single. You should have a husband." Marty's lips tightened over his teeth and his eyes narrowed. Sabrina swallowed hard and kept moving through the parking lot.

"And all of you are here to convince me?" She raised a dubious eyebrow. "I'm not sure I need one husband, much less five."

"We're not into polygyny." Marty and the others edged closer, fanning out a little to get behind her. Sabrina backed up a few steps, trying to keep them all in view.

"I'm relieved to hear it. It's sweet of you to offer, but I'm fine, really." She backed up a little more, the keys cutting into her palm.

"You should have a man to take care of you, Sabrina. Single women with children are an affront to God. You'll never enter Heaven." Marty voice approached reasonable, but his eyes glowed with an unhealthy zeal.

"Hey, you know, I'm not really worried about it." Where had she parked her damn van? "Thanks for the concern though."

The men moved closer, trying to circle her before she could reach her car. The wind blew the scents of cold blacktop and spilled gasoline past her and she wished she'd parked closer to the building. *So much for getting more exercise. I should've taken kickboxing.* Her eyes darted around to see any visible weapon she could use to hold them off other than her keys, but she saw nothing. Not even a damn snowball.

Winter's continued grip on the Rockies sent a cold breeze eeling down her back as her heel came down on a patch of black ice. Her foot shot out from under her and she slammed to the cold pavement on her butt. Cold seeped in through her pants and filled the crannies of her heart.

Glory be, I'm so screwed.

Fear surged as the men closed on her. How would she

get home to her daughters? How could she face them after these men did…whatever they were going to do? She wouldn't allow herself to even name the heinous acts groups of men did to women in the dark.

"Now we're gonna teach you why you need a man."

Marty's expression shifted to rabid as he reached for her. She gritted her teeth and tightened her grip on the keys. If they chose to do this, she'd make sure they'd remember how hard they worked to get her to submit.

"Five men against one woman is a little unorthodox and unfair, don't you think?"

The deep masculine voice floated out of the darkness of the alley they'd left behind. Her attackers turned to look over their shoulders, their bodies tense.

Sabrina couldn't see much at first, just a blacker shadow among the rest. A tall male form emerged into the edge of the light wearing a long black trench coat with a wide hood over his head. He had leather gloves on his hands and heavy black boots on his feet to protect him from the spring cold in the mountains. The hilt of a very large sword rose over his left shoulder, held there by an ornate leather strap embroidered with oak leaves across his chest.

Oh Goddess, who the hell is this?

"Your religious leaders might look askance at your behavior this evening. Hounding women doesn't seem an honorable pastime."

"Who are you?" Marty snapped.

"She needs to be taught a lesson. She needs a husband." Sabrina swore Mr. Frustrated had been dropped on his head as a child.

"Mayhap she does, but this is not the way to convince her," the dark stranger remarked, amusement in his voice. "Did your fathers teach you nothing about wooing? Flowers, chocolates, perhaps even sweet poetry or jewelry. But never threats or fear."

"Hey, man, we saw her first." She knew that voice.

4

Timmy Lewis's pockmarked face looked ghastly in the weak light. "Go find your own woman."

Nice to know she held some value to the local male population.

A deafening silence settled around them. No one moved for a few seconds, but the energy in the little parking lot shifted from tolerant amusement to icy disdain. In a flurry of motion, the stranger swept the feet out from under Mr. Frustrated, slammed Timmy into one of his cronies until they slumped to the ground, held the fourth man in a choke hold, and had a long dagger blade pressed against Marty's throat by the time he stilled.

He'd positioned himself between her and the others and she got a good look at his back. The sword in its leather scabbard hung to his hips and she thanked her lucky stars it remained sheathed. The wide expanse of his shoulders assured her he could wield it, probably faster and stronger than the propeller on an airplane. His arms, one holding the gasping man and the other holding the dagger, never wavered.

"Now would be an excellent time to gather your friends and retreat to your mothers' skirts." The words came out in a growl and Sabrina shivered. "Go. Now."

The stranger released the man he held, and Mr. Frustrated, Marty, and Choke-Hold scrambled to retrieve their two fallen comrades and retreated back toward Main Street. The hooded man watched them go, big, powerful, and menacing in his stillness. When their footsteps faded from hearing, he turned to her and offered her a gloved hand.

"Let's get you home, Ms. Foxglove." His voice encouraged trust.

Sabrina looked at his hand then up at his face for a long time while she waited for her heart to stop pounding. She'd just watched him kick ass on five guys in an icy parking lot, and he expected her to trust he meant her no harm?

On the other hand, he looks fast enough to catch me if I run.

Biting her lip, she reached out to grasp his hand. The warm leather engulfed her frozen fingers and she felt dwarfed by his size. Her hand looked like it belonged to a small child's in his and he tugged her up, guiding her away from the black ice.

"Thanks." She tried to pull her hand away as soon as she gained her feet.

His grip tightened and he dragged her closer to his hooded face. "They were right in one respect. It's not safe for you to be walking alone at night."

"Thank you for the reminder." Goddess save her from nosy men. Her reactionary anger surged. "And you just helped so much by embarrassing them in front of their friends. Now they'll be after me because of it." She shook her head and tugged at her hand again.

"There are greater concerns than that now." He released her, gesturing with his free hand toward her van. "Perhaps we could discuss them on the way to your home."

Sabrina followed the line of his arm with her eyes then looked back into the darkness of his hood.

"What makes you think I'll let you in my car with me?" She snorted. "I don't even know you. Yeah, you beat off those guys, but it only proves you're much stronger than me. Why would I trust you?"

"I just saved you." He gestured, palms up, as if his words explained everything.

"So? I said thanks. Who are you? And how do you know my name?"

He hesitated for a moment, nonplussed. Then he pushed back his hood to reveal his face in the weak light of the bare bulb.

Good heavens, he's beautiful.

Long, straight hair parted haphazardly and fell to his shoulders, the front strands pushed behind his ears to keep it out of his eyes. The eyes were some light color, but she couldn't tell which one in the darkness of the parking lot. They had heavy lids and crow's feet at their corners, telling of his experience. A goatee framed his elegant lips and deep laugh lines at their edges gave him a humorous expression, though he didn't smile. He had eloquently arching brows, one higher than the other in amused query.

"My name is Darius Winterbourne, Chamberlain of the Summer Court, and I've been sent to prepare you for the Court's arrival."

"Wait. The Summer Court, as in the Sidhe, the Fae peoples of the Goddess?"

"Yes."

Sabrina snorted and shook her head. "Is this some sort of joke? Because I follow the old beliefs? Gah! Look, it's not funny. Thank you for what you did, but I'd like you to leave me alone now."

Darius frowned. "I do not joke, Lady Foxglove. I came to prepare you for their arrival."

"The Summer Court is coming here. To Cloudburst, Colorado."

"Yes."

"Why?"

"Beltane is in a week's time and—"

"I *know* when Beltane is, I honor the old ways. I meant, why would the Summer Court of the Fae come *here*, to Cloudburst? It's a flyspeck on the map." *Smaller than that, really.* "Wouldn't it be more fitting for them to celebrate Beltane at, say, Stonehenge, or somewhere more grand? Heck, the Grand Canyon would make more sense if they wanted to come to the US."

"It is the job of the Fae to heal and restore the sacred places of the Earth and to ensure the chain of blessing isn't broken, even in flyspecks like Cloudburst." He raised his chin to look down at her. "They are coming here to strengthen the connections to the Goddess. You are the most powerful resident witch and they depend upon you to uphold the traditions and rituals of Beltane. They will come this year to oversee your practices and bolster the protections."

"Oversee *my* practices?" Sabrina gaped in disbelief. "I haven't done the traditional rituals in over four years and I don't plan on doing them now. The last time I *participated* in the High Beltane rituals, I got a daughter out of the deal. You heard what some folks think of my single-mom status. I don't need any more children, thank you." Even when she'd been on the pill, the magic of the rituals had produced a baby. She couldn't take the chance again, especially when she hadn't renewed her prescription. *What's the point? I'm not having sex anyway.*

"Children are a great blessing of the Goddess."

"Maybe, but with it comes great responsibility and I don't need more of it. Thanks again for your help and good night."

Nodding to him, she spun on her heel and took three quick steps toward her van. She'd almost reached it when the five men cornered her. Why couldn't she have seen it then? She rotated her keys in her hand and inserted one into the door lock. Her nose filled with the scents of leather and pumpkin spice as a warm gloved hand settled over hers. Anger and fear blazed within her. *What is wrong with this guy? Can't he take a hint?*

She leveled him with a narrow-eyed glare. "Take your hand off me."

****

Darius felt the surge of energy around Sabrina as she snarled the words and the hairs on the back of his neck stood up. Holy Goddess, this little witch had much more power than he'd been led to believe. If she focused all her magic on him, she'd very likely overpower him. She didn't seem to have the skill to do it, but he decided against testing her just yet.

"Forgive me, Lady Foxglove." He bowed his head as he removed his hand.

Her shoulders relaxed when he stepped back, but her pale eyes flashed with angry electric purple sparks.

"Perhaps we can speak of this more at your home. It's cold out tonight and we have much to discuss."

The tension returned to her frame and her eyes widened. "You think I'm going to let you come to my house? I don't even know you. I won't endanger my family. Heck, you carry a huge sword over your damn shoulder."

"It's imperative that I speak to you about this." He didn't understand her reluctance to accept the great honor she'd been offered.

"Imperative? The only thing that's imperative is I get home to my kids." She opened her car door. "And no, you can't come with me."

Bloody frustrating woman!

He caught the door before it slammed shut behind her.

"Lady Foxglove. Please." Damn, it grated to have to beg. "There isn't much time and the Court will be arriving in a few days. You must be prepared."

"Tell them to change their plans." She shrugged. "I don't have time to entertain the Court. I have brownies to bake for school. I have garlands to make and ribbons to buy. Plus, I have a job. I can't just take time off. We don't get paid vacation at Mazie's. Send them to the Grand Canyon. Now, let go of my door."

"I cannot!" His temper cracked at her stubbornness. "This is not my honor, but yours. The plans have been laid and it is your destiny to fulfill. I'm merely here to make certain all is prepared for the Court's arrival."

"Don't snap at me just because you didn't check with me first. I have a life and responsibilities that don't include you or the Summer Court." She shook her head and the ponytail of mahogany brown hair slid over her wool encased shoulders. The urge to sift his fingers through it took him by surprise. "Look, success is about communication and you can't have one without the other. So far, your track record is dismal."

"Communication goes both ways." Darius tried to wrestle his temper under control. Where was his famed unruffled demeanor? "I'm here, now, to speak to you about this great honor and event so we might arrange the procedures and protocols. We have a week before the event should occur. Certainly we can come to some sort of arrangement in such time?"

She took a deep breath to deny him, but thought better of it when he raised his eyebrows. She pressed her sensuous lips together in a tight line. He'd like nothing better than to enjoy the feeling of them on his lips or even on his cock, but only if they stopped producing protests. He'd silenced many a woman in such a pleasurable way in the past.

"Okay, fine." Sabrina dropped her head a moment. "But tomorrow. I can't do anything tonight and you're *not* coming home with me. Tomorrow I'll meet you at the Cloudburst Coffee Shop on River Street at 10:30 in the morning. That's the best I can do."

Tomorrow cut a full day off their prep time, but resolution filled her expression, and he had to take what he could get. Besides, his mother had often told him you got more flies with honey than with vinegar.

"Thank you, Ms. Foxglove. I shall meet you at the Cloudburst Coffee Shop on the morrow."

"Okay. Good. See you then."

He released the door and she slammed it shut. The motor hesitated to start in the cold, but eventually caught and Sabrina Foxglove, the Cloudburst witch, drove out of the parking lot, leaving Darius to watch the retreat of her vehicle with a frown.

No one had ever turned down such an honor before. Certainly not when delivered by him. Why hadn't she folded under his charm?

He sighed and raised his hood above his head, protecting it from the fat flakes of snow settling over the black pavement of the little parking lot. Her obstinacy diluted his interest in her, regardless of her beauty. Women should be biddable, accommodating, amiable.

But damn, she is lovely.

His mind recalled Sabrina's lush curves despite the disfiguring wool jacket and thick fleece pants. He could imagine full breasts with rosy areoles and tight nipples flushed with heat from his kisses. Her coat had only hinted at the generous ass beneath, but he could see it gripped in his hands as he thrust into her welcoming heat from in front.

His cock stretched his leather trousers in response to his thoughts and he reached down to adjust himself to a more favorable position. He considered the woman upon whom all his immediate future plans were based.

Sabrina Foxglove had been blessed with strength of will and great power, unlike most of the witches he'd met in the past. Her determined resignation when faced with five opponents of greater stature than herself had impressed him. She should have used a simple persuasion spell to direct their attentions elsewhere. *Perhaps she's untrained.* Experienced or not, she remained a potent witch. *And sexy as hell, too.* When there'd been no other choice, she'd stood her ground with honor. She hadn't cried or whined or begged, qualities he loathed in the fairer sex.

Darius fastened his hooded coat around him and melted back into the alley darkness. The wind threatened to remove his hood, but he held it down with his gloved hands. *Why is it still winter here in this little town?*

Sabrina would change her attitude toward him and the

Summer Court when he had a chance to explain at their meeting tomorrow. She'd see the true honor in what she'd been offered and show proper gratitude for his help. He imagined the type of gratitude he'd like. He could see her lavender eyes staring seductively up at him while her lips stretched over his hard phallic flesh and her tongue polished the head.

Ah, perfection.

He'd hoped to have such an opportunity this evening, but Sabrina proved to be more obdurate than he'd expected. Of course, she'd been accosted by those idiots and frightened. His sudden appearance may have scared her even more. Women didn't trust men who appeared out of the dark. She'd feel differently in the light of day when his good looks and charm seduced her.

Satisfied everything would be settled the next day, Darius lengthened his strides down the quiet snowy street. Silence of winter's last gasp enveloped him, the only sounds the crunching of his footsteps. *Damn, it's cold.* He shivered a little, looking forward to a hot bath and a warm cup of rum to see him through the night.

He stopped as if he'd run straight into the snow-draped brick wall beside him.

Where the hell would he sleep?

CHAPTER TWO

Morning came with the usual routine of getting Sabrina's six-year-old ready for kindergarten and her four year old at least dressed. Tansy happily dressed herself and combed her hair without much direction, but Holly dragged her feet and found almost anything else to do when faced with her mother's need to get ready quickly.

"Holly, are you dressed yet?"

"I'm getting there!"

"Don't 'get there', do it."

"Mom, can I have pigtails today?" Tansy asked as she brushed out her dark brown locks.

"Yep, come here."

"Thanks, Mom." Tansy handed her two hair ties.

"Holly, are you dressed yet?"

"Getting there, Mom!"

Despite Holly's slowness, Sabrina managed to get everyone fed and ready in time to hustle into the car. Tansy jabbered excitedly about the May Day party at school in a few days, and Holly informed them she'd become a rainbow sparkle pony.

"Well, even rainbow sparkle ponies have to buckle up their carseats before we can go."

"Okay, Mommy."

The drive to school filled with conversation about habitat needs of such mythical creatures and Sabrina grinned at her daughters' imaginations. She kissed Tansy goodbye before the girl scampered through the new flurries of snow to her classroom. *One down. One to go.*

"Ready to go shopping, Holly?"

"Ready."

Sabrina and Holly went to the grocery to prepare for the Beltane feast at the end of the week. Holly happily helped pick out fruits and vegetables while going on about what rainbow sparkle ponies liked to eat. Sabrina tried to focus on her daughter's words, but her attention split between getting all the things on her list and the upcoming meeting with Darius Winterbourne at the coffee shop.

The whole encounter behind Mazie's seemed like a dream, a figment of her overactive imagination. Surely Marty, Timmy and the others hadn't been so demonstrative in their displeasure of her marital status. And no one really carried a sword anymore, did they? Had she made a date with a dream guy? *More like a nightmare guy.*

"Hi, Sabrina. How are you today?"

Sabrina jerked out of her thoughts to wave at her neighbor up the street. "Good, thanks."

"Mommy, can we get star squishies?" Holly held up a star fruit.

"Not today, honey."

Sabrina's thoughts returned to Darius. He'd certainly been tall, dark and mysterious. Not to mention incredibly handsome. She didn't think her imagination could have come up with anything so beautiful on its own. She recalled his sharp brows, sultry grin, and the way he held her hand in his in perfect detail.

"Mom, can I watch a movie when we get home?" Holly perused the gum at the checkout aisle.

"You'll have to ask Matilda. She's coming early

because I have an appointment today."

"Well, tell Matilda I can watch the Rescue Fairy."

Sabrina laughed, shaken from her musings. "We'll talk about it."

"Thirty-three, eighty seven, Ms. Foxglove." The cashier waved at Holly, making her giggle.

"Thanks. How's school going this year?"

They finished their shopping and returned home in record time despite the slick, snowy roads. Most people in Cloudburst knew how to drive, but the Spring Breakers who showed up in droves often made the short commutes an exercise in stunt driving. Sabrina's gratitude for the end of Spring Break Season held no bounds.

Matilda Middleton, Sabrina's babysitter, met her at her door and happily took charge of Holly while Sabrina put the groceries away.

"Mommy, I want to watch the Rescue Fairy!"

Sabrina shot a look at Matilda. "Are you okay with a movie? I have the appointment this morning and then work till seven. I'm sorry it will be so late."

"It's not a problem, Sabrina. I'm saving up for a car and need all the extra money I can get."

"If you're sure…"

"Yeah, it'll be fine." Matilda waved her off. "I can get Tansy after school, too."

"Thanks so much, Matti."

Sabrina kissed Holly goodbye and jumped back into her car for the trip to the Cloudburst Coffee and Spa. Only newly opened, the Cloudburst had taken off like wildfire. Moira Callahan had a special gift for knowing what the customers needed each day, and Sabrina had always found the coffee shop soothing when stressed. Sabrina had come back often and struck up a friendship with Moira.

Sabrina pulled into the parking lot and turned off the car. Snow peppered the windshield in dry, cold flakes rattling with the sound of sand grains. The heat immediately decreased and her breath fogged the windows. *What the hell am I doing?* Who went to meet a big guy with a huge sword spouting about the return of the Fae for Beltane? She should call the cops and go back to her normal life.

"Yeah, and they'll so believe you," she muttered. She didn't need to paint herself as a lunatic. Not even the local coven would support her.

"Ugh!" She thumped her forehead against the steering wheel. "Why do I do this to myself?"

Jamming her tuque onto her head, she got out of her minivan and hurried into the Cloudburst to get out of the weather. The interior of the coffee shop had a warm and comfortable décor with brass accents and fixtures, cozy armchairs and couches guarding elegant glass topped tables, and polished, resined wood floors. Moira had decorated her establishment with a retreat in mind and comfort settled around Sabrina's shoulders.

Everyone who entered felt welcomed and protected. Moira had added a back room where the patrons could order a massage from her business partner. An odd combination, true, but Sabrina appreciated the eccentricity, and Moira insisted there was more than one way to relax. Why drown your sorrows when you could have them rubbed out of existence?

Too bad I can't rub out this problem. She stifled a giggle. She sounded like an old Mafia movie.

Sabrina paused inside the door, allowing the scents of cinnamon and hot cocoa to soothe her as she scanned the few patrons already taking advantage of the warm interior. She loved this place and no matter what Darius Winterbourne might want, she felt safe here. Most of the bar stools and chairs sat empty, but her eyes found Darius's broad-shouldered form reclining on a loveseat against the brick wall across from the counter, his sword conspicuously missing. Her tension returned and she took a deep breath as she wound her way through the other chairs toward him.

He turned his head and her steps faltered. *Holy Goddess, he's better looking than I remember.* Eyes an amazing color of deep teal never wavered from her as she approached and her heart pounded with each step. Wearing an expression mixed of frank assessment and sensual desire, Darius Winterbourne embodied a predator, a man used to getting his way every time.

I'm not giving up my way of life just to appease your lofty opinion of yourself, pal. What had he called himself? The Chamberlain of the Summer Court. Talk about arrogance.

Still, she shivered with feminine appreciation of his virility. What would it be like to have a man so powerfully built look at her with real desire? Her ex hadn't given her such attention except during rituals when drunk on lust. Oh, he'd desired her body, but the woman inside? Not so much. She inwardly smacked her forehead and squared her shoulders as she stopped before Darius's reclining form.

"Well met, Lady Foxglove." His warm voice wrapped around her and she damn near melted where she stood.

"Mr. Winterbourne." Sabrina sat down on a plush arm chair across from him and tried to find some composure.

Irritation flitted across his face, but disappeared before she could catch more than a glimpse.

"Call me Darius, please. We will be working too closely to stand on titles."

"You're making an assumption, Mr. Winterbourne." Sabrina leaned back and crossed her legs to give herself a little more armor against his smooth ways. "I told you I'd hear you out and here I am. I didn't promise to suddenly drop everything for your needs."

His irritation flashed again until she said the word "needs." Then sly, seductive amusement flooded his face and exhilaration shot through her.

"My needs are another matter entirely and I'm certain we'll get to them eventually. I'm here today to discuss the matter of the Summer Court's visit."

She didn't know if she wanted to laugh in disbelief or smack him for his audacity. She settled for a roll of her eyes.

"Focus, Mr. Winterbourne. What exactly do you want and what does it have to do with me?"

He opened his mouth to make a no doubt smart-ass comment and she held up her hand. "Rein it in, please."

He chuckled, sitting forward to lean his elbows on his knees.

"As you command, my lady." He inclined his head. "My petition is the same as last night. Beltane is a week away. The Summer Court has chosen your fair little town as the location where they shall perform the healing ceremonies to strengthen the wards, and you're the only witch here who can perform the rituals correctly."

"That's debatable," she mumbled, but he didn't seem to hear her.

"Come now, Lady Foxglove, you must understand what a great honor this is. The opportunity to serve the Court in this way is not offered lightly."

Sabrina snorted. "I thought I'm the only witch in Cloudburst who could correctly perform the rituals. It doesn't sound like selection so much as desperation. I'm the only one you know of here, so I'll have to do. Right?"

His patronizing smile never slipped. "They would not have chosen Cloudburst were it not for you."

"Baloney!" She grimaced and flicked one hand. "Got oceanfront property to sell me in Arizona, right? Nice try. Tell them to visit Sedona, then. I'm sure the Vortices are in need of a good realigning."

Darius's smile began to fade and he took a breath to say something as the waitress appeared beside him, her gaze fixed on his handsome visage. Sabrina smiled, grateful for the interruption, and ordered hot coffee and a blueberry scone. *Gather your wits, because this guy will run all over you if you let him.* Darius's ridiculous demands to host the Summer Court of the Fae ranked up there with cleaning out the sediment trap in her shower. *Yeah, not going to happen.*

Darius turned his brilliant smile on the waitress and she fluttered and simpered, twirling one lock of hair around her pencil with a giddy smile. Sabrina sighed, hoping the girl wouldn't forget her order. Darius played up the charming, handsome, and virile male. She suspected women fell all over themselves to attract his sparkling gaze.

At last, the girl flounced away, her hips swinging in invitation, and Darius watched her retreat with a satisfied smile on his face. Sabrina shook her head in bemusement. *You're just mad because he doesn't look at you like that.*

Why the hell would she want him to look at her favorably? She wanted nothing to do with men. *Selfish, manipulating, responsibility-avoiding bastards.* Darius fit in just right. She bet he'd slept with more women than the flakes of snow falling outside the coffee shop windows.

Yeah, but think of how experienced he'd be.

She stifled a groan.

Darius's gaze fastened on her like a magnet and he cocked his head in inquiry.

Crap, he can't read thoughts, can he?

"Where were we?" His question accompanied a smug smile.

"You were just getting ready to suggest the Court should go to Sedona for Beltane."

The warmth in his smile dimmed and she countered his hard look with lifting her chin. He spread his hands with mock regret, but his eyes remained chips of jade stone. "Would that I could, my lady, but once the Court has determined the place for the rituals, it cannot be changed. I'm afraid it's Cloudburst, or nowhere."

"Nowhere, then."

He sighed. "Listen to me, Lady—"

"No, you listen to *me*, Mr. Winterbourne." She used her best mommy-voice. "I have a family, school obligations, and a job right now. I don't have time to entertain the Summer Court for Beltane. I have to bake brownies for my daughter's kindergarten class, for goodness sake. I have no place for the Court, in my life *or* in my house, and besides, I haven't done the High Beltane rituals in four years."

"I'm sure it will only take a little brushing up—"

"I don't *want* to 'brush up' on the rituals. You're not hearing me. I. Am. Not. Doing. The. Rituals."

Darius's expression solidified into impassiveness and Sabrina crossed her arms over her chest in mute challenge. She wouldn't be pressured into having sex for the Fae. She'd given up on the complex rituals after her ex Tommy left, and it suited her just fine. No male of any race, particularly one claiming to be from the Sidhe, would convince her to open up the hideous box of memories associated with Beltane. *Not to mention threatening pregnancy.*

Goddess, it'd be like running straight into the past.

Suddenly, Darius's face softened and calculated compassion slid into his eyes. Sabrina had seen such a look on Tommy's face enough times to know what would come. He'd play on her compassionate side just to get what he wanted.

Here we go.

"I understand your frustrations and life's complications." He smiled sympathetically. "It won't take any extra time. These rituals are ingrained in you. They'll fit within your schedule seamlessly. I'm sure we can work something out."

Sabrina seethed. *How typical. Doesn't listen to a thing I say. Doesn't care about my needs or my priorities. Just figures a little charm and he'll get his way. Bastard.*

Fighting to keep her anger under control, Sabrina clenched her hands into fists and stood. Spinning to leave, Sabrina collided with the waitress holding her order. The girl squeaked as she dumped the hot coffee down Sabrina's belly. Searing pain accompanied the deep brown stain and Sabrina gasped, jerking back. She lost her footing and toppled over the chair she'd just risen from.

Oh glory! Her head slammed into the edge of a nearby table and brilliant points of light shot across her vision as pandemonium erupted around her.

"Oh my gosh! I'm so sorry!" The waitress set down her tray and reached for Sabrina.

Sabrina hissed as agony flooded her awareness. She yanked her sweater away from her skin and tried to focus through the ringing in her head. Tears blurred her eyes as she struggled to breathe, her ability to inhale momentarily curtailed. The waitress tried to mop up the coffee on Sabrina's belly with her bar towel, but she succeeded in only irritating the reddened skin.

Sabrina moaned and writhed away, batting futilely at the other woman's hands as her head swam from the lack of oxygen. A shadow loomed over her, darkening her fading sight.

"Breathe, Lady Foxglove." The rich voice penetrated her addled brain and she looked up into teal green eyes filled with concern.

What did he say? She frowned and shook her head in confusion.

"I said breathe. Remember to inhale."

I can't... Sabrina's mind raised the white flag and surrendered to the darkness.

****

Darius's gut contracted as Sabrina's eyes rolled up in her head and her body relaxed completely. But she still didn't inhale.

Mumbling choice curses under his breath, he laid one hand over her burned belly and the other on her forehead, hoping he could coax her back into consciousness. The waitress fluttered with incoherent distress beside him and he sent a mental command to retreat back far enough to stay out of his way. She stumbled away, wringing her hands, and he turned his attention back to the wounded witch.

Anger stirred at the vivid red welts already forming on her creamy skin. *Stupid serving woman.* His protective instincts swelled and he closed his eyes, ignoring the fear shouting against Sabrina's ability to survive the nasty blow to her head.

Don't be melodramatic. It's only a faint.

Except she still hadn't taken a breath. Panic screamed at the edges of his awareness and he hoped he could reach her despite their short association.

Bloody hell, woman, inhale!

CHAPTER THREE

Sabrina stood at the foot of a suspension bridge extending into the mists, the cool wetness of spring dripping off the struts of the bridge. Silence of the senses surrounded her. No sounds, tastes, smells or textures shook the stillness. Only foggy sight offered any indication she still existed.

Sabrina frowned.

This had to be a dream because nothing like this stood in Cloudburst. The hazy silhouette of a great tree awaited her at the far end of the bridge, but the distance of the span escaped her estimation. She grasped the guy ropes and squeezed to find some sort of physical purchase, but her hands felt numb.

Where am I and how did I get here?

Memories sifted, as insubstantial as the mists around her. She shook her head to focus her thoughts, but everything swirled away as substantial as smoke.

Something was wrong.

Sabrina sought to inhale, to find the scents of spring, but she couldn't breathe. Panic gripped her mind and her hands tightened on the ropes. *Oh Goddess, I can't breathe!* She bent at the waist and tried again, squeezing her eyes shut, but her lungs refused to expand.

Dear Goddess, am I dying? Is that why I'm at the edge of the bridge?

I can't die! Who would care for her children? Who would protect them?

She wanted to wail her distress, but she had no air to expel sound. She bowed her head and tears fell, scalding her cheeks in fiery trails.

The ropes under her hands vibrated and she stilled, opening her eyes. Raising her head, she stared into the misty expanse of the bridge. A figure materialized half-way along the span, more solid than the rest of this world, and extended his hand out to her. She swallowed hard.

Darius? What is he doing here?

Even in his hazy state, he looked noble and strong. She wanted to believe his appearance meant safety and protection, but standing in the center of the bridge he only represented the unknown.

"Come with me, Sabrina."

How does he have breath here and I don't?

"You must focus, my lady. You must make the first step. Come back with me."

Sabrina shook her head in confusion. Back with him? *Back where?*

His expression tightened with frustrated concern. "Take the step. Trust me."

She wanted to scoff, but sound required air. *Trust him? I don't know him.*

"Please, Sabrina."

Something in Darius's voice encouraged her, coaxing her to move forward. She bit her lip and extended her foot onto the flimsy bridge, hoping it would hold her weight.

"That's it." Darius remained still, his hand offering her shelter and security. "You can do it. Just take my hand."

The bridge swayed in a dangerous arc and she froze on the rickety board, panic dragging at her gut. *I can't breathe,*

I can't breathe. The mantra repeated in her mind, eradicating all other thoughts. Sabrina closed her eyes and bowed her head, her hands squeezing the guy ropes until her knuckles cracked.

"Sabrina, look at me." She shook her head again. *I can't breathe.* "Look at me, *acushla.*"

She forced her eyes open. Darius smiled with none of his usual slick charm.

"Good, my lady. Reach for me, now." His fingers flexed a little, urging her forward. "Just a few more steps."

She wished she could take a deep breath to buck up her courage, but she couldn't make her lungs work. Panic surged, but she focused on Darius's face, his expression tight with worry. *Why is he worried? Don't ask questions, just keep walking.*

Sabrina loosened her grip just enough to slide along the prickly ropes, forcing her feet from one worn plank to the next. She kept her gaze locked on Darius' eyes despite her pounding heart and burning lungs. Tears streamed down her cheeks as she pushed herself onward until she could reach his outstretched fingers.

Sabrina gritted her teeth and flailed for his hand, desperate to reach him. When his warm fingers closed around her frozen skin, relief flooded through her as he drew her into his embrace.

"There you go, *acushla.*" Darius gathered her into the folds of his coat as he wrapped his arms around her. "You're safe now. I've got you."

As soon as she touched him, her lungs expanded and blessedly sweet air filled her chest. Her belly burned and her head ached, but everything paled before the wonderful ability to simply inhale. *Never taking it for granted again.*

"I couldn't breathe." Her voice rasped no louder than a whisper, but any sound made her happy.

"I know, *acushla*, but you're all right now. Come, let's get to solid ground."

Darius shifted his body to escort her the remaining steps to the terminus before the great tree, never releasing her waist. She kept her gaze focused on the hazy branches, but the scents of autumn leaves baking in the sunshine and pumpkin spices filled her nose. As much as she loved spring, the scents of the harvest season gave her comfort, and his natural scents, mixed with the leather he wore, brought the harvest alive.

Goddess of all, he smells wonderful.

"Sorry?"

Crap. Did she say it aloud? "I said it smells wonderful here now that I can breathe."

"I'm glad you can. I thought I'd lost you." Darius's voice sounded remarkably serious.

"Lost me? So I *was* dying?" A sick feeling hit Sabrina's stomach as she reached the tree, touching its marbled bark. "I was that close?"

His teal eyes held no humor. "You stopped breathing when you hit your head."

Sabrina frowned. "I hit my head?"

"In the coffee house."

She looked around at the misty environs. "Where are we now, then?"

"At the bridge."

A rather obvious answer, but she realized he'd capitalized the first letters: The Bridge. She swallowed hard. "Like the Rainbow Bridge of Norse beliefs?"

"The very same."

Sabrina looked back over her shoulder at the rope bridge disappearing into the mists. "I stood on the other side. I was on Tír na nÓg."

"Yes."

"Oh, Goddess, my children." She clutched his shirt.

"They are well, little witch, and so are you. But we must come back to the conscious world or there will be more trouble than just a little headache."

26

"What headache—"

Pain bloomed like fireworks, lighting Sabrina's head and her belly on fire. She gasped with the shock of it, opening her eyes. Worried faces filled her vision as sensation came back. The hard floor seeped cold into her shoulder blades while agony clawed at her stomach. She rolled her head and a sickening, wet sound filled her ears as if she lay in viscous liquid.

"I'm here, *acushla*. Focus on me, just me."

Darius's voice grabbed her attention and she swung her gaze to him. She moaned as the room kept turning without her.

"Tír na nÓg," she whispered.

"I know, *acushla*. But not yet." He didn't smile as his hand rubbed against the pain in her belly. "You're needed here."

Everything hurt and the pain created a morass of sensation swamping her. Sabrina tried to focus on the individual points of agony, but they bled into each other.

"I hurt."

"I know." Darius's voice sounded soothing, but not patronizing.

"Why?"

"Do you remember the coffee?"

Sabrina searched her memories, but she couldn't find anything about coffee, only the drive to... *Where am I now?*

"No."

"The waitress dropped some coffee on you when you got up to leave. It burned you and you fell over a chair and hit your head."

None of his words sounded familiar. "Am I burned? Is that why my tummy hurts?"

A soft chuckle issued from him at her choice of words. "It's not a bad burn. You'll be tender for a day or so, but it's not serious."

"Is she going to be okay?"

Sabrina looked up at Moira Callahan. She held a phone in her hand and spoke to Darius.

"I think she will be fine, but she needs to go home and rest."

"I have to get to work…"

"Not today, you don't," Moira said. "I'm calling Mazy and letting her know you won't be in for at least a week."

"Wise choice, Ms. Callahan." Darius reached for Sabrina's skull.

Irritation filtered through the pain in Sabrina's head. "You did this on purpose…"

He dropped his hands as outrage filled his expression. "I did nothing of the sort, Lady Foxglove." Darius raised his chin and looked down his nose. "It was an accident."

"You just want me to host the…dignitaries." At least she had enough wits not to name the Summer Court in front of everyone. "Best way to do that is get me out of my job."

"I doubt a concussion and a first degree burn is the best way to get you to host anyone," Moira said drily. "And Tess said it was an accident when you two bumped and the coffee spilled."

Moira would never lie to her and Tess seemed honest enough, but she knew the Fae and their minions. She wouldn't put it past Darius to have finagled Tess's coffee slosh. Sabrina narrowed her eyes at him, but his expression didn't change.

Moira reached for her arm. "Come on, Sabrina. Let's get you home so you can rest."

Darius dropped his imperious attitude to help her up, and she resolutely ignored how much she enjoyed feeling his hands on her. *I don't like his delicious scent or the warmth emanating from his body. At all.*

Moira raised her eyebrows, but said nothing as Darius picked Sabrina up and carried her toward the front doors. Sabrina tried not to blush while the other patrons stared at their passing. She wondered when she'd be able to come back to the Cloudburst after this little episode. Everyone would be talking about it for months.

"How'd you get here, Sabrina? Did you drive?" Moira asked.

"Yes." She squirmed in Darius's arms. "Did anyone grab my purse and coat?"

"You have your coat on, hon, and I have your purse." Moira lifted her bag. "You shouldn't be driving with your injury. I'll give you a ride to the hospital in my Jeep."

"No, no hospital. I'll be fine."

"Sabrina, concussions are serious."

Sabrina held up her hand. "I'll be fine at home."

Moira didn't look convinced. "Are you sure you'll be all right alone with the girls?"

"Yes, I—"

"She won't be alone. I'll be there to help look after her." Darius's voice rumbled against Sabrina's shoulder.

"No, you don't have to." She didn't want him anywhere near her home when she felt so vulnerable.

"I *want* to, Ms. Foxglove. And it's no trouble. I'll be happy to stay as long as you need."

Sabrina glared at him while the women who'd overheard sighed with "awwws" and "ohhhhs" at his *kindness*, but she knew his game. His innocent look only added to her frustration.

The sneaky bastard just got into my home and got a free place to stay.

"All right then, we'll get you home in a blink."

Moira led them through the kitchen to the back rooms of the bar and gathered her purse, coat, and keys. She hustled them out the door to her snow-dusted Jeep parked beneath a small overhang. Darius set Sabrina in the back seat and climbed in beside her while Moira stepped out to sweep the windshield. Sabrina wondered where he'd put his huge sword, grateful she didn't have to hold it for him in the car.

Oh, man, that sounds bad. Can I hold your big sword, Darius? She had to stifle a giggle. *Thank the Goddess he can't hear my thoughts.*

"All ready?" Moira asked as she started up the Jeep.

"Yes." Darius brushed her shoulder with his as he sat back, and she inhaled a scented gust of warmth from his jacket.

Sabrina turned her face before he noticed how much she enjoyed it. She let her gaze drift out her window, hoping the drive home would be quick so she could get away from Darius's sensual allure.

They left the town and headed across the railroad tracks, bumping over two sets of them laid side by side. Her gaze followed them where they merged together in a synchronicity of rails and ties. Sabrina wondered if her life would ever find such a connection, the perfect blending of two life-lines into one continuous path.

She laughed silently at herself. *Not likely after Tommy.*

She turned her head just enough to glance at Darius's noble profile.

And not likely with this peacock, either. He's a player and the Fae's minion. Definitely not *husband material.*

Sabrina tried to ignore the flare of pain from her burned belly. *Why am I even thinking of husbands? Marty Robinson must have rubbed off on me after his last threat.* She sighed and closed her eyes. *A woman needs a husband like a zebra needs a frying pan.*

****

Darius heard Sabrina sigh and experienced two equally strong and conflicting emotions. His balls tightened up in lust at the same time as concern burned through him for her well-being.

Damnation, Winterbourne, don't get so attached to this little witch. Just get her to do her job and forget her.

But he didn't like her experiencing pain and his anger still simmered at the other woman's clumsiness. Sabrina had almost died, nearly ruining the task he'd been sent to accomplish. The Summer Court would arrive in six days and if she'd stayed on the other side of the bridge...

The drive to her home continued in silence and they turned up a short driveway after no more than a few minutes. Sabrina's lavender eyes opened when they stopped, but her expression held exhaustion. Darius stomped on a surge of anger as they exited the vehicle. *I have no business feeling sorry for her. She accused me of engineering the accident.* Despite his indignation, Darius hurried around the Jeep to help Sabrina out. She took his hand, but she refused his offer to carry her. He tried to ignore his disappointment.

When she tried to pull out of his grip, he tightened it, giving her a stable point on the slippery ground. At least, that's what he told himself.

The door to her home opened and a young, plump woman gasped in dismay when she spotted Sabrina hobbling up the walk.

"Oh, my God! What happened?"

"It's okay, Matilda," Sabrina soothed, but Darius caught her swaying.

"She got burned and hit her head. She needs to rest." Darius helped Sabrina past the fluttering woman and into the house.

The scents of vanilla and pine flowed around him and soothed some of his concern. Pine boughs tied with golden ribbons decorated some of the flat surfaces around the main room, and warm light gilded the comfortable furniture. Warm, earthy colors filled Sabrina's home and small toys lay strewn about the throw rugs.

"Oh, my God. Is she going to be all right? There's blood in her hair!"

Matilda's voice had reached a screech just as they

rounded a corner into the living room where a little girl dressed in a purple shirt with a big yellow daisy emblazoned on it played with dolls. When she saw her mother, she jumped up and squealed, "Mommy!"

"Hi, Holly." Sabrina's smile wavered. "Can you help Mommy get to bed?"

"Why is there blood in your hair?"

"Is there? I must need to wash it."

"Who's he?"

The child eyed Darius, her expression guarded. She assessed him like one would examine a feral animal.

"He's…" Sabrina grimaced. "Too difficult to explain."

"I'm here to help your mommy because she's not feeling well."

Sabrina snorted her derision, but didn't correct him.

"Why?" The little girl trailed along with them as Matilda directed them to Sabrina's bedroom. "Why isn't she feeling good?"

"She hit her head on a table," he said and Matilda gasped.

"Oh, my God, does she have a concussion?"

The repetition of the phrase grated on Darius's nerves. He clenched his jaw and took a deep breath of Sabrina-scented air as he called upon his Chamberlain training. He had to appear calm and distract the fluttering creature.

"I don't believe so, but the wound looks worse than it is. Just a little cut at the back. We need attend to it and then she can rest."

"Mommy, are you okay?" Holly's voice sounded fearful and something in Darius's chest clenched.

"I will be, honey. I just need to get some sleep." Sabrina took Holly's hand.

"Okay, I'll help you get to bed." She released her mother's hand and ran to the bed, jerking back the covers. Matilda helped when they proved too heavy.

Sabrina leaned on Darius as he assisted her across the

room. While she'd stayed upright, her skin turned ashen and he sensed she suffered more pain than she let on.

She sat down with a sigh and closed her eyes, her mouth tightening. Darius wished he could help her, but his healing skills had always been meager, and the only real cure would be rest.

Kneeling before her, he took a deep breath. "Sabrina, look at me, please."

At his gentle command, she opened her eyes. The pupils dilated evenly with the light and she appeared able to track his movements.

"We need to clean your hair and then you can rest. It will hurt." They grimaced at the same time and a ripple of amusement shifted through him. "Do you have any frankincense or lavender oil?"

She started to nod, but halted the motion. "Yes, in my bathroom cabinet."

Darius looked over his shoulder at the plump woman. "Can you get it for her?"

"Oh!" Matilda bit her bottom lip. "What does it look like?"

"Small brown glass bottle with a purple label that reads lavender." Sabrina's shoulders slumped as her strength waned and Darius's concern ratcheted up another notch.

"How are you feeling?"

She rolled her eyes toward him. "How do you think?"

He gave her a half-smile. "Well enough to give me some sarcasm."

"No, not even that well." She sighed and knuckled one eye. "I just want to sleep."

"Here's the lavender!" Darius wished Matilda would stop speaking in exclamations, but he took the bottle from her and gently applied the fragrant oil to Sabrina's wound.

She hissed with pain and his gut clenched. She bore his continued ministrations stoically as he helped her to the bathroom and washed her hair in the sink. Crimson stripes swirled to the drain against the white porcelain and Darius wished he could turn back time to change the events.

If you did, you wouldn't be here in her house, where you were meant to be from the beginning.

He'd much rather have seduced his way into Sabrina's house than overruled her with her friends' encouragement, but he'd take what he could get. She'd proven a formidable opponent when it came to determination.

Darius wrapped a towel around Sabrina's shining brown locks and carried her back to the bed with Matilda trailing after them, wringing her hands. All the fight had fled from Sabrina's frame and she settled easily into the sheets. The lines of strain around her eyes and mouth worried him, but in uncharacteristic concern, he sent a prayer up to the Mother Goddess in hopes She would help Sabrina mend quickly.

"Get some rest, *acushla*," he whispered before he laid a gentle kiss on her brow.

One lavender eye opened in surprise. "What was that for?"

"For luck and blessings. Now rest." He offered a smile to take the sting from his words.

She looked at him a moment longer before her eyes closed and she settled into sleep.

"What should we do now?" Matilda's voice seemed too loud for the bedroom and he drew her out into the hallway.

"I suggest you let her rest. Sabrina will mend more quickly. Perhaps you could prepare a simple luncheon for us to be saved for when she awakens?" He pushed a gentle compulsion into her thoughts and she nodded, worriedly.

As the babysitter retreated into the kitchen, Darius prayed Matilda's fears, and his own, remained unfounded.

CHAPTER FOUR

Sabrina woke to the sounds of a bass drum pounding in a slow rhythm and pain throbbing in time with it. She moaned, adding a new sound to the steady thumping. She opened her eyes and scanned the bedroom. Swarthy shadows cloaked the room and the silence beyond her own rustling movements told her the sun had set for the day. What day was it? She couldn't quite recall, but she remembered…what? Sabrina rifled through the images in her head, but she kept coming back to a bridge in the mist and a pair of amazing teal eyes. *That doesn't make sense. Where the heck did I go today?*

She tried to find memories of the day, but nothing came to mind and she groaned in frustrated pain. Why in the Goddess's name did she hurt so bad?

Her sound must have been louder than she thought because the door opened and soft light from the hallway pushed back the darkness. The vision filling the doorway made even less sense than her memories, and she wallowed in confusion for a few moments.

Tall, broad, and unquestionably male, the figure slipped into the room on silent feet and clicked on the reading lamp beside her favorite chair. More light flooded her room, highlighting the tawny shoulder-length hair and teal eyes of the man beside her bed.

Teal eyes...

"How are you feeling?" His voice reminded her of comfort and protection, the rich tones soothing her concerns.

"Hurt..." She didn't think the sound could reach to his ears, even standing beside her, but he crouched and brushed a hand across her forehead.

"I know, *acushla*. I will help as much as I can." He settled his weight on the bed beside her and grasped her head between his warm, broad hands. "Close your eyes for me."

Sabrina didn't argue and settled back into her pillow, trying to ignore the pounding throb in favor of his physical heat. With the warmth came his scent, spicy and male, seeping into her consciousness and adding another level of comfort. She wanted to wrap herself up in it, but her headache broke through the pleasure.

Heat from his hands increased around her head and sweat popped out on her skin. It pushed away the pain, but the pressure built until something snapped, and the pain drained out of her. Sabrina sighed in relief and all her tension slid away as she melted into the bed.

"Feel better?"

"Yes, thank you." She opened her eyes. "What time is it?"

"It's close to midnight."

"What are you doing awake?"

"Checking on you." Darius smoothed the hair back from her face. "Are you hungry?"

She almost shook her head, but thought better of it. "No, but I am thirsty. Is there any tea?"

"Not yet. Shall I brew some for you?"

"I can—" She started to rise, but he pushed her back down.

"Be at ease, Lady Foxglove. I have some small skill at preparing tea." He gave her a sexy, lopsided smile. "Perhaps you'd allow me to care for you a little longer."

"I don't really have any choice, do I?" Sabrina eyed his self-assured expression. "You're here now. You're not likely to leave short of me physically throwing you out, and I'm in no condition to throw anything."

Darius shrugged. "I suppose you could always use a banishment spell, but it would seem rather ungrateful since I have helped you."

"Banishment spell?" Sabrina bit her lip. "What are you talking about?"

He cocked his head. "You don't know about banishment spells?"

"No. Would it really get rid of you?"

He nodded. "Much like they say revoking permission prevents vampires from entering your dwelling."

She'd ask about vampires later. "How does it work?"

"If you don't know the spell, I won't teach you now."

"Why not?"

"Because it's imperative I stay and help you ready yourself for the Court's arrival." He crossed his arms over his broad chest.

"I don't know you, Mr. Winterbourne. You're a stranger and I'll do everything in my power to protect my children." She gritted her teeth as she prepared to get up.

"Peace, Lady Foxglove." He laid a warm hand against her shoulder. "I mean you and your children no harm."

"How do I know that? Words aren't very substantial when I know nothing about you." She shook her head slowly to keep from jarring it. "I'm sorry, I'm used to doing everything myself, and it won't change just because you think you can do better."

Darius's expression turned mutinous, but he tipped his chin up and placed a hand over his heart. "Upon my honor, my family name, and place as the Summer Court's

Chamberlain, I swear I mean you and your family no harm, and I shall do my utmost to help and protect you all."

A ripple of energy swirled around them and spread throughout the room at the end of his vow.

Sabrina blinked. "Did you see that? What was it?"

Darius grasped one of her hands. "I made a solemn vow and the Goddess accepted it. I'm now under oath to do as I promised." He squeezed her hand. "And you're not alone. I'm here to help."

"And convince me to do the rituals," she remarked drily, grimacing.

"It's immaterial at the moment. For now you must rest and recover before you're able to do anything."

"I'm not an invalid, Darius."

"No, you have a head injury." He released her. "Allow someone to help you so you may return to your regular routine. Is it not customary to have one's friends step in to offer support?"

"Yes. But I've only known you…a few hours." Sabrina gasped and tried to rise. "Oh Goddess, what about Tansy?"

"Peace, Sabrina, she is safely in bed. Matilda picked her up at school while I stayed to watch over you and Holly." He again kept her in the bed. "They were well cared for while you rested." He frowned and studied her for a few moments. "Where is the girls' father?"

Old patterns of anger and hurt rose in her mind, rumbling through her gut and tensing her shoulders. *Probably off fucking some buxom bimbo without stretch marks.* The unhappiness churned in her gut until she felt as if she'd throw it up. *Let it go, he's not worth it.* But the fury remained.

"I don't know. He left after Holly turned six months old."

The silence between them thickened with unspoken anger and disgust, but Darius only nodded sharply. "Was he your husband?"

"No."

"And he left *after* Holly, your youngest, was born?"

"Yes." Sabrina turned her head away from him and closed her eyes. She'd been a fool. She'd thought they were in love and believed Tommy wanted her for her. But he'd walked away because her body had changed with the pregnancies. He'd told her he'd only been "trying" the Goddess's path. *Yeah, he'd only been "trying" it for two and a half years, two children, and then ran off with Merrilee Fuckstwice. But I'm not bitter.*

"Perhaps it's something to be grateful for."

"What?"

"A man who leaves a woman and children is lower than pond scum." Darius's teal eyes glittered in the dim light. "But a man who leaves his wife and children is only good for cannon fodder in a losing battle."

Despite the old anger, Sabrina laughed. "I'll have to remember that."

His face creased into a smile. "In the meantime, just rest while I fetch the tea." He patted her arm and rose.

Sabrina watched him saunter out of her room, wondering for the hundredth time what motivation bubbled around in his head. It made no sense to injure the person he wanted to perform the rituals, but he'd definitely manipulated his way into her home, something he'd expected when he first arrived. On the other hand, he'd saved her from Tír na nÓg without hesitation and swore to protect her and her children before the Goddess.

It's simply because he can't have a dead witch to perform the rituals.

She couldn't argue the point, but her gratitude for his help remained. And he continued to help even now.

Sabrina worried the debate back and forth until Darius returned carrying a tray with her favorite tea set and a little bowl. He set the tray on the chair and helped her sit up higher on the bed.

"How is your head feeling now?"

"Better. Tender near the gash."

"It will be for a few more hours."

"Hours? Not 'days?'" She flattened the covers over her lap and Darius set the tray on the flat space.

He gave her a funny look. "I expect you to heal yourself faster given all your obvious ability. Besides, we don't have days before the Summer Court arrives. You must be ready for Beltane."

Sabrina sighed and set down her cup. "You just don't get it, Darius. I'm not doing the rituals. For one thing, my head isn't going to just miraculously heal in time. And for another, there's no suitable male counterpart for the full rituals." Tommy's betrayal burned brightly for a moment, but she shoved it aside. "Most of the men around here are either married or don't follow the Goddess's path, and I draw the line well before any of those options."

"The Summer Queen will find a suitable male to impersonate the May Lord, Sabrina. The only thing required of you is to be the May Lady."

"No. I'm done with the High Beltane rituals." She leaned back and closed her eyes. "We're just going to do our usual. Light the fire, give it our offerings, and wind the little May Pole in our backyard. It'll have to do for the Goddess this year."

"It's not the Goddess who insists, but the Summer Queen." Darius clenched his jaw. "You don't understand. Once this honor is given, it cannot be revoked. You've been chosen for the rituals."

"And *you* don't understand. Unlike you, I don't live in the world of the Sidhe. I live in this one and after the Summer Court leaves, I'm going to have to deal with the consequences, not the least of which will be some of my neighbors. You saw what Marty and the others think of an unwed mother. I'm not getting married just to appease them, but I won't chance *another* pregnancy just to satisfy the Elves."

"Children are a blessing."

"Yes, they are, but those blessings take a lot of time, effort, and attention, and I only have so much I can give. I already have two blessings and they're enough for me to take care of on my own." Sabrina stopped, frustration and pain making her head throb. "Look, Darius, I appreciate the vote of confidence from the Summer Court, but I'm not the witch for the job. You'll just have to find someone else or go elsewhere."

She set the tray away from her body on the unused side of the bed. "I'm tired. I'll talk with you more about it tomorrow. Please turn off the light when you leave." She rolled onto her side with her back to the door.

She hated letting anyone down, but she'd made a decision after Tommy left. She'd live quietly, celebrate simply, and take care of her children honorably. Bitter experience taught her men remained undependable and the only one riding a white horse and saving her was her. Darius didn't really need Sabrina Foxglove to do the rituals. Any witch who followed the sacred ways of the Goddess would do.

I'm sure Merrilee Fuckstwice would be happy to perform them.

Anger, pain, and loneliness mixed into a bitter brew and crashed over her. Tears squeezed out of her eyes. No matter what, she wouldn't give in to more pain and humiliation.

****

Darius closed the door to Sabrina's house softly and settled his cloak around him as he traversed her frozen yard. Her resolute stubbornness surprised him and he'd started to wonder if she could be convinced at all. Her

41

voice had been full of pain and betrayal, but he didn't think it all stemmed from the near-death experience she'd had at the coffee shop.

Whatever betrayal she'd experienced, it had pushed her away from the healing rituals and the development of her own natural gifts. Darius suspected it had to do with the man who'd walked out on her and his lip curled in disgust at the cock-swinging churl who'd mounted Sabrina and run from his responsibilities. Darius had no problem with recreational pleasure, but running from responsibilities sickened him. He had no patience for it.

So now he stood in a frozen forest in the dying grip of winter waiting to speak with the Summer Queen of the Sidhe. He'd received a message from Her Majesty while he'd prepared Sabrina's tea and he had no idea how he'd tell the Queen of Sabrina's refusal. He suspected Her Majesty wouldn't take it very well. He doubted anyone turned the Queen down, not and lived happily ever after.

He could almost hear Her Majesty's voice saying, "You're in a position to take care of things like this. I do not care how, just make it happen." And he would, he simply needed a little more time. When the Queen of the Summer Court called for an audience, any Chamberlain worth his mettle would never refuse.

The air around him shifted from biting winter cold to a soft, spring breeze. Frost under his boots melted and the ground grew fragrant. The surrounding trees sprouted new life from embryonic buds and a soft glow permeated the dark forest, pushing back the cold shadows with healing warmth.

Darius shifted into a bow as the Summer Court materialized around him. Tall forms of the Queen's most favored courtiers filled the widening space around him between the softly glowing trees. Scents of hyacinth and honeysuckle replaced the winter pine immersed in damp cold. Darius closed his eyes and bowed lower as sibilant whispers of the Court took the place of the soughing wind.

"Be welcome, Chamberlain Winterbourne. What new developments have you to tell Us of our Beltane ceremonies?"

Darius rose and opened his eyes to gaze upon the Summer Queen. Girlishly slender and smooth of skin, Her Majesty never seemed to age. Her ancient green eyes twinkled with continued amusement at his surname. Taking a Winterbourne as her Chamberlain had been her way of thumbing her nose at the Winter Court. Though younger than most of her Royal Elven cousins, the current Queen had assumed the throne when Titania stepped down after the Midsummer's Night Dream debacle in the early 1500s. Darius had been appointed her Chamberlain soon after.

Well, "soon" as Elves figure it.

"I have not made too much progress, Your Majesty, but it is early yet and I've only just gotten into the witch's good graces."

Her Majesty cocked her head. Today her white-golden hair had been gathered up in a complex chignon wound around a delicate gold filigree circlet with emerald oak leaves, the symbol of her house. The air around Darius cooled a little as the Queen rose from her throne and closed the distance between them.

"Only now, Chamberlain? It seems to have taken more time than necessary."

"Yes, my Queen. The witch, Sabrina Foxglove, has no love of strangers or men in general." He chuckled and inclined his head toward her. "I found her cornered by five men."

"Blessed be!" The Queen settled a warm, elegant hand on Darius's arm. "Is she all right?"

"Yes, Your Majesty. I arrived just in time, but it made her less than welcoming."

"She had no gratitude for your efforts?" The Queen raised an eyebrow as she led him toward a small intimate garden she used for private audiences.

"I'm sure she did, but I was a stranger and far larger than her five would-be assailants."

"We are certain you shall make strides soon. When will she begin the rituals?"

Darius hesitated and the Queen leveled him with a narrow-eyed stare. "Chamberlain?"

"The Lady Foxglove is proving rather obstinate. She has refused to do the rituals, but I'm sure it is merely a matter of time before she comes around." He offered a placating smile in hopes the Summer Queen took it at face-value. "She had an unfortunate accident, which caused a head injury."

"Oak and holly, this woman does seem to carry unfortunate luck." The Queen appeared more amazed than sympathetic. "How does she fare the last you saw of her?"

"Very well, Your Majesty. My own small healing talents combined with her natural gifts seemed to have sped her healing along. It shouldn't be more than a day or so."

"Good. Beltane is five days from now and the rituals must be performed." Though she represented the warmest season as the Summer Queen, ice crystallized below her words. She smiled benignly. "We are counting on you, Chamberlain, to make sure the witch is ready for Our arrival."

"Yes, of course, my Queen." Darius smiled, but the Queen must have noticed something because she scrutinized him again.

"Will this be a problem?" she asked sharply.

"No, Your Majesty." Goddess, he hoped not.

"Come now, Chamberlain. We have seen how you entice the fair sex with your gentlemanly ways and smooth speech. Surely one human witch is no match for your powers of persuasion."

That's debatable.

"As always, I shall endeavor to convince her."

"Be sure you do. More than the wards hang in the balance." Her smile contained more threat than goodwill. "Thank you for your report. We shall contact you again soon."

Darius stopped as the Queen drifted away from him, taking the warmth, light, and softness with her. He found himself standing at the edge of Sabrina's backyard, the dark silent trees cold sentinels around him.

Bollocks. What else depended upon his task? He'd just have to redouble his efforts to convince Sabrina and use his famous charm. *You gather more flies with honey.* He just hoped his mother's words would be enough.

CHAPTER FIVE

Morning arrived with less pain than Sabrina expected, but more than she wanted. She tried to recall if she'd taken any aspirin or even had any in the house, but only the teal eyes of her new houseguest filled her memories. *He's not important. You have too much to do to worry about him.* She gingerly tested out the back of her head for injuries, but other than a bruised tenderness, her head felt fine.

Sabrina sat up slowly, careful not to jar her head lest her brain slide out her ears. A dull ache settled behind her eyes, but no nausea or dizziness assailed her. *Thank the Goddess.*

To her surprise, she found a tray with a pot of tea beside her bed, the teapot cool to the touch. She smiled at Darius's thoughtful effort and dragged herself to the bathroom. Showering took more effort than usual, but she made it through without collapsing in an exhausted heap and dressed with methodical precision.

Please, Goddess, make today an easier day than yesterday.

Feet firmly ensconced in slippers, Sabrina ventured out of her room. Each step made her head throb a little, but she made her way to the kitchen. The girls were already up, chattering away with someone. Had Matilda come early?

When Darius's laugh echoed through the house, Sabrina hesitated as a mixture of emotions swirled within her. She liked to hear a male voice and his rich baritone brought comfort of alarming proportions. But she didn't want to feel anything about this man. He'd be gone as soon as she convinced him she wouldn't perform the rituals, and growing attached to his presence in her house simply asked for trouble.

Face the day and see how it goes. I can kick him out after breakfast.

She resumed her trek to the kitchen, but paused on the threshold as tenderness overtook her. Darius sat with her daughters at the table helping them make May Day wreaths out of pine cones, glitter, pine boughs, and brightly-colored ribbons. Holly's looked like a rainbow had been denuded over an evergreen tree while Tansy's resembled a spiky wheel with all the cones.

"Did you really do this when you were little, Darius?" Tansy asked as she sprinkled more glitter over a cone.

"Yes, my mother helped me and my brothers make these wreaths for every door of our home." He held the glue for another ribbon on Holly's wreath.

"Why did you put them on the doors?" Tansy doused the wreath with more glitter.

"To protect the home with the good luck of the Goddess. Each wreath would gather up the good energy and push it into the home, but would project the bad energy back to the senders."

"Do you put them on all the doors of the house?" Tansy examined her wreath for defects.

"Yes, every door to the outside."

"We have three doors in this house," Holly said. "But only two wreaths. What about the other door?"

"I'll just have to make another wreath with your mother."

Making a Beltane wreath with the handsomest man she'd ever seen? Excitement shot through Sabrina. *Get a hold of yourself. It's not like you're eighteen and at your first bonfire.* But the joy remained despite her rebuke.

Darius held up Holly's wreath. "I think it's done, except one thing."

"What?" both girls chorused.

He winked and dug around in the pocket of his pants, pulling out a small leather pouch. "No Beltane wreath is complete without a crystal charm to hang in the center."

"What kind of crystal, Darius?" Tansy's gaze remained riveted to his hands.

"The best kind is quartz. Clear quartz channels the Goddess's energy, reflecting the light of Her love and the harmony of Her grace into the home, and deflecting the negative energy from outside sources."

Darius held up two perfect crystal points as clear as water. "These two crystals were given to me by my mother for me to pass on to my daughters." He handed one to each girl.

Heartfelt warmth hit Sabrina's gut, followed by surprise. Why would Darius give such treasures to her girls? She almost protested, but a surge of energy wafted through her kitchen. Joy and comfort danced in the dust motes from the sunlight streaming through the windows. The crystals held a great deal of power. *Damn, they have to be ancient to hold so much energy.*

"Wow."

"It's so sparkly!" Holly held it up to the light. "Can we put it on the wreaths now?"

"Of course, Miss Holly. Here." Darius held out a bright red ribbon. "Thread the ribbon through the hole drilled in the end."

Holly took the ribbon and tried to feed it through the small hole, her tongue sticking out between her lips. Sabrina smothered a laugh. She'd forgotten how cute her daughter looked when concentrating.

"I can't get it through the hole. Can you help me, please?" Tansy held up her ribbon and crystal.

"Certainly, Miss Tansy." Darius took the proffered ribbon and showed it to her. "The easiest way is to fold the ribbon in half." He threaded the end of the satin through the crystal. "See? Grab the end now."

Tansy pulled and the ribbon slid through.

"Show me!" Holly thrust her ribbon and crystal at Darius, but he gave her a mock glare and she subsided. "Can you show me too, please, Darius?"

"Much better, Miss Holly." He took her crystal and showed her how to thread the ribbon.

Warmth suffused Sabrina's chest. Darius looked so handsome working with her girls, his pants and arms covered in little sparkles of glitter. She wished this could be reality, a happy family scene of a man working with his children to decorate for Beltane. *But reality is he's only here as long as I do the rituals then he's back to the Summer Court.* The hard thoughts stole some of her warmth.

She sighed and Tansy looked up.

"Mommy! Look what Darius is helping us with." She proudly held up her spiky wreath.

"Oh, it's lovely, Tansy." Darius met her gaze and smiled. Her heart fluttered and she told herself to stop mooning over what she shouldn't want. "Are you ready for school?"

"Mom." Tansy rolled her eyes. "It's Saturday, remember? I don't have to go to school until Monday."

Saturday? A huge weight lifted off Sabrina's shoulders and she sighed in relief. "Oh, good."

Holly laughed. "Come on, Mommy. You can make a Beltane wreath with Darius for the door."

"Let me get some tea first, okay, honey?" Sabrina shuffled for the coffeemaker.

"Let me get it for you, Lady Foxglove." Darius rose and beat her to the counter. "I didn't know you were awake. I would have brought more tea to you."

"Thank you, but I can't lay in bed forever. I have many things to do."

"Such as?" He raised a dubious eyebrow, igniting her temper.

"Since when did I have to clear my schedule with you?"

"Since you knocked yourself unconscious and gave yourself a concussion." He stared her down as he poured her a mug of tea. "Head injuries are no laughing matter. You must rest today and possibly tomorrow so you have the strength for Beltane."

Sabrina narrowed her eyes. "I'm not doing the rituals."

"Let's break our fast and wake up fully before we discuss it."

Anger surged inside. "Don't treat me like a child, Darius. I'm more than capable of making my own decisions, whether I'm fed or not. Do me the courtesy of remembering that."

Irritation showed in his teal gaze, but he inclined his head and handed her the mug. "Would you care for honey?"

As long as it's real honey and not this fake sweetness you're offering me now.

"Yes, please."

"Go sit down. I'll bring the honey."

Know my kitchen so well, do you?

"Thank you." Sabrina took the unoccupied chair against the window. The weak spring sunlight warmed her back and she looked at the creative devastation strewn across her table. "Your wreaths look lovely. Where will you hang them, ladies?"

"I want to put mine on the front door." Tansy held up the spiked wreath.

"No, I want to!" Holly thrust the ribbon-festooned wreath at her mother.

"Ladies—"

"Perhaps we should let the Goddess decide, eh?" Darius cut off the argument before it escalated. "She usually knows the best place for all the decorations. I'm sure She'll make it very clear where She wants each wreath. Until then, can you help me make breakfast for your mother?"

Sabrina looked on in wonder as her children jumped up to prepare a meal for her. Darius directed them like a general, mustering a clean up of wreath materials and doling out KP duties. In less time than it usually took Sabrina to make tea, the table had been cleared and a plate of toast with fresh huckleberry jam sat before her.

Darius cooked omelets for them while the girls chattered at him about projects at school and favorite movies. He responded as if they were visiting dignitaries, due all respect and attention. Again, Sabrina's heart tightened and she wished she could wake up to this every morning.

"Very well, girls, let your mother eat and get your rooms picked up." Darius set two plates down on the table. "A great deal needs to be done before Beltane and we must help your mother prepare."

"Okay!" The girls took off for their rooms.

Sabrina gaped after them then turned her amazement on Darius. "What did you do to my children?"

"How do you mean?" He frowned.

"They're never willing to clean up or help with meals." She gave him a mock-suspicious look. "You didn't sprinkle them with fairy dust?"

Darius laughed, his teal eyes sparkling and she tried not to enjoy the effects. "Not at all. In fact, they offered to help me as long as I helped them make the wreaths."

"Are you sure that's all you offered?" She waved her

hand over her plate. "Not ponies or unicorns or even chocolate lollypops?"

"I assure you, Lady Foxglove, on my honor, I have given them no more incentive than spending the day preparing for Beltane."

"Humph." She suspected his motives for such preparation were far from noble. What better way to get her to do the rituals than have her children cajole her? But she found herself happy for his help and his "parental" manipulation. It was nice to have someone else harangue the kids. *Don't get used to it.*

"What preparations do you usually make?" Darius sipped his tea as if they'd shared breakfast hundreds of times.

Sabrina rubbed her head and tried to think. "Give me a moment. My head still hurts."

"How much?"

"Sorry?"

"How much does it hurt?" He set down his mug and stood, reaching for her head.

"More of a dull ache than anything. Oohhhh…"

The moment he touched her, comfort and heat permeated her skull and soothed the pain. She hadn't realized how much it hurt until he relieved it. She relaxed her shoulders and leaned into his warm hands, grateful the pain had stopped.

At last he stood back and tipped her chin up. Sabrina reluctantly opened her eyes.

"Better?"

"Yes, thank you."

Darius smiled the same sincere smile she'd seen the day before. "You are welcome."

Damn, she wanted to fall into those eyes, let him tell her everything would be all right and believe him. *Why can't life be so easy?* But she knew better. She'd be alone again in a few days.

Sabrina jerked her attention back to the subject at hand. "Okay, what I usually do is make sure there's enough firewood for the fire, attach the ribbons to the May Pole, and make two dozen Deviled Eggs."

"Eggs seem like an odd feast item for a fertility ritual of the Goddess."

"Maybe, but they taste so good and we have to do something with all those eggs from Easter."

Darius raised his eyebrow. "You celebrate Easter?"

"Yes, at least dyeing the eggs and hiding them for the girls. And we have baskets full of goodies to enjoy."

"Oh? What's in your basket, Sabrina?"

The way he said her name sent fire into inappropriate places. Her pussy tingled and her heartbeat sped up. *What is wrong with me? All he did was say my name.*

She cleared her throat and sucked down her tea to buy some time. "I prefer chocolate and essential oils, but sometimes all I get are jellybean eggs."

He leaned toward her, his gaze smoldering, and some part of her wondered how the morning had gone from comfortable to sexy. "I'd be happy pack your basket with chocolate and essential oils, Sabrina. I find it very endearing you choose to celebrate all the holidays." His gaze dropped to her lips and her pussy clenched.

Kiss me, kiss me, kiss me.

Darius tilted his head and reached out to tuck a stray strand of hair behind her ear. A small smile curled his lips as he cupped her cheek with his hand and drew her to him.

Darius brushed his lips against hers and her arousal hit the ceiling. He tasted of crisp autumn mornings, her favorite time of year, and she wanted to fall into his sweet flavor. She would have kept kissing if she hadn't heard the furnace rattle and the girls loudly discussing who would put which wreath where. Reality intruded and Sabrina jerked back, her face hot.

Darius wore a similar dazed expression and they stared

at each other for a few moments, trying to recollect their thoughts.

What's wrong with me? He's a seductive player, a gigolo, and all he wants from me is to do the rituals. None of this is real.

"What are you doing?"

****

What am I doing?

Darius hadn't meant to kiss Sabrina, but the image of her celebrating Easter with her daughters, dyeing and hiding eggs, filled him with a yearning he'd never experienced before. She'd looked so happy and relaxed, and he couldn't resist tasting her joy.

The rattling furnace and her children's voices had startled him, but he would have kept kissing her if she hadn't pulled away. She tasted of fresh jam and sweet tea, and he'd become addicted in those few moments of touching her lips.

What is wrong with me? She's a human witch and I'm the Chamberlain of the Summer Court. The odd yearning must have been a remnant of his memories of celebrating Beltane with his family. It had to be. The idea he might be falling for this little witch after knowing her a total of two days stretched the boundaries of belief.

"Forgive me, Lady Foxglove, I don't know what came over me. Please accept my profound apologies."

She ran her fingers over her lips and his cock flexed with interest. Those lips had tasted so sweet and he resisted the urge to lean over and take them again. *Calm yourself and focus on the task at hand.* The reprimand lost power when another voice reminded him such actions could influence her cooperation in performing the rituals of High Beltane.

I still could.

"If you think you can sleep your way into getting me to do the rituals, you can tuck your cock right back into your pants, buster, 'cause sex has never swayed me." Sabrina rose from the table, her breakfast unfinished.

Anger surged, only because she'd hit the truth dead on, but he smothered it. His motives strayed far from pure and even the Summer Queen had suggested he seduce Sabrina's cooperation.

"Wait, Lady Foxglove." He caught her wrist as she tried to pass. She stopped and stared down at him, anger swirling in her lavender eyes. "I never intended to coerce you with the use of intimate relations. As I said, I don't know what came over me. Please, come back and sit down. You need your strength."

"For Beltane, I know."

"No, for running your own household." He gave her a half smile. "You strike me as a woman who rarely takes a break from her hectic schedule. Please." He stood and pulled out her chair. "Come back and finish your breakfast. Food and rest are the best for fast healing. Please."

He'd never said please so much in his life, but he'd never wanted anyone's company as much as he wanted Sabrina's. In just two days, he'd grown attached to her and found himself wanting to help her more than do his duty.

And therein lies trouble and despair.

Sabrina hesitated, her expression suspicious, but she returned to her chair and picked up her fork. Darius breathed a subtle sigh of relief.

"Why are you here, Darius?" Sabrina grasped her tea mug and held it like a shield in front of her.

"To help you."

"Yeah, but why? What is your motivation? Do you think making my children like you will convince me to do your bidding?" Her expression remained flat and he hoped he hadn't walked into a trap.

"I'd never use your children against you." The idea

curdled his stomach. Even he'd never sunk so low.

"Then why? You hardly know me. I'm sure you've met hundreds of single mothers. What makes me different from all of them?"

What, indeed?

"I don't think I can explain it to your satisfaction. Duty requires me to convince you and I'm nothing without my duty." *And the threat from the Summer Queen.* "However, I respect your reasons for choosing not to do the rituals, and your persistence in declining the honor."

"I hear a monumental 'but' coming."

"Not at all. I won't coerce you into doing the rituals."

"You won't?" She raised an eyebrow.

"No, but I won't give up trying to convince you." He winked and grinned. "I'm convinced you must do the rituals. You're convinced you won't perform them. We shall see who wins the battle of wills over the next few days."

"And if you don't convince me?"

"We'll cross that bridge when we come to it." In truth, his gut clenched in concern at the idea, but he nodded gamely and hoped for all involved she'd agree to his request.

"Mommy! I wanna hang my wreath on the back door, but Tansy said she's gonna put hers there." Holly's wail preceded her appearance in the kitchen, her face creased in a scowl.

Sabrina sighed and swallowed some of her tea. "Do you remember what Darius said, girls? He said the Goddess would make it very clear where each wreath should go."

Darius's chest tingled with pleasure and he rubbed the warm spot between the muscles in surprise. *Don't be ridiculous. If course she remembered what I said.* But the pleasure remained.

"But, Mom..."

"Don't 'but, Mom' me, Tansy." Sabrina plucked the

wreath from her eldest's hands and stopped in the center of the kitchen, closing her eyes. "Hmm. I think this one should go on the back door to the yard because the cones will ward off dangerous spirits." Tansy lifted her chin and gave her sister a superior smirk.

"That's not fair," Holly grumbled.

"And yours, Holly, I think should go on the door to the garage so it's the first thing we see when we get home and the last thing we see as we leave. All those cheery ribbons will definitely be good luck."

Darius admired the way she'd pleased both girls and deflected an argument. Not unlike the efforts he often had to make among the courtiers at Court.

"Let's hang these on their hooks."

"Does mine go on the sucker hook?" Tansy asked, marching toward the sliding glass door.

"Suction, and yes. We'll hang it there. Did you attach a hanger ribbon?"

Darius cleared the table as Sabrina helped the girls hang the wreaths on the doors. When Holly complained her wreath hung wrong, Sabrina lifted her up so she could rearrange it to her satisfaction. Darius enjoyed watching Sabrina work with her children and the yearning returned stronger than before. He wanted this, to be part of a family again, complete with squabbles and intrusions. While the Court offered a similar experience, the smiles meant less than nothing and promises broke like spider silk. He could depend on few, and truly trust no one. Particularly not with his heart.

"Do you like it?" Holly's voice broke Darius's reverie.

"Sorry?"

"Do you like it, Darius?" She dragged him over to the garage door and proudly pointed at the garish wreath.

"I think it's perfect, Miss Holly." The little girl beamed and he swore some ice melted off his heart.

"All right, who's up for making Deviled Eggs?"

Sabrina called.

"Meeee!" Holly raced back into the kitchen and joined her sister and mother at the table.

Darius watched in amazement as Sabrina organized the girls into specific tasks. Holly got to crack and peel the eggs while Tansy crushed the hard yolks with a fork. The girls laughed and chattered all the while and by the time Sabrina spooned the yellow concoction into the egg white halves, Holly's fingers matched her wreath.

"Go wash your hands, Holly."

"Mom, I have egg on my hands, too." Tansy scowled at her gritty fingers.

Sabrina sighed as she finished the last of the Deviled Eggs. "Wash your hands in the kitchen sink."

"I can't reach it."

"I'll help you, Miss Tansy." Darius steered the girl to the sink by her elbow then lifted her until she could reach the faucet.

"I like having you here. You're nice to me and my mom and my sister." She smiled up at him as she scrubbed her hands. "Not like Tommy."

"Who's Tommy?" Darius tried to keep his tone casual.

"He lived here before Mom brought Holly home. I'm glad he's gone, but Mom was sad." Tansy shut off the water.

"Is she still sad?"

"Sometimes, but not as much as when Tommy left. I'm glad he did, though."

Darius held back a growl and gently set Tansy down to dry her hands. "Tommy didn't treat you well?"

"No, he didn't play with me at all. And he liked to drink stinky water a lot."

"'Stinky water?' What's that?"

"I don't know, but it comes in a tall bottle and has a pirate on the front. It looks like ginger ale, but it doesn't smell like it." She wrinkled her nose and stuck out her tongue. "Tommy used to drink it all the time."

Darius didn't know the libation Tansy described, but he suspected it had to do with the common love of alcohol amongst the humans. The Elves tended to swill wines of various types, but eschewed the other forms of fermented liquids.

"Do you drink the stinky water?" Tansy waited for his answer with a serious expression and Darius hastened to reassure her.

"While I'm not familiar with that particular beverage, I don't believe I drink such things." He smiled at the relief playing across her face. "I do like apple cider and grape juice, though."

"Really? Me, too!" Tansy darted back to the kitchen table. "Mom, Darius likes apple cider and grape juice just like me."

Sabrina glanced up from sprinkling the eggs with paprika. "Does he? That's wonderful, sweetie."

"I like him a lot better than Tommy. He does stuff with us."

Resignation filled her lavender eyes, but she smiled at her daughter. "I like him better, too, Tansy."

An unreasonable amount of joy and pride washed through Darius and he resisted the urge to preen under her praise. Instead, he surveyed the platters covered in red, gold, and white eggs, daunted by the sheer number of them.

"What more needs to be done here?"

"We'll cover them with plastic wrap and throw them in the fridge." Sabrina pointed to the long narrow box on the table as Holly returned far less colorful.

"Can we do the May Pole ribbons now?"

"Yep, it's the next thing."

Darius wanted to ask more about the man who'd been in Sabrina's life before, but the moment disappeared before the excitement of picking out the colorful ribbons for the pole. While her children argued the merits of each color,

Sabrina measured out the proper lengths for the pole in her backyard.

"How many are we gonna do this year, Mom?" Tansy asked as she surveyed the different colors.

"Well, we need one for each of us, one for Darius, and one for the Goddess."

Holly grabbed a brilliant yellow ribbon. "I want yellow."

"Very well done, Miss Holly." Darius examined the ribbon. "A fine choice."

"Are you really going to dance around the May Pole, Darius?" Tansy picked up a summer green ribbon.

"If your mother invites me, I'd be honored." He reached for a navy blue ribbon and glanced at Sabrina. "Am I?"

"We'd love to have you at our Beltane celebration, Darius. Which color would you like?" Sabrina grasped a coral pink ribbon and measured it out.

"Navy for the vast night sky."

"Oooh, pretty." Holly set it next to the length of yellow. "Look, Mommy, it looks like a bumblebee. What color do you want?"

"I think I'll take this lovely pink one, and..." She picked up a lavender ribbon. "This one will be for the Goddess."

Darius had a sudden vision of Sabrina dancing before the bonfire wrapped in nothing but her rich hair and the ribbons from the Pole. Her hips and breasts swayed seductively and his cock thickened with joyful anticipation. Oh, to be her mate for the night of glorious celebration. The yearning returned full force and he pressed his hand between his pectoral muscles.

"Are you all right, Darius?"

Good heavens, could she see the swelling in his trousers?

He cleared his throat and tried to smile. "Yes, of

course. Shall we affix the ribbons to the Pole?"

"I'll get my coat!"

"Me too!" The girls took off to find their outer garments and Darius hoped to find his composure as Sabrina gathered up the ribbons.

"Can you grab the stepladder, Darius? It's just inside the garage."

He'd never been so grateful to be sent on a mundane errand in his life. *Get a hold of yourself, man.* Between the odd yearning and the sexual attraction he experienced around Sabrina, he swore he'd lost his mind. The last time he'd been this out of control, he'd been a boy of twenty years. At two hundred and eight, he expected more decorum from himself.

The bracing cold and manual labor should do the trick. He gathered the stepladder and his cloak before they all trouped outside, the girls running through the patchy snow with exuberance. Darius took a deep breath, hoping to cool his arousal as they set to work, the girls shouting instructions in between gathering little sticks for the fire.

Sabrina's cheeks turned rosy in the frigid air as she worked and the weak sunlight peeking through the clouds sparkled off her hair. Instead of dousing his ardor, his mind filled with images of warming her up beside the fire and teasing her with hot tea or chocolate. His cock saluted to the idea and strained the seams of his pants.

Dammit, she's just a human witch. Whom he liked, admired, and respected. He thought again of Tansy's explanation of Tommy and his fury rose to engulf his arousal. *At least my cockstand has retreated.* But the idea of someone leaving a woman like Sabrina prompted an old anger. A rage he kept burning for the man who'd left his mother with three sons.

And what makes me any different?

Darius had never committed to a woman and promised to stay. He'd only had one night liaisons with the lasses to avoid such entanglements. He wanted the pleasure without the concern of breaking a promise like his father had broken to his mother. Darius didn't believe in celibacy, but he did believe in commitment, and he'd never give his until he found the one woman he couldn't live without.

And it's not bloody likely. The only commitment he needed from Sabrina concerned the rituals. Afterwards, they'd be free of each other.

He resolutely ignored the hollow feeling following his thoughts.

CHAPTER SIX

Sabrina finished the supper time dishes and hung her apron on the hook in the pantry as she thought over the day. It had been productive with the Beltane preparations. The girls had been delighted to have Darius's help, and Sabrina had to admit she enjoyed it as well. He'd helped tie the ribbons to the May Pole, chop vegetables for the crock pot stew, and decorate the house with pine boughs filled with dried flowers.

But the best part had been when he chopped the wood for the fire.

Sabrina gripped the edge of the sink as she closed her eyes in remembered pleasure. Darius had removed his shirt as the day warmed and the pale sunlight glistened on his shoulders. Sabrina had forgotten what she'd been doing when he swung the axe. Each motion made the muscles of his back, shoulders, and arms ripple in the light and she damn near swallowed her tongue.

No man should be so beautiful.

The grace and power in his body as he chopped the wood sent juices flooding to her pussy and she'd wished for a moment to see him naked, proudly erect, and hot for her. She had to shove her hands into the snow to keep herself from overheating or reaching out to stroke his back.

You're just overreacting to being celibate for so long.
Still, the rumble of his voice filtering through the house as
he spoke to her daughters before bed sent pleasure skipping
through her. She dried her hands and followed his voice to
Holly's bedroom where he read her a story.

Sabrina paused on the threshold, reluctant to interrupt
the tableau before her. Darius read a llama rhyming book
and Holly giggled in delight at the funny pictures. Sabrina's
heart melted, aching with the wish for his presence to be
reality instead of temporary.

*What's wrong with me? I've never needed a man
before and I won't start now.*

But when he kissed Holly goodnight on her forehead
and tucked the blankets up to her chin, Sabrina's throat
closed and she had to look away before she cried.

"Mommy, Darius read me the Mama Llama book and
he did funny voices."

"Funny voices?" Darius jammed his hands on his hips
and gave her a mock glare. "I'll have you know mah accent
doesna change jest ta please ya." Each new iteration of his
voice sent Holly into fits of giggles and Sabrina chuckled
along with her.

"See? He's funny, Mommy."

"Yes, he is, but looks aren't everything."

Darius gasped in dramatic horror, setting Holly off
again.

"Fine. Perhaps I shall just go chop more wood for the
fire." He raised his chin and stomped toward the doorway,
winking at Sabrina as he passed.

Her face heated and she wondered how he knew what
she'd been thinking of earlier. She sat down on the bed and
kissed her daughter goodnight, tucking the blankets around
her shoulders.

"Mommy?"

"Yes, Holly."

"I like Darius. He's fun." Holly smiled and wiggled deeper into her covers. "I wish he could stay."

Me, too. "I like Darius, too. Get some sleep. I love you."

"Love you, too, Mommy."

Sabrina switched off the lights and closed the door most of the way, her mind churning over her houseguest. *Wishing him to stay is ridiculous. He's a player, a charmer, and temporary.* Reality stuck its barbs firmly into her happy bubble and she retreated to the kitchen to brew some tea. *Maybe an electric tea.*

Darius sat at the table, his hands wrapped around a steaming mug and his expression far away. Sabrina thought she saw sorrow in his eyes, but his face smoothed into a smile when he caught sight of her.

"Are they abed?"

"Yes, finally." Sabrina pointed at the second mug on the table. "Is that for me?"

"Yes, I thought you'd like it." Darius gestured to the chair beside him at the table. "Come sit for awhile, Sabrina."

"Thank you." She took the chair and ran her hands through her hair as she inhaled the sweet scent of peppermint tea. "Peppermint. Perfect for a trying-to-be spring night. And my favorite."

"Is it?" He offered his charming smile. "I've always liked its soothing qualities. I'm glad to know I chose well."

"You've been a great help today. Thanks."

"My pleasure."

"Yeah, right." Sabrina snorted.

"No, truly, Sabrina. I enjoyed decorating with your children and you. It's been a long time since I've prepared for Beltane in such a simple way." When she raised an eyebrow, he added hastily, "I mean not for the Court. Like we used to at my home, with my mother and brothers."

"You have family?" Sabrina sipped her tea and let the

mint soothe her.

Sadness briefly flashed across his face. "I no longer see them very much, but my brother still holds our estates outside of the Fae city of Na'ersindel." He shrugged. "We have drifted apart with the death of my mother several decades ago."

"I'm sorry, Darius."

He dismissed it with a wave. "No matter. It's in the past. Today has been a good day. Thank you for including me."

Sabrina chuckled. "Well, I couldn't exactly exclude you when I didn't feel very well this morning. And there's no way I could've chopped the wood with my head pounding."

"Speaking of which, how are you feeling now?"

"I'm fine. I think the swelling's gone down, too."

"Let me see."

He rose and stepped behind her, his hands sliding over her scalp as he searched for the lump. She hissed when he hit a tender spot and he murmured an apology, tucking her hair behind her ears. She allowed herself to enjoy the tender gesture.

"It is much reduced," he agreed, but remained behind her with his warm hands on her shoulders. "I'm relieved you're all right."

"Me, too." Sabrina closed her eyes as his fingers caressed her shoulder muscles. "Ooohhhh, that feels great."

"Why are your shoulders so stiff, Sabrina?"

"Maybe it's because I'm a single mom in a dead-end job trying to make ends meet and periodically accosted by determined men with conflicting beliefs." She shrugged. "Just a theory, of course."

His seductive chuckle rumbled behind her. "Oh, is that all?"

His understanding of her sarcasm startled a laugh out of her. "Yes, that's all."

Darius gave her one last rub then trailed his fingers over her neck and shoulder as he moved to the counter to grab the teapot. Sabrina suppressed a shiver of pleasure and tried to concentrate on the heat of her mug rather than his hands. *Your focus needs focus.*

"And if you could do anything, Sabrina, what would you do in your dead-end job's stead?" He returned to the table and refilled his mug before sitting down.

"I don't know."

"What?" He raised his eyebrows. "Surely you have dreams and aspirations."

"You mean in a perfect world where dreams come true and happily-ever-after exists?" Sabrina laughed derisively. "There's no such place."

"Come now, don't allow bleak reality to steal your hopes." Darius grasped one hand and stroked the back of it with his thumb. "If you could do anything, what it would be?"

Sabrina sighed and closed her eyes, trying to remember a time when she believed in dreams. *Long before Tommy Two-Faces and Merrilee Fuckstwice.*

"I've always wanted to have an herb garden where I grow my own herbs and brew my own oils, creams, and poultices." She pictured the whole set up in her mind. "I'd set up a shop where I could offer Cloudburst some homeopathic remedies for health and beauty using home-grown ingredients." She bit her lip and opened her eyes. "I know it sounds hokey, but I've always wanted to do it on a larger scale than just for my kids."

Darius grunted with thoughtful appreciation.

"Where would you choose to have this shop? In town?" He sipped his tea, hiding his expression.

"No, there isn't any space for rent and I couldn't afford it anyway."

"Do you have another place in mind?"

She wished she could judge his thoughts, but he gave

nothing away and she hoped he wouldn't laugh at her outright. Sabrina rubbed the handle of her mug.

"There's this old abandoned gold mine on Oro Creek two miles up our road from here. It's got an old mill with a working waterwheel right on the creek." She squirmed in her chair and refused to meet his too discerning eyes. "The bones of the structure are still sound and clearing there has great energy. My girls and I go up there every summer to pick wildflowers and herbs."

"What's stopping you from doing this?"

Sabrina snorted. "You mean other than not having the money to renovate, much less purchase the property?"

He grunted again, but she couldn't decipher the sound. "Why have they called the town Cloudburst if their mine produced gold?"

"The first settlers who came here weren't miners, but families just trying to find a safe place to live. When they first settled, the rain storms here were fantastic, but short. So they called the town Cloudburst for the weather. Later they found gold in them thar hills and named the creek Oro. I don't know what they named the mine."

"Who owns the mill now?"

"I don't know. I'd have to do some research in the town records." A derisive laugh escaped her lips. "What am I talking about? I don't even have the funds to consider buying the land. There's no real point finding out how to purchase it."

"There's always a reason to find out such information, just in case."

"Just in case, what? I win the lottery?" Sabrina laughed again and shook her head. "I can barely make ends meet by working at Mazie's. I can't afford to set money aside to buy land."

"You know, if you do the rituals, you may ask a boon of the Summer Court. Perhaps you could ask for the funding for a land purchase."

Cold horror filled Sabrina's stomach and she swallowed hard. "No way. I'm not taking any favors from the Fae. I've heard the stories of what happens to people who receive the Fae's 'gifts'. You've heard of Rip Van Winkle, right?" She waved her hand over her mug. "No thanks."

"Master Van Winkle irritated the Fae rather than received a boon." Darius gave her a sardonic look.

"Still, I'm okay without any Fae favors." She smothered a yawn with the back of her hand and her head throbbed with the remainder of her concussion. "I think I'm going to go to bed. I'm tired and there's more to do tomorrow."

Sabrina grasped her mug and carried it to the sink. She jumped a little as Darius brought the teapot to the counter beside her.

"How is your head feeling? Any pain?"

"A little, but I'm sure it will be better after I sleep."

He frowned. "Go get ready for bed. I'll turn out the lights and tuck you in."

Sabrina chuckled. "I'm a big girl, Darius. I can tuck myself in."

"I'm sure you can. The Goddess knows you've had no one to offer you such comfort." His smile made her wonder how she'd ever done without someone tucking her in. "Go ready yourself for bed and I shall be there anon."

"Darius…"

"Please, Sabrina." He grasped her shoulders and stared her down. "I just want to be sure your head is on the mend."

She searched his eyes, looking for his motives. Had she heard real pleading in his voice? *Don't be ridiculous. He's just making sure his pet witch isn't going to fall over dead before I do what he wants.* At least he'd been honest with his intentions.

"All right." She almost added he shouldn't get any

funny ideas about crawling into bed with her, but some traitorous portion of her suggested it wouldn't be so bad. *Shut up.*

"Go on. I'll be there in a trice."

Sabrina retreated into her thoughts and her bedroom, wondering when she'd started to like him. When he treated her children with respect? Or helped them prepare for Beltane? Or had he been more subtle, using a small spell to shift her regard?

Ha, fat chance. I'd notice.

She threw her clothes in the laundry hamper and pulled her fleece pjs on just to discourage her traitorous voice. No way he'd be getting any nookie through those babies. By the time she'd settled into the bed, Darius appeared at her door and knocked softly.

"May I come in?"

"Yes, I'm ready for you." *Geez, can I sound any more sexually interested?*

His chuckle told her he'd thought the same thing. "Good. How is your head?"

"It's not pounding, but the headache has settled into the background." She shrugged. "It'll be gone in the morning."

"Let me take a look."

He settled on the bed beside her and reached for her head, his spicy scent enveloping her. She closed her eyes and drank in the heat of his body along with the energy of his presence. Warmth from his fingers digging gently into her hair caressed her face and she fell into it with a sigh. Behind her eyelids he glowed with healthy energy, although the swirls of color moved somewhat sluggishly as if he hadn't reached his full potential.

She'd had this sort of experience before with a few of the people in town. Everyone had a distinct energy signature, but some showed tarnish where their physical or mental health suffered from one malady or another. She'd always been sensitive to those who needed healing, often knowing exactly which herbs or creams to use to relieve the symptoms.

With Darius, it appeared he needed something to invigorate him, but not something physical. From what she'd seen earlier, he hadn't required physical energy. *No, not at all.* Instead, he seemed to need a mental spa day, something to recharge his internal batteries, as if his lifestyle had run him down.

"Are you tired, Darius?" She opened her eyes to scan his face.

"Sorry?" He looked startled. "Tired?"

"Yeah, you know, like you need a break from the stresses of life."

He chuckled, but the warmth had drained from his laugh. "Not at all. Visiting your world is no travail for me."

"Just the difficulties of convincing one stubborn witch."

His eyes smoldered for a moment before he winked. "'Tis a challenge, to be sure, but a welcome one." He frowned. "But I'm afraid my small magics aren't enough to relieve the last of your pain. Perhaps you could help me by augmenting my abilities with your own."

"What?"

"I have a little healing magic, but as you know, most of the Goddess's strengths are passed through the maternal lines." He stroked her hair and she resisted the urge to close her eyes again. "I have more ability than my brothers, but in truth, my magical strengths are greatly reduced by my sex. If you could lend me the energy, I could help you heal yourself."

Sabrina stared with amazement. "Heal myself? I wouldn't even know how."

"That's why we must work together." Again, he stroked her hair. "I know how to direct the healing energy, I just don't have enough of it."

"You want me to give you energy?"

"Yes."

"How?"

He sat back and took her hands, staring into her eyes. "It's a simple enough procedure, but it requires honesty and trust between those transferring energy."

"And I don't know you very well."

"Precisely." Darius nodded with a rueful smile. "However, desire can take the place of trust, at least for short bursts."

"Desire? As in 'sexual' desire?" *Oh, please Goddess, don't let him know I'm remotely interested in him. He'd use it against me.*

His rich laugh flowed over her, warming her as much as his hands. "Much as I'd prefer such desire, this is merely the intention for the transfer to work long enough for your pain to be vanquished."

"Oh. So I have to want it to work bad enough to override the trust issue."

"Yes."

Sabrina mulled the idea over in her mind. "Can I trust you enough not to do damage with the energy I give you, particularly to me?"

She felt the surge of his anger before it suffused his expression, but it cut off as his logic caught up with his emotions. "Ah, you have no reason to trust me, but I might remind you I've helped you heal this head injury for the last few days without your extra energy. And I made the vow to protect you before the Goddess. I don't wish to hurt you, Lady Foxglove. Far from it."

Something about the way he said the last convinced her. More than just the words, her gut told her he meant them with every fiber of his being. *Ha, you're probably just tired and wishing a handsome man like this could truly feel something for you.*

It wouldn't hurt if he did.

"All right. Let's try it so I can get some sleep. What do I need to do?"

"First, close your eyes and try to mesh your energy with mine. I'll be looking to receive you."

"Oh, something easy, then." She snorted as she closed her eyes.

He chuckled. "No more lip, woman. Focus."

Pleasure bloomed through Sabrina's chest at his humor and his energy signature glowed clearly in her mind's eye. It swirled in warm earthen colors: brown, gold, orange, yellow, crimson, and pulsed to the beat of his heart. Her own energy looked bluish-green to her, almost the same color of Darius's eyes. With the recognition of the similarity, her energy surged into him, locking on the gold and yellow swirls until they turned a summer green.

"Holy Goddess!" Darius's exclamation surprised her and she opened her eyes, losing the connection.

"No, no, I'm sorry, Sabrina." He smiled at her with wonder. "It was amazing and so well done. Please, try again."

"Are you sure? I don't want to hurt you or anything."

"No, you were fine. I simply wasn't prepared for the strength of your offering."

"I'm sorry, Darius. I don't know how to dial it back."

"Fear not, I'm ready for you this time. Try again." He squeezed her hands with reassurance.

Sabrina bit her lip, but closed her eyes and reached out with her energy again. This time when the swirls changed color, Darius inhaled sharply but didn't pull away. She tried to modulate the flow of energy to him, but she had no idea if she'd succeeded in stemming the current.

"Well done, Sabrina." Darius placed his hands on her head again and soon the throbbing stopped while her vision filled with green light.

She sighed and relaxed, completely losing grip on her energy flow. The throbbing pain didn't return, but the heat of Darius's hands faded, and she opened her eyes.

"What happened?"

He smiled. "It's done and you should be feeling better. True?"

"Yes, no more pain."

"Excellent." He patted her hand and stood. "Then I shall bid you good night and leave you to rest."

"Thank you, for everything, Darius. I really appreciate it."

He paused on the threshold of her room. "You're welcome. Sleep well, Sabrina."

She belatedly realized she hadn't made up a bed for him. "Where will you sleep?"

"Your divan was very hospitable last night."

"Div—oh, the couch." Why did it seem so gauche? "At least let me get you some blankets." She threw off the covers and pushed her feet out of bed.

"No, no, it's not necessary." He strode back into the room and stopped in front of her. "Please, get back into bed. I'm quite comfortable there."

"But *I'm* not comfortable with you on my couch without any pillows or anything. I have to be the worst hostess ever."

You can always offer him space in your bed.

"I'm perfectly comfortable and I have all the amenities I need."

Darius set his hands on her shoulders, giving her more warmth than she expected. Heat flooded her body and she had the sudden urge to throw her arms around him and lean her head against his chest. Sabrina met his teal gaze and sank into the seductive comfort swirling in his eyes.

He's just playing you. Yeah, I don't care.

"Darius…"

He leaned in and her nipples pebbled with the anticipation of his kiss. But he diverted his motion at the last second to brush his lips against her forehead.

Disappointment surged as he pulled back and gave her a gentle smile.

"Be at ease and rest, Sabrina. I shall see you in the morning."

He left the room without another word, switching off the light as he sailed out the door.

****

Sweet Goddess, I turned her down.

Darius flopped onto the divan and wondered when he'd lost his mind. A beautiful woman had just offered herself to him and he'd walked away. *What's wrong with me?* His cock wanted to know the same information as it throbbed hungrily against his fly. Sabrina made him hard as diamond, but he couldn't take advantage of her after they'd shared her magic.

Even if the Queen suggested I do the same.

Something about using sex to coerce Sabrina into performing the rituals made his stomach churn. She'd been used for sex enough times in her life and he wanted no part in betraying her trust. He'd get her to agree, but he'd do it honestly, through offering his help and being respectful.

This little witch and her charming daughters had gotten to him, filling his heart with real joy and comfort for the first time in decades. He knew his duty and he'd see it done, but he wanted her to perform the rituals because she wanted to, not because he'd demanded it of her. Anything else would brand him lower than pond scum.

Darius turned out the rest of the lights and toed off his boots, before returning to the sofa. He pulled up the blankets and closed his eyes, trying to court sleep. But his mind swirled with the delicate scent of Sabrina's hair and the gloriously sensual touch of her magic when they'd communed.

He hadn't expected her power to be so strong or so

pleasurable. He'd never communed with anyone outside his family before, but her magic had slid over him like a tailored glove, meshing with his own abilities perfectly. He'd only wanted more. His suggestion to try again had been made more from desire than from encouragement.

Even now his cock rose in response to the sensation memory of her glorious energy.

Quiet, you. Go to bed.

He resettled his body against the cushions and closed his eyes, but the arousal followed him down into his dreams. He found himself standing in Sabrina's room beside her bed as she slept. She'd thrown off the covers and lay on her back in nothing more than a gossamer silk nightgown. The finely woven fabric cupped her breasts, offering the barest hints of dark areolas and taut nipples. Another dark smudge marred the cloth at the juncture of her thighs and his cock flexed happily against his trousers.

"Holy Goddess," he whispered. He could no more stop himself from bending to kiss her than he could stop the rain.

Sabrina smiled sleepily and opened her eyes. "Darius."

"Shh. Let me pleasure you, *acushla*." He traced her neck and shoulder with kisses as he slowly pulled aside her nightgown.

When he exposed one full, plump breast to his lips, he sucked the nipple into his mouth, laving it with his tongue. Sabrina moaned and writhed beneath him with sensual, sleep-slowed motions.

"Oh, yes, Darius. Please."

The pleasure in her voice sent blood rushing to his cock, impossibly hardening it more. Her rich taste against his tongue took his breath away and he couldn't get enough of her. He thrust his hand under her gown and stroked the other breast, reveling in the taut nipple against his palm as she gasped.

"Oh, Goddess, that feels wonderful."

Encouraged by her response, Darius released her nipple and gently worked the silk up over her hips to expose her legs and mound. To his delight, she kept it neatly trimmed and short, a perfect triangle pointing to the treasure between her thighs. He watched her hand slide down her body and stroke over the lips of her pussy as if she ached for stimulation. Darius just about swallowed his tongue and he groaned as his cock flexed.

"I want you, Darius." Sabrina's hand swept through her short curls and the scents of sex and aroused woman filled his nose.

"Sweet lady, I'm going to savor your nectar and drink my fill of your cream." He fell head-long into her perfume, pressing his nose into the hot flesh between her legs.

"Oh, my glory..." Sabrina wriggled her hips, spreading her thighs wider to allow him access to inhale her hot, sweet scent.

He'd never smelled anything as exquisite as Sabrina's womanly juices. Her scent varied from sweet to tangy and back, alternately teasing and soothing his palate. He shifted his weight onto his belly and spread her fleshy lips apart with his hands. Her pink pussy glistened in the light of the bedside lamp and wept her juice as he watched.

It was too tempting. He sealed his mouth against her weeping slit and stroked the hot flesh with his tongue. Sabrina wailed with pleasure, her hands grasping his head as her fingers stabbed into his hair. Her soft lips and tight opening caressed his tongue, drawing it deeper into her as he stroked her.

Darius delighted in the sounds she made and the involuntary motions of her body as she succumbed to the pleasure he offered her. He licked her clit, stroking it until it hardened beneath his tongue then sucked it into his mouth, tugging on it. Sabrina keened her approval and her fingers dug into his scalp as she raised her hips, thrusting them imperatively at his face.

"Oh, Goddess! Please, more, Darius, more!"

"Your wish is my command, *acushla*."

Her honey flowed at the sound of his voice and he slowly inserted a finger into her quaking pussy as he sucked on her clit. An earthy groan erupted from her lips at the intrusion and her inner walls tightened around his hand. He teased her by gently tugging his finger out then returning it with measured motions.

Darius increased the pressure of his mouth on her nubbin as he inserted his hand harder and faster. Sabrina whimpered in time with his thrusts, rocking her hips to receive more and more of his attention. Her heady scent intensified as she built her orgasm, the sounds she made increasingly desperate.

"Come for me, *acushla*. Give me your cream."

His voice sent her over and she wailed, tightening on his finger like a vice as she ground her pussy against his face. He lapped up all her sweet nectar, reveling in the delicious flavor filling his mouth as she keened her ecstasy to the stars. He sailed with her, his joy at her pleasure nearly disguising the rising need in his groin. Pride and delight echoed through him as she slowly came down from her high and his rigid cock demanded his attention.

Licking her juices off his lips, he crawled up her body, dragging her nightgown with him until she allowed him to pull it over her head. Darius paused to admire her seductive curves even while his cock pulsed with insistence. Her glorious breasts rested above a generous swell of hip and belly, and he drank in her lush beauty.

"You are lovely, my lady."

Sabrina sighed and gazed at him with languorous eyes, satiation filling her smile. "I'm glad you think so."

"Oh, I'm certain of it."

Her gaze dropped to the front of his trousers and a sultry smile curled her lips. "You seem in need of some relief. Can I help?"

He didn't think he could get more turned on, but her husky voice and mischievous smile pushed him close to the edge. He jerked away and shucked his clothes in record time, not wanting to miss a moment of her silky skin against his.

"Holy Goddess, you're beautiful." Sabrina's soft exclamation warmed the dark corners of his heart as she perused his body with her gaze.

"Perhaps you'd permit me to offer this beauty in exchange for your pleasure." He returned to her on the bed, crawling over her body to settle atop her.

"Wait, what? So I get both the beauty *and* pleasure?" She quirked a brow.

"Oh, very well, if you insist."

Her laughter ended in a low moan as he lavished her throat with licking kisses and worked his raging cockstand against her mound. She shifted beneath him, sending pleasure surging through his body from nuts to nose, and he added his own moan to hers.

"Sweet Goddess, you are magnificent, *acushla.*" Darius dropped his head to suckle her nipples, reveling in the pebbled tips teasing his tongue. Sabrina gasped and writhed harder, making his cock demand relief.

"Darius, I need you."

"Where do you need me, *acushla?*" He gritted his teeth to hold back from thrusting his aching dick into her hot sheath, but he awaited her answer with iron willpower.

"In my pussy. Now!" She emphasized her demand with a thrust of her hips.

Oh, thank the Goddess. "As you wish."

He rocked back, positioned his tight head against her weeping slit, and slid slowly into her. They both moaned long and hard as he came to rest, fully seating himself in her liquid warmth. Flames of pleasure licked from his balls up his spine and he shivered with their searing heat.

"Sweet mercy, you're so damned tight."

Darius dragged his cock out of her warm grip and pushed back in so slowly he thought his head would explode. Her sheath gripped him with erotic contractions, squeezing and releasing his shaft with sensual need. Each pulse left him with less willpower than the last and he felt his control slip, the pleasure swamping him.

"I'm going to fuck you, Sabrina, until you cannot remember anyone else ever giving you such pleasure."

"Oh, Goddess, yes, Darius. Give it to me. Fuck me hard."

Her husky voice blew his control to hell and he surged forward, slamming his cock into her tight pussy. Each thrust dragged his release closer and closer, but he held on, hoping to last long enough for her to reach another orgasm with him.

His demure mother of two became a wanton wench, writhing and demanding more cock from him, and he reveled in it. Darius pounded her hard, building their orgasms with each thrust. Her groans and wails only spurred him on, swamping his mind with delirious bliss until he only had enough sanity to make one last demand.

"Come with me, *acushla!*"

He punctuated his order with a fierce arch of his hips and the pleasure broke over him as Sabrina screamed. A bubble of emotion deeper than lust welled up with his release, cracking the ice around his heart.

"I love you, Sabrina!" His roar accompanied his release, hot jets of cum filling her tightening sheath until he couldn't distinguish where he ended and she began. Stars cascaded behind his tightly closed eyes and he came to land with a soft thump on his back.

What the—

Darius opened his eyes to find himself still dressed, lying tangled in the blankets on the couch. Sticky heat covered his belly and soaked his trousers as he panted with the remnants of the orgasm still thundering through his veins.

A wet dream...

He scrubbed his hands over his face as he tried to gather his wits. Should he be grateful or disappointed he woke up alone? His cock didn't care, now quiescent in his trousers, and he rose to find some way to clean himself. He hoped no one had heard him and he strained his ears for sounds of disturbance among Sabrina's family.

Deep relief followed the sleepy silence of the house and he thanked his lucky stars his confession of love had only happened in his dream. Because it couldn't be true. It was impossible, and saying it aloud would have made it real and binding.

Besides, it's not true.

So why did that statement seem to be the false one?

CHAPTER SEVEN

Sabrina stumbled toward the kitchen the next morning with the intent to make a strong pot of tea, but the sight of Darius asleep on her couch stopped her mid-step. He lay with one arm behind his head and another across his waist, anchoring the blanket to his body. His bare chest rose and fell with his breath and she covered her mouth to keep from drooling.

Men should not *be so gorgeous.*

Her gaze followed the line of hair from between his pectorals down to his belly button and beneath the blanket. She stifled the urge to lift the cloth to see if he lay as naked below as on top and shook her head at her audacity.

Too bad he's not the guy who will be my partner for the rituals.

The thought drew her up short. Since when had she even considered performing the High Beltane rituals? She wouldn't do them ever again. She couldn't.

Despite modern medicine's advancements in birth control, the magic of the High Beltane fertility rituals blew such prevention away. And it would be even more potent with the Summer Court's attendance. *Plus no one would pause to don a condom, and I haven't taken the pill in years.* Her gaze strayed to Darius's glorious chest. *I don't need more children. Even if they're his.*

She took a step closer to the couch, not sure if she just wanted to inhale his scent or touch his handsome chest. Unfortunately, the girls started arguing over who'd get to help make the brownies. Darius blinked awake and Sabrina found herself pinned by his teal gaze.

His lips curled into a sweet, seductive smile, stealing her ability to think or speak or, hell, even breathe. She had the unwanted wish to have him smile at her every morning, but she mentally slapped herself.

Don't be sucked in by his good looks and charm.

But, oh how she wished it to be real.

"Good morning, Sabrina. Did you sleep well?"

Not as well as I would have with you pressed up against my back.

"Yes, thank you. Would you like some breakfast?"

"Certainly." He shifted to sit up then realized he wore nothing and paused, a sultry smile creasing his lips. "Forgive me, my lady. I'd forgotten my state of undress." He wrapped the blanket around his chest as he scanned the floor for his discarded clothes.

"It's okay, Darius. I've seen a naked man before." *Just not one as fine as you.*

"I'm sure, but in light of your children being in the other room…"

"Oh. Right." *Duh! What is wrong with me?* "Let me to get you a robe or towel or something."

"Thank you, that would be very kind. I'll take advantage of your bathing room as well."

The idea of him naked with hot water sluicing down his body made her breasts tingle as her nipples tightened to hard points. *Sweet blessings, I'm so messed up.*

"Yeah, I'll just get one for you." Sabrina retreated to the linen closet to keep her composure intact, but she had to take a few deep breaths to calm herself down.

When she returned with a towel, she almost offered to help him wash his body down, but she slapped her inner trollop and only smiled.

"I'll get breakfast started while you shower."

For a moment it looked as if Darius might say something and hot desire flashed across his face. But he smothered it with a friendly smile and nodded his thanks. Sabrina told herself she wasn't disappointed in the least.

Yeah, right.

Fortunately, the girls provided enough of a distraction for Sabrina to actually make some sort of meal and calm down from the raging lust attacking her usual composure. Darius returned to the kitchen fully dressed and completely unruffled, smoothly greeting her daughters and hearing their plans for the day.

"Mom, can we go roller-skating today? Melanie said her mom would take her. Can we go, too?" Tansy begged with big blue eyes.

"I wanna go, too, Mommy," Holly piped up.

"What about Darius? We can't just leave him here. It would be rude."

"He can come with us. Please?" Tansy grabbed Sabrina's hand and bounced a little.

Sabrina involuntarily sought out Darius's gaze and swallowed hard at the desire suffusing his expression beneath the polite smile.

"Well..."

"Pleeeaasse?" both girls chorused together.

"All right, as long as we get our chores done before we go."

"Aw, Mom—"

"Hey, there's still more things we need to do before Beltane, and tomorrow is a school day." Sabrina admonished her daughters with the 'mommy look' and they sighed theatrically. "Unless you don't want brownies for your class on Tuesday and you don't need hot apple cider and poppyseed cakes for the celebration." She shrugged nonchalantly.

"No, no, we want them," Tansy said quickly.

"Good. Let's get to work, then."

"Can I help with the apple press this time, Mom?" Tansy helped her clear the table of dishes and load them into the dishwasher.

Sorrow bloomed from somewhere deep inside and Sabrina took a fortifying breath. Tommy had always done the press with Tansy and Sabrina had refused to touch it since he'd left. Tansy kept asking each year and Sabrina didn't have the heart to refuse her again.

"I think..."

"I'd be happy to take on the task, Lady Foxglove, if you'd permit me."

Sabrina looked back at Darius as he handed his dishes to Tansy. She hadn't heard him get up from the table.

"Oh, yes. Sure, you could." *At least it would be more fun to watch him pump the crank than Tommy Two-Faces.* Name-calling was beneath her, but it made her feel better. "Thank you."

"It's my pleasure to help with your holiday preparations." He smiled so sincerely she almost believed he had no ulterior motives.

"Yay!" Tansy squealed and launched herself into Darius's arms, startling him. "Thank you. Mom never wants to do it."

"Oh, why not?" He raised an eyebrow at Sabrina and she grimaced.

"'Cause Tommy always did it and she doesn't like to think about him."

"We shall have to make newer and better memories of the apple press so your mother doesn't have to think of anyone but us doing it."

A curious mixture of relief and excitement skittered down Sabrina's back as Darius winked at her over Tansy's head. A wicked part of her whispered, *Can he do it naked? That would wipe out all my previous memories.* She shut the thoughts down before they flooded a blush across her cheeks. She marshaled her youngest daughter into getting dressed and focused on peeling the apples to distract herself.

Now if only those memories could be renewable, year after year.

She tried not to wish for such destructive things, but the insidious hope grew as the day wore on.

****

Darius had never had so much fun with an apple press as he did with Sabrina and her daughters. The little ladies had enough enthusiasm for twenty of his family members. Apple chunks and bits of peel found their way onto every flat surface of the kitchen as well as dotted his arms up to his elbows. Holly's face wore streaks of cinnamon like war paint and Tansy's pigtails hung in clumps from the sweet juice. Everyone laughed and carried on while Sabrina made poppyseed cakes around them.

Darius's belly ached from all the laughter and his heart swelled with the love emanating from this little house in Cloudburst, Colorado. He tried to think of a time when his family had ever been this happy preparing for Beltane, but he'd rarely seen his mother smiling after his father left. Beltane had been a time for stately and reserved celebration of renewal, not this joyous, messy outpouring of laughter. Envy knocked at the door of his heart and he wished he could do this each year with this family, watching as the girls grew into ladies and helping them celebrate.

But he'd be somewhere else, contracting a new witch to serve the Summer Court in rehabilitating some sacred site for the rituals. The idea no longer held the thrill of adventure it once did, and disappointment festered in his gut.

They cleaned up the mess they'd made and Sabrina pronounced it good enough to go to the skating rink. She called Moira to have her car returned and promised to drop her off at the coffee shop on the way to the rink. Darius wasn't sure he wanted to face whatever activity they had in mind, but the girls bounced with excitement as they dressed to go.

"Don't look so worried, Darius. It'll be fine." Sabrina patted his shoulder and smiled.

He scoffed. "I'm not worried."

"Of course." She winked and helped the girls prepare.

When Moira Callahan arrived, she gave Darius an inquiring look as if questioning his continued presence, but she did no more than nod courteously and handed the car keys to Sabrina.

"Feeling better?"

"Yes, much. Thank you for bringing my van, Moira. I really appreciate it."

"It's no problem. Talia says we could close for a week and we'd still be able to offer everyone a Christmas bonus this year." Moira winked. "I told her I'd only be gone an hour or so."

Sabrina laughed and the sound warmed Darius from the inside out. "How were the roads?"

"Good. The sun came out and melted them."

"I hope it stays out long enough to dry them or we'll have black ice."

The ladies murmured in commiseration as they herded the children out to the van he'd seen the first night he met Sabrina. He'd never heard so many female voices talking all at once. He swung his cloak over his shoulders and hoped he could give a credible answer should any question be directed at him in the hubbub.

Fortunately, such an event never came to pass as they dropped Moira off at the Cloudburst. The woman paused long enough to look at him then at Sabrina with speculation, but she merely smiled and said goodbye. Darius hoped she wouldn't meddle in Sabrina's business. He'd seen the look countless times and it usually meant trouble.

Goddess knows I deal with enough meddling busybodies in the Court.

He'd staved off several attempts at trapping him into a marriage of position. More for the lady than for himself. He had no intention being caught by matchmaking humans any more than he did the Elven versions.

His position at Court didn't allow for much of a family life and he'd never found one woman more attractive than any other. They came in such a variety, he thought he'd never get tired of sampling them.

Until now.

Darius watched Sabrina negotiate the van through the streets of the town with confidence and skill despite the pedestrians out braving the sunny but cold weather. The girls chattered about the skating rink with an enthusiasm Darius found endearing. Holly declared herself a warrior princess who would skate to rescue her loved ones while Tansy reminded her she needed a sword to be a warrior.

"Right, Darius?" Tansy eyed him for confirmation.

"The weapon does not make the warrior, Miss Tansy. Some choose to fight with tools other than steel." He smiled at her frown.

"You mean like the guy in Mom's favorite TV show?"

"What?" Darius had never kept up on the myriad forms of human entertainment.

"You know, the show about that guy who saves the world with a paper clip, duct tape, and a pocketknife." Sabrina winked at him in the rear-view mirror. "He generally doesn't kill people and he finds creative solutions to problems using science and knowledge of the natural world. He thinks outside the box."

"Yeah, he's so cool. I wanna be him when I grow up."

"Well, I wanna to be a warrior," Holly said.

"He *is* a warrior," Tansy insisted.

"No, he's not."

"Yes, he is."

"Okay, ladies, let's move on. We're here." Sabrina pulled the van into a large parking lot and found a place to stop. She twisted around and eyed them all with a patented "mommy look." "Now, here's the deal. We're going in there, but you need to be on your best behavior or we'll get back in the van and go home. Got it? No fighting. Are we clear?"

"Yes, Mom." Both girls nodded.

"Good. Let's go, then."

They piled out of the vehicle and Darius inhaled the crisp spring air. The temperature had warmed since he'd arrived, but spring hadn't gotten a foothold yet. Tansy requested to hold his hand as they crossed the gravel lot to the front doors of the skating rink and warmth filled his heart. He'd never had a child interested in spending time with him and he liked the simple joy of it, especially with Sabrina's children.

The scents of fried food and popcorn hit his nose as soon as they stepped inside the large squat building. Laughter and high pitched squealing filled the spaces between the heavy beats of the music playing over the PA system and Sabrina directed them over to a table near a central area. Beyond some half-walls people of all ages swirled more or less gracefully over a flat, glossy wooden floor. All seemed to be wearing ugly heeled boots with a set of four wheels attached.

"Okay, let's go get our skates." Sabrina helped the girls remove their coats and took Holly's hand. "What size do you think you wear now, Holly?"

"Seven."

"C'mon, Darius. I'll show you how to skate." Tansy

grabbed his hand and pulled him toward a counter where a pimple-faced teen set out the tan wheeled boots. "What size are your feet?"

"I'm afraid I don't know, Miss Tansy."

"I bet they're really, really big."

Sabrina looked over her shoulder at them and raised an eyebrow, but said nothing. Darius shrugged and followed them to the counter. While Sabrina paid their entry fee, he helped the girls choose their skates.

Tansy seemed perfectly at ease with the wheeled monstrosities and quickly slipped her feet into them as Sabrina returned to them with an amused smile wreathing her lips. Holly promptly sat down on the floor and pulled off her shoes, but she had trouble keeping the skate close enough to get her foot into it.

"Here, let me help you, Holly."

Sabrina crouched beside Darius as he eyed the plethora of roller skates lined up on the counter. His gut told him these were meant for fun, but they resembled torture devices and he couldn't imagine a reason to wear them.

"What is the purpose of these, pray tell?"

Sabrina laughed. "It's to go as fast as possible around in circles while trying to keep your balance." She grinned. "You're telling me you've never done this before?"

"No." He scowled.

"Mommy, can you tie my skates, please?" Holly raised one foot.

"Sure, honey." Sabrina winked at Darius. "Just put the skates on your feet."

"They look ridiculous."

"Just wait until you're rolling around in circles." Sabrina laughed as he gaped at her in horror. "Don't worry, I'll be with you."

"I'm not sure—"

"Oh, come on. I thought you were a warrior. Warriors accept any challenge."

"Not the stupid ones." His shook his head.

"Stupid warriors or stupid challenges?"

"Challenges."

Sabrina sighed. "Look at it this way. It's an exercise in balance and dexterity. Warriors need practice, right? Think of it like fighting on ice. Your feet will be unstable. Can you keep your balance while rolling, or sliding?" She held up a pair of skates to Darius.

He took the awful beige, heeled shoes and fit them to his feet, trying to ignore the goad to his pride. Scuffs and scars marred the stiff leather. He took better care of his fine leather boots. With the boots laced tight, he stood, testing his balance. His left foot shot out to the right, and his right foot zipped backwards until he damn near dropped to his knees.

"Whoa!" Sabrina grabbed his wrist and provided a steady anchor. "Easy, there, Skippy. I'll help you." She, too, wore skates, and far more effortlessly than he did.

"How are you able to remain still?"

"See the toe rest on the skates?" She tilted one foot up. "I just point my toe down and it keeps me from rolling."

Darius tipped his own foot forward and found he'd stopped rolling. "At least there's something useful."

"See? So let's go have some fun with the kids."

Sabrina pushed off and gently rolled a little way on the muffling carpet. He followed after her, stumbling and skidding with the uneven footing. Ahead, on the smooth wooden floor, children of all ages slid by in smooth glides. *Surely if they can do this, I can.*

"Look, Mom! I'm flying." Sabrina's oldest daughter flew by, her arms extended before her.

"I think you need a cape, Tansy," Sabrina called with smile.

Tansy twirled gracefully, her hands on her hips and skated backwards. "I don't need to have a cape. I already have wings. See?" She flapped her arms up and down as she rolled along.

"You're as fleet as a falcon, Miss Tansy," Darius said. Sabrina arched her brow and smiled at him. "What?"

"That was kindly done." She offered him her hand as she stepped onto the floor.

"She has a strong spirit. Much like you, Sabrina." Surprised pleasure flashed through her expression before she turned her face away. Satisfaction filled his chest when her fingers tightened on his.

****

Skating turned out to be a comedy of errors and Darius found it easiest to watch Sabrina and her children from the edges of the rink. He took pleasure in exchanging the hideous skates for his comfortable boots. *Bloody awful things.* Holly and Tansy were masters at the sport and Darius grudgingly admitted admiration for their coordination. Sabrina floated like an angel across the wooden floor and he caught himself gaping like a fool.

Sabrina's mahogany brown hair waved behind her in a silken tail, a few wisps escaping the band holding it at the nape of her neck. He knew the softness of those tresses and his fingers ached to trail through them again. When had she become more beautiful than most of the Fae lasses with whom he'd dallied? She didn't have their willowy physique, her beauty more grounded in an earthy solidity he preferred. He liked her strength and resourcefulness as well as her unwillingness to bow to every one of his wishes. She represented a challenge and it interested him far more than a biddable female.

Watching her laugh with her children struck a chord in his chest and he rubbed a hand over his heart with a groan. An odd mixture of yearning and hope bloomed inside, followed swiftly by fear and despair. When had he started wanting a family? Why did this little witch affect him so strongly? Her very humanity made it impossible for them to be together. He'd outlive her by centuries—he already had—and he had his duty to the Sidhe Summer Court. He couldn't set it all aside for one human witch.

But the yearning refused to abate when Sabrina and her daughters rolled off the rink's floor, laughing and chattering about how fast they could go. Sabrina's eyes sparkled with love and joy for her children, and Darius wished she'd look at him with such emotions.

Like she did in my dream. He kept strong control over his wayward cock and hoped his expression remained relaxed and pleasant.

"Mom, can we get some hot cocoa and cinnamon buns afterwards?" Tansy looked up hopefully as she worked on removing her skates.

"I don't know."

"Pleeeese?" Holly piped up. She tried to jump up and down, but her skates shot her feet out from under her and she toppled backwards with a frightened squeak.

"Steady, Miss Holly." Darius caught her and cradled her in his arms. A sudden protective instinct gripped him and he squeezed her gently. "It seems wiser to take your skates off first then you may jump."

"Okay. Thank you." Holly's politeness always surprised him. He'd never encountered such good-natured children.

We were never so polite until after Father left.

The old anger tried to rise again, but he stuffed it away. Holly's and Tansy's father had run out on them as well and he'd be damned before he left them in the lurch.

What am I thinking? I won't be here past Beltane. But he wanted to stay for more than just their mother's hot body. He wanted to stay to teach them about… *What? What do you know more than Courtly intrigue and manipulation?* He shoved the snarky voice away. He wanted to stay with Sabrina and help her raise her children.

He had no idea where the certainty came from, but it left a warm spot in his chest and he smiled as he helped Holly sit down. "Would you like some help with your laces?"

"Yes, please."

"Very well. Have you learned to tie them yet?"

"No. Mommy ties them for me 'cause I don't know how."

"Would you like to learn?"

Holly looked at him for a long moment then nodded. "Okay."

"Let's do it using your shoes. Are you right-handed or left?"

"Right." Holly waved her little palm at him.

"Very well. Sit before me and I shall show you how to tie your shoes."

Holly settled between his legs as he leaned around her and showed her how to make a loop and wrap it with the other lace. She focused on his hands and practiced a few times, making messy but functional bows.

"Look, Mommy, I can tie my shoes!" Holly jumped up and pointed her toes at her mother.

"That's wonderful, Holly."

"Darius showed me how." The triumph in Holly's voice delighted him almost as much as the surprised pleasure on Sabrina's face. "Thanks, Darius. I'm gonna get my coat."

He climbed to his feet and brushed off his trousers as Sabrina watched her daughter run off to the table. He liked helping her family, and an fantastic idea took hold in his chest. He wanted to help them more than just for these few days.

Mayhap I should look into the abandoned mine site and see if there's a way to purchase it.

"Thank you."

Darius blinked in surprise. Had she heard his thoughts? "Sorry?"

Sabrina gestured at Holly chattering with her sister as they zipped up their coats. "For teaching Holly how to tie her shoes. I really appreciate it, and so does she. So, thank you."

"My pleasure, Lady Foxglove." Not quite as pleasurable as her gratitude, but close. "I'm happy to help."

She smiled and his heart swelled again, but he resisted the urge to rub his chest. "I'm going to go warm up the car for the drive home."

"Do you wish me to come with you?" He hoped to have more time alone with her.

"No, I can do it. Please watch over the girls. I'll be right back."

"We shall be waiting."

Her grin filled him with satisfaction and he hoped he wouldn't miss it when he left.

CHAPTER EIGHT

Sabrina's breath puffed out in front of her as she hurried across the parking lot. The sun had set while they skated and the air had turned chill. Pleasure and excitement kept the cold at bay as she paused to pull out her keys. Darius's simple acts of kindness were slowly winning her over.

It could all be a ruse.

True, but she'd seen him with the girls when he didn't know she watched and he'd been so attentive and kind. *Now if only he could be so real with me...*

The parking lot echoed with voices of people walking to the skating rink and cars creeping across the gravel. Sabrina misjudged the distance to the door of her van and knocked the keys out of her hand. Grumbling, she crouched to retrieve them then screamed as something crashed into the door above her head. She dropped to the ground and scrambled backwards, bruising her hands on the gravel.

A dark shape spun and lunged after her, tackling her legs. Sabrina shrieked and kicked with all her strength, but whoever held her only tightened his grip. Fear mixed with fury swelled in her gut and she swung one fist at her assailant's head.

He must have seen it coming because he ducked and it bounced harmlessly off his shoulder.

"Let go of me!" Where were all the people she'd heard? Hadn't anyone seen him grab her? "Help! Help!"

"Shut up, you stupid slut." The man slapped her across the face in an effort to quiet her, but she screamed even louder while dizziness made the world wobble.

"Who are you? Leave me alone." Had anyone heard her? *Please, Goddess, send someone.*

"Quiet, bitch! You should be home minding your children."

Something about the voice seemed familiar. She swung her hand at his face again. He dodged and she swept his hat off, exposing his head. The meager street light cast enough of a glow to identify her attacker.

"Marty? What the hell are you doing? Leave me alone, dammit."

Another blow to her head caught her broadside. "Your mouth needs to be beaten out of you by your husband. I'm looking forward to doing the job."

"What are you talking about?" The dizziness had gotten worse and she couldn't find much coordination, but she struggled and shoved at him even as her strength waned. "I don't need a husband."

"Yes, you do. A husband could make sure you're home safe where you belong." He pushed her down to the ground with one hand and tore at her jacket with the other. "You should be looking after the children and taking care of the house, not out flaunting your body like a common harlot."

"Flaunting my body? Are you insane? I just took the kids rollerskating!" She shook her head but the dizziness only worsened. "I don't need a husband." She tried to sit up.

"Yes, you do." Marty slammed her back down just before he found the waistband of her jeans and yanked on them.

"Mommy!"

Tansy's voice made Marty pause and look up, and Sabrina's stomach sank. Her children stood wide-eyed a few feet away and she groaned, trying to get up. A furious roar filled the parking lot and another dark shape slammed into Marty, lifting him up and away. Sabrina lay on the ground, the cold, damp gravel seeping into her head, back, and hips, and tried to make sense of what she heard. Marty cried out in cadence to the meaty thuds as someone beat the living daylights out of him, but she didn't have the energy to look.

"Mommy, Mommy! Wake up, Mommy."

Sabrina opened her eyes to look at her daughters. Both their faces held fear and she tried to smile.

"I'm okay, ladies. Just a little bruised and dizzy." She sat up slowly, hoping the world would stop spinning, and gathered her daughters into her arms. Both started to cry and wrapped their arms around her. "Shh, shh, it's okay. I'm right here." She wished someone could tell *her* everything would be all right as she squeezed her girls.

May Marty Robinson rot in hell for what he did.

Sabrina tried to look for the bastard, but the cars blocked most of her view beyond her daughters' heads. The dizziness made it difficult to keep her eyes open and she closed them, rocking her children gently. Angry and stern voices sounded off in the background, but she just murmured nonsense to her frightened children, and tried to will away some of the developing pain in her head.

Please, Goddess, just get us home safe.

She jumped as another body wrapped itself around her and the girls, and she struggled a little until Darius's familiar scent reached her addled mind.

"Easy, Sabrina, it's me, Darius." He cradled them all in his embrace. "Are you all right?"

Sabrina opened her eyes, but had a hard time focusing. "I'm fine." His lips pursed and she knew she hadn't convinced him, but he didn't gainsay her. "I'm just a little battered and bruised, and I really want to go home."

"Then home we shall go."

"He hit her." Holly's voice held tears and anger.

"Yes, I know, Miss Holly, but I made him stop."

"Why did he do that?" Tansy wiped her tears with the back of her hands.

"It doesn't matter. He won't be doing it ever again." The fury in Darius's voice made Sabrina shiver. "Did you kill him?"

The rumbling chuckle held no humor. "No, but I wanted to. Lt. Fitzroy of the Cloudburst Police arrested him and put him in his car after I subdued him. He will not be seeing you for a long time."

"Good. Never seeing him again would be too soon." She squeezed her daughters once more. "Help me get up and let's go home. I'm done being social."

"Do you need to go to the doctor, Mommy?" Tansy's lower lip trembled, but no more tears fell.

"No, no, honey, I just need to get home."

"Maybe she's right. We could always—"

"No!" Sabrina almost shook her head, but the pain stopped her. "I'm sorry. I didn't mean to snap. I just really want to get home where we'll all be safe."

"I'll keep you safe, Sabrina."

She had her doubts. With his upcoming departure, they'd be in the same boat they'd always been. Her alone and the only defense for her children. She thrust the thought away and leaned on him, taking what she could get.

Somehow, they made it to the van and Holly found the keys in the slushy gravel. Sabrina sighed in gratitude as she settled into the passenger seat while the girls fussed around her, their voices ringing with worry. She wanted to comfort them and tell them everything was all right, but her energy level ebbed low and she couldn't find the words.

"I love you, Mommy." Tansy peered into her face, her

breath puffing the cold interior.

Oh, dammit, I didn't turn the heat on. "I love you, too. Tansy. Don't worry. It will be okay."

"Is Darius gonna take us home, now?"

"I hope so."

"Why aren't you driving, Mommy?" Holly touched her shoulder.

"Because my head hurts. Get clipped in, now."

Darius spoke a short time with Lieutenant Fitzroy then climbed into the driver's seat of the van. Sabrina grasped his arm as he turned the ignition.

"What did he say?"

"Your assailant has been arrested and will be taken to their holding cells. Tomorrow, you'll need to come down to make a statement against him, but tonight I'm taking you home."

"Okay, good. Maybe we can have some hot cocoa when we get there."

"I don't want hot cocoa. I want some tea." Tansy leaned forward and rested her hand on Sabrina's shoulder. Sabrina laid her hand over her daughter's.

"Sounds very good, Miss Tansy." Darius threw the van into gear.

Yes, it does. Sabrina closed her eyes and leaned back against the headrest. Now she just had to make it through Beltane and everything would get back to normal.

****

Darius cursed his clumsiness as he hit another slippery patch in the road and they skidded a little. He had no idea how difficult driving on icy slush could be until now, but he'd be damned before he let Sabrina stay at the roller rink after Marty Robinson attacked her.

Fury flared again and he made sure to slow his motions as they turned a corner onto Sabrina's street. When Darius had seen the bastard on top of Sabrina, he'd thrust the girls at the nearest bystander and launched himself into the fray. He'd been prepared for a real fight, but Marty Robinson had no formal fighting ability and had immediately started whining and crying beneath the force of Darius's blows. *The mewling blighter used his weight and strength against a weaker woman, bullying her.* Darius had only stopped from beating him to a pulp when it became obvious Marty couldn't match his warrior skills. Darius had given him a few injuries of his own. The man would be feeling his decision to attack Sabrina for a long time.

Before he'd let him up, Darius had snarled a warning to leave the Foxgloves alone. He courted Sabrina now and wouldn't tolerate anyone poaching on his turf. She and her daughters were under his protection and if the little puke got anywhere near them, the consequences would be far more dire than just a beating. Marty had whimpered his understanding when Darius shook it out of him.

Fortunately, Lieutenant Henry Fitzroy, an off-duty police officer for Cloudburst, had taken care of the girls while Darius took down Marty. He witnessed the whole event and had no compunction against arresting the stupid bastard. Fitzroy promised to keep an extra eye on the blighter if anyone came to bail him out, but he'd need Sabrina's statement to hold him longer than twenty-four hours. Darius promised to bring her to the station the next day.

Right now, he just wanted to get his family home where they'd be safe.

They are not *my family.* But he wanted them to be. He wanted it more than he wanted anything else in his life. Seeing Sabrina fighting an attacker enraged him beyond reason and he'd damn near killed the man for daring to harm his woman.

Darius gritted his teeth against the furious howl wanting to break loose and slid the ungainly van into its place before Sabrina's garage, praying he wouldn't crash into the door. It took him a moment to figure out how to open the garage, but Tansy pointed to the black box on the sun visor. He thanked her and told her to open the door while he helped her mother inside. Holly raced inside to turn on the lights as Tansy held the door wide, and Darius carefully pulled Sabrina out of the van. She'd fallen asleep and his heart leapt at the idea she may be badly injured.

If she is, I'll kill the bastard before he makes it out of the jail.

Sabrina moaned as he shifted her into his arms and he kissed her forehead.

"Easy, *acushla*, I've got you. We're home and you're safe."

"Head hurts."

"I know. We'll fix it soon."

"Put me to bed?"

"Not right now. I think you have a concussion. Again."

"Why is everyone hitting my head?"

He chuckled at the plaintive tone in her voice. "I don't know, *acushla*, but we have to keep you awake for a short time. How about the divan?"

"The div—Ugh, just call it the couch, ok?"

Darius kissed her forehead again and set her down on the *couch* before he removed her boots and helped her out of her jacket. He dragged the fleece afghan he'd used as a blanket over her and checked her eyes, losing his smile.

"I think you may have avoided another concussion, but we'll have to check after I help the girls with supper."

Sabrina sighed and struggled to get up. "I can do it. Just give me a minute."

"Peace, *acushla*, you need to rest. I'm happy to make the meal. Just rest."

"Wait, you can cook?" She eyed him narrowly. "I thought you had servants for that sort of thing."

"Only when I'm at Court." He winked as he tucked the

blanket around her again. "Stay put. I'll have Tansy bring you some tea."

Sabrina sighed and settled back into the divan, holding her head away from the back. He suspected she had another bump to add to the one she'd gotten at the coffee shop and his anger flared. How dare the little bastard touch Sabrina just because she spurned him? Didn't he know it came down to female choice?

Darius forced himself to calm down as he marshaled the girls into making the evening meal and bring Sabrina tea. Tansy willingly helped, but Holly wanted to stay by her mother's side and Darius couldn't blame her. *I want to stay there, too.* And not only for a single evening.

He refused to examine those thoughts and focused on the girls. Sabrina read them a goodnight story on the couch and his heart clenched while watching the girls snuggle with her. He wanted this, wanted it so much he could barely see straight, but he knew his responsibilities lay elsewhere.

Darius tucked the girls in, but Holly sat up and held his hand for a moment before he could leave her room.

"Are you gonna take care of my mommy?"

"Yes, I am, Miss Holly."

"I mean more than just tonight. She likes you."

Warmth mixed with sadness in his chest. "I like her, too."

"So are you gonna stay for a long time?"

The earnestness in her eyes damn near unmanned him. How could he tell this courageous little girl he'd only stay long enough to convince her mother to protect the world? *Correction: to convince her mother to perform sexual rituals to restore the wards.* Even the description curdled his stomach.

"I'll stay for as long as I can."

She frowned. "That's not very long, is it?"

What could he tell her? "Probably not. I'm sorry."

Holly shook her head. "Don't be sorry, just don't hurt my mommy. I don't like it when she's sad."

"I don't, either." His words rang with so much truth, Holly patted his hand and settled back into her pillow.

"Good. G'night, Darius."

"Good night, sleep tight, Miss Holly."

He returned to the living room where Sabrina diligently sipped her tea, but he saw her head nod as exhaustion stole her energy.

"How are you feeling?" He sat before her and she opened her eyes. Lines of fatigue creased her face and he wished he could take some of it away.

"My head hurts and I'm sleepy."

"Shall we try to take away the pain?" He grasped her hands around her mug and let the heat of them seep into him.

"You mean the whole *merging magics* thing?" He smirked at her dry tone. "Yes, please. I really don't need to feel like I've been hit by a bus tonight."

"Very well. No 'bus-impact' sensations."

Sabrina laughed and some of the sorrow from the conversation with Holly dissipated. "Close your eyes and reach out for me."

The first time they'd tried this, he'd damn near shot straight to orgasm with the power and pleasure of her energy. This time he knew what to expect, but he still moaned when the surge flowed over him. Her magic felt like hot velvet wrapping around him and pushing away any weakness he'd ever experienced. Strength pulsed through him, banishing any aches or pains, and setting his cock on fire. It felt as if someone had wrapped their hand around his dick and stroked softly.

Focus! You're supposed to help her with the pain.

Her discomfort appeared like hole punched in a masonry wall, broken bits of brick and mortar littering the space around it. His skill pertained to removing the shattered bricks, replacing them with whole stones, and filling in the mortar around them. Each time he repaired her wall he found himself drawn deeper into her magic and spirit. He hadn't meant to connect so profoundly, but sharing the magic tightened her grip on his heart.

When the wall appeared whole once more, he "swept" up the broken pieces and "pasted" the excess energy into the "mortar", then withdrew from her energy signature. Part of him didn't want to let such glorious energy go, but he reminded himself he could only borrow it for a time, not keep it.

A soft sigh from Sabrina made his eyes jerk open and he scanned her face for any signs of discomfort. Her expression remained soft and relaxed, and relief poured through him. *Thank the Goddess her pain is gone.*

"Feeling better?"

"Very much, thank you." Sabrina gazed up at him and his cock rose with the heat in her gaze.

Don't be ridiculous. That's your own lust talking.

It didn't stop him from leaning forward and sweeping his lips across hers, nor did it abate the cockstand straining his fly. Even as his mind screamed a warning, Sabrina tilted her head and opened her mouth. If Darius's eyes hadn't been closed they would have rolled back in his head from the pleasure blooming inside him.

She tasted of tea and sweet woman, and he couldn't get enough of her. The warning faded into the background and he gave in to the arousal swamping his mind. Sabrina's answering moan only fueled his desire and he deepened the kiss, stroking her tongue with his.

Darius pushed her down against the flat cushions and covered her body with his. The hard ridge of his cock pressed against her hip and pulses of exquisite pleasure spurred him on. Her woman's scent filled his nose and he couldn't stop tasting her smooth skin and lips. He caressed her breast through her shirt, the taut nipple thrusting up against the cloth.

She tasted better than his fantasies of her suggested and he wanted more. More touch, more kisses, more time. *Please, Goddess, give me more time with her.*

But reality crashed through the arousal as a small voice called from the bedrooms and they both froze. Darius reluctantly let Sabrina up when she pushed against his chest, and the moment disappeared.

Darius rolled onto his back and watched Sabrina attend her daughter, trying to calm his cockstand. How could he let it go so far? He had a job to do and then he'd return to the Court. He shouldn't lead her on or even entertain ideas of permanence. He'd be leaving in a few days.

But what if I don't want to return to Court?

The question both thrilled and scared the hell out of him.

****

Sabrina mentally smacked herself as she tucked Holly back into bed. *Get a grip. He's only here for a few days. Don't get attached!* But the sensation of Darius's lips on hers still fluttered through her head.

You don't want another man in your life. Men leave.

Somehow, her heart remained unconvinced. She returned to the living room where Darius sprawled on the couch and tried to analyze her feelings. Unfortunately, her mind kept replaying the kiss she'd shared with him and like a delicious cookie, she wanted more of it. He lay on his back with his eyes closed and his head supported with one burly arm. She wanted those arms around her, holding her tight.

Stop wishing for things you can't have.

"Thank you for helping me tonight. I really appreciate it."

Darius turned his head and opened his eyes. "You're

106

welcome, Lady Foxglove."

So they were back to being polite. *It's for the best. He's leaving after Beltane.* The reminder didn't settle the yearning.

"How are you feeling? Has the pain abated?"

She ran a careful hand over her skull. "Yes, no lumps this time." She bit her lip. "Darius?"

"Yes?" Those teal eyes stole her sanity, and her nerve.

"I'm going to clean up the kitchen and head to bed. Is there anything you need before I turn in?"

He remained silent so long she had to clench her hands into fists to keep from fidgeting. The expression on his face remained stoic, but his continued regard suggested he sorted through various responses. At last he gave her a half-smile and shook his head.

"I don't need anything, thank you. Let me take care of the mess in the kitchen. You've had a rough day and deserve to rest."

A combination of disappointment and irritation flashed through her. "It's okay. I can take care of my own house."

"Yes, I'm aware you can. But tonight you don't need to. Come. Sit down at the table and I'll bring you a cup of tea." He rose with languid grace and reached for her hands to draw her into the kitchen, but she pulled back.

"Why are you being so helpful?"

Darius paused, frowning. "Why do you ask such a question? Can't friends help friends?"

"Are we friends, Darius?" Sabrina preceded him into the kitchen. "Or am I just a witch you need to get a job done? Is this just more manipulation?" She had to distance herself, no matter how much it hurt.

He sighed. "Sabrina."

"No, just listen to me." She turned on the tap for hot water and leaned over the sink as she gathered her thoughts. "I don't understand your motivations here. You help me heal whenever I get into trouble, you spend time with my girls decorating for Beltane, and you stand up for me against Marty Robinson. Why? Why are you being so nice? What do you get out of it?"

"You think I'm only doing these things for a reward?"

"It's crossed my mind, yes." She filled the basin with soap. "Darius, you're from the Summer Court, and you can't tell me you don't jockey for position to remain within the Queen's good graces. You make calculated moves to get what you want from whomever you need it. What will I owe you at the end of all this?"

His jaw clenched. "Nothing, Sabrina. I'm not expecting you to 'owe' me come the onset of Beltane." He crossed his arms over his chest. "I made no secret I would try to convince you to do the rituals, but I never intended to coerce you through kind actions. I've been happy to help you and your daughters."

"You have helped, and I'm grateful." Sabrina shut off the water and stared at the suds a moment. "But you can't keep fighting my battles for me, or them."

"What do you mean?"

"Marty Robinson is a bother and a prick, but you've now embarrassed him twice, and gotten him arrested once."

"*He* got himself arrested, Sabrina."

"But he won't blame himself or you, Darius. He'll blame me, and I have to live in this town after Beltane."

"He won't be bothering you again."

Sabrina narrowed her eyes. "Why not?" She tipped her head. "What did you do to him?"

"Nothing. He's been arrested and the police are aware of his penchant for violence against you. Plus I informed him if he ever came after you again, I'd personally see to it he paid with more than a beating and incarceration."

"You threatened him?"

"Merely a warning."

"And how are you going to uphold your warning? You're outta here come Thursday."

"Sabrina—"

"No. Look, I appreciate everything you've done for me and the girls." She took a deep breath against the pain arrowing through her heart from the words she needed to say. "But no more saving the day, no more heroics. Let's just get through the week so you can get back to your life and I can get back to mine."

Goddess, it hurt to push him away. It hurt more than when Tommy left with Merrilee. Sabrina turned her head toward the sudsy water and fought back her tears.

Why the hell am I crying? I barely know this man and he can't mean so much to me.

She sniffed hard and wiped a hand across her eyes, leaving a streak of bubbles along one cheek. Before she could brush them away, Darius stood beside her, his hand cradling her face and his thumbs smoothing her skin.

Goddess, why does he have to be so handsome and kind? He used to be arrogant. What happened to that guy?

****

Darius swore someone had stabbed him in the chest with the pain radiating from his heart. Not only had her words struck him, but her tears buried the blade deep. Everything within him cried out to make her stop crying, to ease her pain, to soothe her hurt.

Even if he was the source of it.

"Please, *acushla*, don't cry."

Sabrina sniffed mightily and closed her eyes. "What does that mean?"

"What?"

"*Acushla*. You keep calling me that. What does it mean?"

Surprise hit him. How long had he been using the endearment? "It means 'dear heart' in Gaelic."

She sniffed again. "Ah. I suppose you use it as part of

your arsenal to seduce women to do your bidding."

Anger replaced the surprise, but he beat it back. "No. Actually, I've never called anyone *acushla* before." But her accusation didn't stray far from the truth. "You're the first."

"Oh, come on." She scanned his face. "Really?"

"Really." He'd never let anyone as close as Sabrina had come. Close enough to question whether he really wanted to continue being the Chamberlain for the Summer Court.

She studied his expression for a long time, each breath brushing softly against his lips and enticing him to kiss away her doubt. He wanted this woman, wanted her bad enough he waited for her to come to grips with what needed to be done rather than push her.

I'm a fool.

"I can't do the rituals, Darius. I already told you why."

He gritted his teeth and pushed his frustration down. The Summer Queen had insisted on Sabrina and her little town, but she still refused to step up to her responsibilities. *Well, not entirely.* She did have two little girls from the last two times she'd done the rituals. *And no man to help her with them.* Goddess, he wished he could be her man.

"A child is a blessing—"

"Says the man who loves 'em and leaves 'em." Sabrina pulled away and plunged her hands into the soapy water. "No, not this time. It's been too long and I don't need more children to raise by myself."

He couldn't deny the possibility of her becoming pregnant. He wracked his memory to find leverage to convince her.

"You are the only one strong enough to do them properly and the Summer Queen has requested you personally." Darius wished he could choose someone else, if only to spare them both some hurt, but the Fae Queen had made her decree. Sabrina Foxglove must do the rituals.

Unfortunately, it had to be her choice. *It's always female choice.*

"Why, Darius? Why has she requested me? She doesn't even know me."

"Theirs is not to reason why. Theirs is but—"

"To do and die. I know the quote. But I'm not blindly following orders."

He sighed. "I suspect she chose you, Sabrina, because she knows of your strength and persistence despite adversity. The sacred site needs your strong magic to protect it from the encroaching destruction."

"Now you're just trying to butter me up."

He paused to gauge her response. Then he did something he'd never done before with anyone.

"Is it working?" He offered her a cheeky grin.

She laughed ruefully. "Maybe a little."

"Sabrina, I know we're asking a lot of you, especially when you find yourself as a single mother. But the sacred site here in Cloudburst needs you and your magic. Both you and it will benefit from your performing the rituals." He rubbed her back in little circles, trying to convey his earnestness. "I suspect once you do the rituals, you'll be far too strong for even Marty Robinson to trifle with you."

"Ha!" She snorted derisively. "He knows where we live and where I work. I doubt it will keep him away."

Fury fired his blood at the thought of Marty Robinson coming anywhere near Sabrina. After Darius's warning, he'd be a fool to make such a move, but Darius wouldn't put it past him.

"Perhaps you need a new place to live and work."

"Ch-yeah. Not likely on Mazie's wages."

"What about your herbal shop?" He kept rubbing her back, unable to resist touching her.

She sighed and paused in her dish washing to close her eyes. "Where would I get the capital to start it? I can't even afford to buy the place I want, much less the time to prepare everything to start selling to make enough to survive." Sabrina shook her head and opened her eyes. "It's a dream, but nothing more substantial right now."

He didn't like the sound of defeat in her voice, but he said nothing. His mind had already started working on a solution to her problem. She simply needed the location and the help to get her business started. Then she'd be able to carry on by herself, even after he left.

Certainly, the Summer Queen would grant Sabrina a boon. *Or me, if she won't ask for it.* He'd make sure Sabrina got her mill and started her shop. Any other solution struck him as heartless as the man who'd left her with two children to raise on her own.

They finished the dishes together in silence and Sabrina wished him a pleasant night, but Darius knew his night would be lonely without her fiery kisses. It didn't matter. He'd be leaving in a few days, but he could still dream of her. And decide what gifts he could leave behind.

CHAPTER NINE

The clatter of female voices woke Darius with a start and he jerked upright, tense for evasive action.

"Holly, get dressed!"

"Working on it, Mom."

"Tansy, do you have a snack in your backpack?"

"Yes, but I can't find my water bottle."

"Did you look in the dish drainer?"

"G'morning, Darius." Tansy waved as she trotted into the kitchen.

"Morning." He scrubbed his face with his hands as he realized the house wouldn't come down around his ears. "What all is going on?"

"It's Monday. Time to go to school." Tansy waved her water bottle. "Found it, Mom!" She grinned at him. "Didn't you go to school?"

It'd been centuries since he'd been in school and he'd forgotten the hurry of getting a family on the move. He gave her an enigmatic smile and rubbed his chin again. Damn, he needed a shave.

"Did you fill your bottle, Tansy?" Sabrina asked as she entered the room. "Oh, good. Now get some breakfast. We have to get going soon. Holly, you better be dressed."

"Working on it, Mom."

"Ugh." Sabrina paused and raised an eyebrow at him. "What?"

Darius realized he'd been caught staring, but her beauty caught him completely by surprise. She'd donned a wine colored V-neck sweater and long, black skirt, neither of which did anything to hide her curves. The skirt flared at her hips and swirled around black leather boots. He'd been caught imagining what she'd look like gliding around the Queen's ball room, the skirt swinging each time she turned.

His cock hardened and he bunched the blanket over his lap.

"Nothing, Sabrina. You look lovely this morning."

She snorted and shook her head. "I left towels in my bathroom if you want to take a shower. The girls' bath needs a good cleaning. But hurry. We need to leave in twenty minutes if I'm going to get Tansy to school and give the police my statement before work."

She swirled away from him, shouting for Holly, and he could barely find a coherent thought as her backside flexed beneath the rippling fabric. Darius wished he could get his hands on her ass, hold it tight as he pumped into her slick pussy. *This is not helping my cockstand!* He cleared his throat and searched for his pants for the trip to the bathing room.

He hurried through his ablutions and tried not to enjoy the scent of her shampoo in his own hair as he dressed and returned to the kitchen. Holly brushed her hair, Tansy packed her bag, and Sabrina ran over the instructions with Matilda. Darius looked for a cup of tea, but he'd barely taken a sip when Sabrina pointed at him.

"What will you do after we go to the police station? Do you need me to bring you back here?"

"It's not necessary, Lady Foxglove." He gave them a vague smile. He didn't think he could stand to be in the same room with Matilda after the evening he'd spent listening to her swear to God every other sentence. "I shall find my own way back."

Sabrina raised an eyebrow. "It's a long way to walk, Darius."

"Worry not, lady. I shall meet you at the school when Miss Tansy gets out."

"All right." Sabrina didn't look convinced but she returned to going over the requirements for the day with Holly.

Darius hustled Tansy into the van while Sabrina kissed Holly goodbye and reminded her to listen to Matilda. Darius wondered how long the child would obey, but he wisely kept his mouth shut and helped Tansy get "clipped in." Sabrina joined them and they drove off to Tansy's school. Tansy chattered the whole way, reminding her mother about the brownies she promised to bake.

"I know, Tansy. They'll get done." Sabrina's voice sounded tired and he wondered if she'd slept well.

"Mom?"

"Yes, Tansy?"

"What was Mr. Robinson doing last night?"

Darius's anger rose at the sound of the solemnity in Tansy's voice and Sabrina's shoulders drooped. He still wanted to beat Marty Robinson all over again for causing such loss of innocence.

"Mr. Robinson was…" Sabrina cleared her throat. "What do you think he was doing, honey?"

"He looked like he was really mad at you, Mom."

"I think he was."

"Why?"

"He has strange ideas of what makes a family and he thinks I'm doing it wrong." Sabrina shrugged, but Darius could see the tension around her mouth as she pulled into the school driveway. "But don't worry. The police took care of him and he won't be bothering us anymore."

"I don't like him. He's mean."

"Don't worry about him. You just head on to class. I love you, Tansy."

"I love you, too, Mom."

Darius's throat closed as Sabrina hugged her daughter, squeezing her eyes tight. She kissed Tansy on the head and sent her off to the kindergarten teacher waiting at the door. Tansy waved and ducked inside, but Darius caught Sabrina wiping a tear from her cheek and his gut clenched.

"Don't cry, *acushla*. She will be fine, and Mr. Robinson is no longer a threat to any of you." He brushed her cheek with the back of his fingers.

"I know, but I'm just so furious at him." Sabrina thumped the steering wheel with her hands. "How dare he frighten my children? I hope the bastard rots in jail for a long time. He stole their innocence."

Darius wanted to make him pay with more than incarceration for such an action, but he had little influence in this town or world. He had to abide by their rules.

A tense silence filled the ride to the police station and Sabrina's ire mounted as they parked in the parking lot beside the police cruisers. She didn't say a word, but energy crackled off her like little sparks and Darius wondered if the whole world could see what he did.

"Are you all right, Sabrina?"

"I'm fine. Let's get this over with."

Darius followed her into the building and the officer greeting people directed her to Lt. Henry Fitzroy's office. The balding man offered them each a chair and settled his glasses a little more comfortably on his nose before fixing Sabrina with a piercing stare.

"Can I offer you some tea, Ms. Foxglove?" He gestured to his little coffee maker in the corner, steaming gently in the cooler air.

"No, thank you, Lieutenant. Can we just do what we need to and move on? I need to get to work."

"Of course." Fitzroy ran a hand over his balding pate

and rose. "Let me just pour some tea for myself and we'll get started. Mr. Winterbourne, would you care for some?"

"No, thank you."

Fitzroy nodded and poured some fragrant tea into stained coffee mug before returning to his desk. He set the mug farther away from himself than strictly necessary for easy consumption, and pulled out a form from his desk drawer.

"Okay, Ms. Foxglove. Let's go over what happened last night. Where did everything start?"

"I left the skating rink to start my van before we loaded up to go home."

Fitzroy wrote swiftly on the sheet. "Um-hm, and then what?"

Sabrina recited the tale of Mr. Robinson's attack on her and Darius held his fury in check. *You can't pummel him any more than you already have.* He still wanted to hit the little prick again. By the end of the recitation, Sabrina's anger shimmered in the air above her head like a halo, but she appeared remarkably calm.

Lieutenant Fitzroy wrote everything down in a concise hand and asked clarifying questions occasionally, but his own energy remained steady. Darius sensed this man had abilities beyond those of the regular population, but he appeared to use them in subtle ways.

"That's all I can remember before Darius pulled Mr. Robinson off me." Sabrina clenched her fists in her lap and stared at a point beyond Fitzroy's shoulder. An angry tear slid down one cheek, but she showed no other sign of her frustration. Darius ached to wrap her in his arms and hold her against his chest, but he didn't want to assume he'd be welcome.

"All right." Fitzroy read over the form then handed it to Sabrina. "Read this and check for any mistakes. If there are none, sign and date at the bottom."

Sabrina scanned the document and signed it. "What

will happen to Mr. Robinson?"

"Right now he's been booked on aggravated assault and his hearing is scheduled for this afternoon."

"Do I have to be there? I have to work."

"No, ma'am. We have your signed statement. It will be enough, plus there was a witness to back up your story."

"Who witnessed it?"

"Me."

Sabrina paused, her eyes narrowing. "How long did you watch before you did anything about it, Lieutenant?"

Anger tightened her shoulders, but Fitzroy gave her a faint smile. "I got there the same time as Mr. Winterbourne. He moved faster than I did."

Sabrina's gaze to Darius and some of the anger faded. "Thank you, Mr. Winterbourne."

"You're welcome." And he'd do it again, anytime she became threatened.

Except I won't be here after Beltane.

Darius suppressed a growl and swore he'd find a way to help Sabrina long after he'd gone.

"Thank you for coming in, Ms. Foxglove."

Sabrina nodded. "Just as long as Marty Robinson stays away from me and my children. He's obsessed with me being a stay-at-home mom. I don't know what his issue is, but he seems to think I need a husband."

Fitzroy snorted. "A woman needs a husband like a man needs a wife."

When Sabrina raised her eyebrows at him, he raised his left hand. "No ring, Ms. Foxglove."

She snorted and gave a sharp nod.

"Thank you for your help, Lieutenant Fitzroy." Darius reached out to shake his hand. "If you have a moment, sir, I'd appreciate some information after I bid my lady farewell for the day."

"I have some time."

"Excellent. Thank you, sir."

Darius escorted Sabrina out to her van as she shot curious looks at him, but he said nothing until they'd reached her vehicle. He'd be damned before he let her go out alone. It irked him he had to let her go to work by herself, but it couldn't be helped. He had errands to run before he met up with her again.

"Are you sure you're going to be okay? I can drop you somewhere on my way to Mazie's."

"No, I'll be fine, Lady Foxglove. Just keep yourself safe and I shall see you at the school when Tansy is released." He brought her hand to his lips and kissed her knuckles. "Be safe, my lady."

Her breath hitched and two spots of rose lit her cheeks as she climbed into the driver's seat. Darius hoped she enjoyed his kiss, but she only nodded and closed the door before driving away. He watched the van depart, wishing he could go with her. He'd stand guard over her if he could, but he suspected she wanted that less than she wanted to be alone. He shook off the odd urge and returned to the police station.

Lt. Fitzroy sat where Darius had left him, but he spoke with a tall man with silver hair cut close to his head. A whiskey colored gaze flashed to Darius, but the tall man nodded to Fitzroy and left through a side door. Darius sensed strength and power from him, more power than even the Elves displayed, but no evil. Again he wondered at Fitzroy's background.

"Come in, Mr. Winterbourne. What did you want to talk to me about?"

Darius returned to the chair he'd left a few minutes before and cleared his throat. "Sabrina Foxglove and her safety."

"Don't worry. Robinson isn't going anywhere, and even if he does manage to secure bail, I have some of my best people keeping an eye on him and his cronies." Fitzroy sat back in his chair. "Which makes me wonder what your connection to Ms. Foxglove is. How are you involved in her troubles?"

Darius raised his hands. "I'm not, really. I'm just visiting her for the Beltane holiday and then I shall return home." He shrugged though his heart sank with the idea. "Did she tell you this was the second time Robinson attempted to harm her?"

"She did. She also said you stopped the first assault as well." Fitzroy fixed him with a piercing stare drilling all the way to Darius's bones. "What are you really doing here?"

"I'm here to help Sabrina Foxglove celebrate the holy holiday of Beltane and make certain she'll be safe after I leave." Darius met Fitzroy's gaze and squared his shoulders. "Which is why I wanted to speak to you. Are you aware of an abandoned mine site on Oro Creek?"

"I know of several. Which one are you interested in and why?"

"I believe it has a waterwheel and a mill along the creek. I've never seen it, but Ms. Foxglove has spoken highly of it recently and I'm curious if it's for sale."

"Waterwheel…I think that's the old Miller homestead." Fitzroy rubbed his chin. "I don't think it's for sale, per se. The land went back to the town of Cloudburst." He glanced up at Darius as he typed something into his computer. "Why do you want to buy it?"

Darius bit back a retort. This man kept the peace in Cloudburst and had no reason to trust Darius. "I want to make certain Ms. Foxglove is safe and has a home she loves. She has spoken to me of this place many times and has hopes of starting her own herbal shop there. I want to offer her the opportunity."

"So, you'd be buying it for her?"

"That's correct."

Fitzroy glanced at the computer monitor then back at Darius, the silence stretching as he rested his hands on the desk. Then he rose and closed the office doors before returning to his chair and leaning his elbows on the desk. "It's my job in more ways than one to make sure this town is safe, Mr. Winterbourne. I've been doing it for a long time and while I'm not as jaded as most small town cops, I still get a hinky feeling when one of my residents keeps getting saved from assaults by a stranger who just *happens* to be in town at the time." He raised his eyebrows and spread his hands. "Now this stranger wants to buy land for the same resident he's rescuing, and *that* land just happens to be the site of some very powerful energies. Energies I suspect you're all too familiar with. So give me a reason not to be suspicious."

Darius stared at the cop and had his own suspicions. *Could Sabrina's dream homestead actually be the sacred site where the rituals must be performed?* It made an ironic sort of sense. What better place for a powerful witch to live than on the sacred site she was meant to protect? Darius chuckled at the Goddess's subtlety.

"Something funny?"

"Just ironic. Are you aware Sabrina Foxglove is a witch of considerable ability?"

"I am."

"Then you must understand how important the Beltane holiday is to those who care for the Goddess's sacred sites. Each site must be periodically protected by renewing the wards and cleansing the energies therein." Darius spread his hands. "That is why I'm here. To help Ms. Foxglove with the rituals surrounding Beltane and secure the protections of the sacred site here in Cloudburst. I suspect the Miller homestead may well be the site where the rituals are to be performed." He crossed his arms over his chest. "In which case, it seems fitting for the witch who does the rituals to also reside there and continue to reinforce the wards surrounding it."

Fitzroy tilted his head, rubbing his chin. "As I recall, Beltane is also a fertility ritual, a renewal of life, not just

121

protections. And to do the full rituals, there must be two people to perform them, the male and female aspects of the divine." The cop paused, his gaze thoughtful. "Are you to be her partner in this ritual, Mr. Winterbourne?"

Darius gaped at Fitzroy, his gut dancing. Partner Sabrina in the High Beltane rituals? *That's absurd.* As the Queen's Chamberlain, the task of arranging the witch to perform the rituals had always fallen to him, but another man was chosen as the May Lord. He'd never wanted the part. And yet he couldn't deny he'd delight in the opportunity to bring Sabrina pleasure in the name of the Goddess.

I'm over two centuries in age and must return to my position as Chamberlain for the Court. And Sabrina deserved someone who would stay with her forever and help her raise the child bound to be conceived. Why then did he want to be that man more than anything else?

He gave a deprecating laugh. "No, Lieutenant. I'm only here to help her master the rituals and the energies associated with them. A suitable male has already been chosen."

"Tommy Hawthorne?" Fitzroy's voice held a sharp edge.

Darius frowned. "No. Who is Tommy Hawthorne?"

Fitzroy shrugged. "A local man who claims to be part of the regional Coven. I suspect the man has more interest in the rituals than actual ability."

"Was this man involved with Ms. Foxglove at any time?"

The corner of Fitzroy's mouth quirked in a small smile. "Several years ago."

"Is he the derelict father of her two children?"

"Could be." Fitzroy nodded slowly, but his expression closed. "Well, if you're really interested in buying the land, you'll need to stop by the town hall and talk to the clerk. They should be able to direct you." Again, he eyed Darius.

"Are you sure this is what you need to do for Ms. Foxglove?"

"Of course." Darius rose and held out his hand. "Thank you for your help, Lieutenant."

"You're welcome, Mr. Winterbourne." Fitzroy shook his hand then released him. "Good luck."

"Sorry?"

But the Lieutenant had already turned back to the pile of paperwork on his desk and picked up his phone handset. Darius took his cue to leave, but he wondered what the man had meant. He'd give Sabrina a place to make her livelihood and let her go. Simple. Easy. Right?

He found the town hall and the clerk, but locating the parcel he wanted took some time. Apparently it had been patented under the name the Copper Queen Mine and Mill, and equated to roughly forty five acres of actual land. The selling price seemed ridiculously cheap for such a sacred site. The humans' attachment to electronics and technology made purchasing the land tricky, especially with his small ability at magic. The trick was to charm the clerk and make the little ones and zeroes line up just right to show the transaction. The actual gold would arrive at a later date. Darius made sure the title to the land stated Sabrina's name and left the town hall with satisfaction curling through his chest.

She'll be safe and the site will be protected. And he'd be back to his life.

A life of fake smiles, jockeying for position, and stilted courtly manners. A life of worrying about whether or not he and his family had the Queen's favor. Darius drew his cloak tighter around him to keep out the bitter spring wind, and the bitter truth. His life had never seemed empty. There'd been a time when he'd enjoyed the pageantry of the Court, the honor of the position, and the influence he wielded within the Queen's realm. Hell, he'd even enjoyed winning the Queen's favor over his elder and pompous brother. He'd reveled in being the best Chamberlain the Court had seen in millennia.

And enjoying the fruits of the witches' gratitude hadn't been bad, either.

But now, it all seemed like empty nonsense after spending time with the Foxgloves. His mind filled with the warmth of Sabrina's kitchen and he pictured laughing with her daughters over holiday meals, sharing mulled wine with Sabrina before a cheery fire, and sharing even more with her after the girls had gone to bed.

Suddenly, his Court life appeared like a shabby façade in comparison to the richness he'd found in the Foxglove home. Fatigue hit him squarely between the shoulder blades and he stopped in the middle of the sidewalk, his chest tight. He was tired of fighting for his position and always kowtowing to the Summer Queen's ephemeral whims.

Bloody hell, how long do I have to do this?

It'd already been nearly two centuries. Dear Goddess, it seemed like a long time. And how much longer would he continue?

What would happen if I walked away?

Nothing. Not really, but duty and honor would be lost, two things his family held dear. Somehow, they'd lost their glossy finish and felt more like shackles attached to his ankles.

The back of his neck prickled and he rubbed it, groaning. A summoning from the Queen. Just what he needed when questioning his duty. He scanned the street ahead and grimaced. Too many people wandered along the slushy sidewalks. He couldn't make a crossing where someone would question his abrupt disappearance. Goddess knew he didn't want the Lieutenant to ask any more questions about his origins.

Darius trotted across the street through the light traffic and ducked into an alleyway between buildings, trying not to breathe in too much of the wet garbage stench. He waited a few heartbeats for the pedestrians to clear before giving into the summoning magic.

His cheeks tingled with the abrupt change in temperature and he sweated under his thick cloak. The Summer Court remained at summer temperatures with no regard for spring in Colorado. The Court solidified around him and he bowed low as the Queen approached him with another lady in tow.

Today she wore a summer green dress with leaf fringed hemline and an asymmetrical cream stripe across the bodice and skirt. Gold embroidery etched swirling designs over it all as she advanced, her bearing as regal as ever. But Darius found her beauty cold and mercurial, and he longed to return to Sabrina's earthy warmth.

Get your mind in the game. Never show weakness before the Queen.

"Ah, be welcome in our Court, Chamberlain Winterbourne. I trust your recent endeavors have been fruitful." Though the Queen's expression remained inquiring, the words disguised an order.

Darius inclined his head. "Yes, Your Majesty. To some extent."

"To some extent?" She didn't frown, but her voice sharpened.

"Yes, Your Majesty." He hesitated as he noticed the other lady hovering beside the Queen, and his stomach sank. "Good day, Lady Winterbourne."

"Good day, Darius." His brother's wife curtsied dutifully, but dislike erupted in her eyes and his gut churned. The Queen rarely invited his family to Court, but his sister-by-law ached to attend and never declined an invitation. "I see you're well."

"Yes, lady, I am."

"It's been a while since you've stopped by Cairnwell to see us." She pouted prettily, but disgust rose in his chest.

125

He'd never liked his brother's wife, and she'd made no secret she thought the Chamberlain position wasted on him instead of her husband.

"Forgive me, my lady. Her Majesty the Queen has set me many tasks that require my attention and I often cannot get away." He gave her his courtly smile as anger churned. She had no interest in his visiting her husband. Darius suspected she'd just as soon prefer him dead so his brother might take his position at Court. "Perhaps there will be time when this current task has concluded."

Lady Winterbourne returned his smile. "That would be lovely. I know Tiberius would like to see you."

Given their last interaction, Darius doubted her words, but he nodded graciously. Tiberius hadn't wanted Darius's position until after their mother's funeral, and Darius suspected his wife had goaded him into it. At the time, Darius had laughed at his brother, knowing his place secure as long as he did his duty to the Queen. Chamberlains were appointed, not inherited. But now he wondered if his brother and sister-by-law might be better suited for the Court antics. Such games had grown wearisome to him.

"Of course. I shall make a note to visit when my duties are concluded." If luck followed him, he might not have to return to the Fae world at all. He wanted out of this cutthroat game, and never more so than now. He just had to find an honorable way to end it.

"Excellent. I shall inform him of your intent. No doubt he'll be overjoyed."

Or sickened and resigned.

"Thank you, my lady." Darius inclined his head, dismissing her. "Forgive me once more, but I must finish reporting to Her Majesty on Court business. If you'll excuse us?"

Thunderclouds of ire brewed in her eyes, but Lady Winterbourne curtsied to him and the Queen, and took her leave. Darius had never been so grateful to see a woman's back in his life.

Her Majesty ignored the Lady and looped her arm through Darius's as she steered him into her private salon and bid the guards to shut everyone else out. She released him as soon as the doors closed and strode to a comfortable chair set beside an arched stained-glass window. She smiled with beguiling friendliness, broadcasting gracious warmth as she settled.

"Please, Chamberlain, tell Us how your task has progressed 'to some extent'." She gestured to a chair and he sat, sweeping his cloak out of the way.

"I have secured the sacred site and have tested the witch's abilities. She is as powerful as you surmised." The Queen's expression remained serene, but she waited for him to continue. "Unfortunately, there have been some complications in an attacker who keeps coming after her. I've neutralized him, but she has sustained some injuries to her person."

Her Majesty didn't bother with the false compassion. "You said this at our last meeting. Does this woman attract trouble, Chamberlain?"

"I don't believe so, Your Majesty, but there is one man determined to see her harmed and he has interrupted my efforts. I've done my best to repair any damage his interference has caused."

"Excellent." The Queen smiled and Darius noted how cold and practiced it seemed compared to Sabrina's easy grins. "So, she has agreed to do the rituals, then."

"Not exactly, Your Majesty."

The smile disappeared so fast he wondered if he'd seen it at all.

"Explain yourself, Chamberlain. We made it abundantly clear this location and witch are needed for the High Beltane rituals. There can be no other. Why is there this hesitation?"

For the first time in his long career as Chamberlain to

the Summer Court, Darius didn't want to placate her. He had the dangerous urge to tell the Queen Sabrina held no interest in the rituals and had enough going on in her life without the Court's intrusion. But good sense and self-preservation prevailed and he inclined his head to Her Majesty.

Goddess, I'm so tired of this game.

"Yes, Your Majesty. I believe we've reached a turning point. It won't be long now. I suspect I will secure her agreement this night, and we shall have the sacred site prepared for your arrival."

The Queen stared at him with thoughtful eyes, but her expression remained serene. Darius had the sinking feeling the other shoe was about to drop.

"See that you do, Chamberlain, or the consequences will be dire." She rose from her seat and turned, raising her chin and looking down her nose at him. "You must convince her to do the rituals or you will lose not only your position in our Court, but also your longevity, your honor, and your sword, which your family prizes so. In addition, the Winterbourne name shall be stricken from our records, and your family shall be banned at Court."

Darius's gut churned and he clenched his jaw. How dare she take everything he held dear from him over another's choice? He'd been nothing but loyal and diligent for all his centuries of service. He'd never considered the Queen banishing his family from her Court over his failure to convince Sabrina. As much as he didn't like his brother's actions and his sister-by-law's covetous nature, he couldn't destroy their hopes. The Court meant everything to them, as it had meant to him once, and he couldn't take it from them.

But he couldn't coerce Sabrina into performing the rituals, either. She'd never forgive him, and he'd never forgive himself.

"I understand, Your Majesty." He bowed to hide his

frustration.

"Ah, Darius." The Queen laid an elegant hand against his arm and he carefully met her eyes, hoping he presented her with an emotionless face. "Perhaps this will sweeten the task for you." She smiled at him and his blood froze with premonition. "We would like you to partner with the witch for the sacred Beltane rituals. As a reward for all your hard work, you have been chosen as the May Lord to honor the Goddess."

Damn, did she overhear the conversation with Lt. Fitzroy? A surge of mixed emotions shot through him. On the one hand, he'd get the opportunity to touch and enjoy Sabrina's glorious body, sinking his cock into her sweet earthen heat. All in the name of the Goddess. But at what price? He'd live up to her fears to save his position and his family's standing at Court. Sabrina would be left to raise his child while he played the endless Court games in a life of empty smiles and gestures.

You'd be as bad as Tommy Hawthorne.

"Thank you, Your Majesty."

The Queen gifted him with a brilliant smile and the strength of her magic flowed over him. But he remained unaffected, the magic sliding away into the air. Her smile did nothing to reassure him and he wondered if the connection he had with Sabrina had rendered him immune to Fae charms.

"It is truly my pleasure to see my favorite Chamberlain rewarded, and perhaps we will further reward you with increased invitations of your family to our Court." Amusement flickered across her face as he gritted his teeth. "I understand they would like to see you."

Not bloody likely. But familial squabbles needed no airing, especially to the Queen.

"So it seems, Your Majesty. I do know my sister-by-law prefers the Court to the country estates."

"And you, Darius? Where does your heart lie?"

Darius stilled. Did the Queen suspect he no longer had the taste for intrigue and Courtly games? "My heart lies in my duty to my Queen, and to the honor of my family."

She nodded, a wise smile curling her lips, and Darius hoped she would dismiss him soon.

"Very well, Chamberlain. The time of Beltane draws near and the seasons wait for no one, not even the Summer Court." She laughed, infusing more of her seductive magic into it, but the energy brushed past him without effect. "Bring your witch to heel and I shall be most pleased with you." The Queen gestured to the door of her private salon and it opened to show him the slushy alley he'd left.

Bowing deeply, Darius backed out into the Rocky Mountain springtime, grateful she'd let him go with such a light sentence.

Light sentence? Bollocks! He still had to convince Sabrina to do the rituals, and he no longer had any idea how.

****

Sabrina tidied up some of the shelves in Mazie's Five and Dime and wondered how she'd make it through Beltane with her sanity intact.

Just keep your mind on work and you'll be fine.

She had no reason to moon over Darius Winterbourne, Chamberlain of the Summer Court, or what couldn't be, but her mind kept filling with images of him. She had no idea what a Chamberlain did, but she suspected it important enough to keep him from staying with her.

And I don't want him to stay. Which is why I'm not doing the rituals. Yeah, she knew all the arguments for and against. She'd been rolling them over in her mind every time Darius said something. So why did she even entertain the idea?

Because I want his hands on me.

She groaned, wishing she could slam her forehead into the shelves without her boss looking askance at her. Could she drown her inner sex kitten?

The bell above the front door of the shop jingled and Sabrina raised her head to see who came in. A woman sauntered inside wearing tight jeans, leather high-heeled boots, and a sheepskin coat belted to her narrow waist. Sabrina didn't have to see her face to recognize her. She'd seen those curves buck-assed naked in her own bed.

Hells bells! Is it quitting time yet?

"Good afternoon, Merrilee. We haven't seen you here in a while." Sabrina's boss waved from the front counter. "What brings you in today?"

"I'm here for Sabrina Foxglove. Is she in today?" Merrilee's voice didn't sound so husky when she wasn't moaning.

"Yes, I think she's straightening the shelves. Do you want me to call her?"

"No, I'll just find her."

Great. Sabrina stifled the urge to bolt for the back door. *Why would Merrilee need to see me? I don't remember any of Two-Face's allergies.*

"Sabrina, thank the Goddess you're all right!"

Sabrina raised her eyebrows as Merrilee grabbed her hand and squeezed, her expression full of relief. Since when did the woman care what happened to her lover's ex? A woman who'd stolen her lover from said ex.

"I heard what happened yesterday at the roller rink and I was so worried." Merrilee scanned Sabrina from head to toe. "Did Marty Robinson really attack you in the parking lot? In front of your girls?"

"Yes." *Gosh, I'm so glad the gossip chain is alive and well.* "But he's been arrested, so it's fine." *And thank you for reminding me of how scary it must have been for my kids.*

"Oh my, I would've been so scared." Merrilee shifted

her weight back on one leg and patted her ample bosom. "But they and you are all right, right?"

"Yes. Thank you for asking." Maybe Merrilee had some compassion after all.

"Good, good." Then a perfectly crafted smile slid across her plump rosy lips. "Maybe he's jealous of your new beau. I hear he's quite the handsome one."

Sabrina felt her burgeoning smile freeze and become brittle. The question raised her hackles. *Is Merrilee in the market for a new man?* They'd never been close enough to share "girl-secrets", even when they'd attended the same coven. But the way she smiled suggested the tart fished for information. *What, tired of Tommy already?*

"Oh? Where did you hear that?" Sabrina turned back to her job, straightening products as she continued down the aisle.

"Well, half the town saw him with you at the rink, skating with your girls." The way Merrilee kept putting the ownership on Sabrina made her ears twitch, as if Tommy had nothing to do with making their daughters. *Takes two to tango, sweetheart.*

"But not you?"

"I don't have kids. I don't need to go there much." Merrilee didn't quite put her nose in the air, but her serene smile and flat belly said enough. No kids. Tommy liked those things especially about Merrilee. *That, and the big tits.*

Sabrina nodded. "How's Tommy?"

Merrilee waved her hand and tossed her head. "Oh, you know, he's okay. Getting ready for Beltane. We're having a big celebration and bonfire in Durango. Are you celebrating this year?"

Tommy's lies stabbed at Sabrina between her shoulder blades, but she'd known they'd been excuses at the time he left. Still, it hurt to think he'd said one thing and done the opposite. Sabrina tried to focus on her work, but Merrilee's question hung in the air between them, and she returned to her internal debate. She'd be celebrating, but not the way she suspected Merrilee Fuckstwice thought.

"Because if you're not, you should come with us."

"Come with you?"

"Yeah, me and Tommy and the rest of the Malachite Coven. We're leaving tomorrow night to spend the day in Durango. Get someone to watch the kids and bring your man. It'll be fun." Merrilee gave her a blinding smile as if they'd been secret friends forever.

In the past, Sabrina might have found the trip to Durango for Beltane an exciting adventure, but the idea of having sex with a stranger in a fertility ritual had lost its luster. *Yeah, two kids will do that.* And she had no desire to be with her ex and his current lover.

"Actually, I already have plans, but thank you." She didn't know which plans she had, but she'd do just about anything to put Merrilee off.

"Oh, well, if you change your mind, you're always welcome. You and your guy." Merrilee sounded truly disappointed.

"Thanks. Have a nice time with Tommy and the Coven. Who is performing the rituals this year?"

A smug smile spread across Merrilee's face. "There are actually three couples from the three attending covens performing the blessings." She flipped her ponytail over her shoulder. "Tommy and I got the honor for the Malachite Coven this year."

"Ready for motherhood?" Sabrina muttered under her breath.

"What?"

"Congratulations on the honor. You must be very excited." Sabrina tried to focus on rearranging baby oil. Between the Summer Court's attendance at her own festivities and Tommy's penchant for fertility, Merrilee might get more than she bargained for.

"Yes. I wish you could come see it."

Ewww! Saw it once in my own bedroom, thanks.

"Are you sure you're busy?"

"Yep, got my own celebration planned." *And I'll be doing it with a man who knows my worth.* Sabrina resolutely ignored the warm glow suffusing her chest from the thought.

"Well, okay, then." Merrilee looked like she wanted to say more, but she swallowed her words when Sabrina turned her attention to the diapers. "I just wanted to make sure you were okay. I'm glad you are. I can't imagine what would happen to those kids if you weren't."

"Fortunately, nothing happened. I'm okay. Thanks for stopping by."

Merrilee hesitated at Sabrina's polite dismissal, but she nodded and waved. "Take care and blessed be."

"Blessed be."

Sabrina watched the woman saunter out into the spring afternoon and tried not to give her a one-finger salute. Disgust simmered just under her skin. First, Merrilee had fucked Sabrina's lover in their bed, then she had the gall to invite Sabrina to watch them fuck for Beltane. Sabrina gripped a bottle of suntan lotion until her knuckles turned white as her stomach churned.

Let it go. She's just a horny little slut. Tommy is perfect for her.

The rest of Sabrina's day dragged on and she tried not to watch the clock. The interaction with Merrilee had left her feeling dirty and she desperately wanted a shower. With a whole bottle of body wash. And her kids could help her scrub the ick away.

Freedom beckoned and she almost skipped to her van when the time came. She let her mind wander over what needed to be done and it slid back around to Merrilee's visit. Sabrina stopped hard as the real reason the younger woman had been concerned for her occurred to her. If

Sabrina had died at Marty Robinson's hand, Tommy would have to take the kids, and Merrilee didn't want Sabrina's kids anywhere near her.

"You smarmy bitch!" The fury in her own voice startled Sabrina and she forced herself to calm down before she drove off the road. "Let it go. Water under the bridge." No amount of fury would change what had happened.

Besides, I have a much better man now.

Except, Darius didn't really belong to her, and he wouldn't be staying after Beltane. Sorrow disproportionate to the situation settled over her shoulders and she sighed. Why couldn't it work out like all those movies she liked to watch? *Like it worked out with Tommy?*

Perhaps she could take what she could get this time and let the rest go. She could pretend the man chosen for the May Lord wore Darius's face. The traditional mask worn for the rituals would help with the fiction. She could make some nice memories to hold on to after Darius left. Hot, sexy memories she could savor for her nights alone.

So I guess I'm doing the rituals. She sighed again, the truth settling into her gut. *Let's just hope I don't get pregnant this time.* And she could pretend Darius cared for her.

CHAPTER TEN

Sabrina found Tansy chatting with Darius in front of the school and tender warmth suffused her heart. Mrs. Lincoln hovered nearby, her eyes trained on the stranger speaking with her student, but Sabrina waved her off as she stepped out of her van.

Darius had said he'd be there to pick up Tansy and his actual presence made her yearning come back. She wished he could be there every day to pick up her daughter from school. *Stop wishing for unicorns. Just do the rituals and hope for the best.*

"Mommy!" Tansy leapt into a run for the van. Darius followed more slowly, a welcoming smile curling his lips. "Today we made May Poles with ribbons to tie on for May Day." Tansy held up a little dowel strung with a rainbow of cloth ribbons. "Now my dolls can celebrate Beltane, too."

Sabrina laughed. "That's right, honey. What a marvelous idea." She hugged her daughter. "Clip yourself in. Let's get home so I can make those brownies for your class tomorrow."

"Can I help, Mom?" Tansy settled in her seat.

"Sure."

Sabrina retreated around the side of the van before

Darius could reach or touch her. She wasn't quite ready to tell him about her decision. Darius climbed in the passenger seat as she settled behind the wheel.

"How did your day go, Darius? Anything exciting happen after I left the police station?"

She ignored the voice accusing her of stalling. She needed to fortify herself before she took the plunge and admitted she'd participate in the rituals.

"Nothing too exciting." Amusement filled his voice, but she didn't know what he found funny. "Your police Lieutenant is very protective of his residents and required me to vouchsafe my presence here."

"He didn't do a background search, did he?" Nothing like getting the Department of Homeland Security involved with a man who lived in the Fae world.

"No, no, nothing so drastic. He simply wanted to ascertain my motivations for being here."

"Did you tell him about the Beltane?" Just what she needed; the whole town knowing she had to have performance sex. *It might put a crimp in Merrilee's tail, heh.*

"I did, but only as a reason for my presence, not in regards to your own participation."

Sabrina sighed. "Yeah, well, I suspect he knows what my participation will be. Goddess, I hope he's discreet."

"The Lieutenant struck me as a man of honor. He won't tarnish your standing in the community."

Would it be so bad for the town to know she fucked for the Fae? *Stop being so crude. It's a high honor to perform the full rituals.* She'd certainly win points with the Malachite Coven. She rolled her eyes. She no longer wanted to worship with them, especially when Tommy and Merrilee remained active members. *There'll be no living with them after Durango.*

And they'd never know she'd done the rituals here at home. *Thank the Goddess they'll be away.*

"I hope he'll keep it to himself. After the day I've had, I don't need any other rude surprises."

"Oh? What happened today?" Darius lost his easy smile.

"Mom! I forgot my gloves at school. We have to go get them." Tansy's voice edged toward panic.

Sabrina smiled apologetically at Darius and focused on calming her daughter. "Don't worry, Tansy. Where did you leave them?"

"In my desk. We have to go back."

"It's okay. They'll be there when you go back tomorrow. No worries."

"Okay." Tansy brightened. "Can we make mint frosting for the brownies?"

"Brownies don't need frosting." Sabrina laughed.

"Please?"

The plans for Beltane and Tansy's brownies distracted Sabrina as they arrived home. Holly had given herself a splinter in her hand from trying to stack more firewood, and Matilda seemed happy to head home. Darius helped Tansy get started on the brownies as Sabrina comforted Holly, then dinner had to be made and the demands of the evening superseded the events of the day. Sabrina forgot about Merrilee and the High Beltane rituals until dinner had been cleaned up and the girls put to bed.

Sabrina settled into her comfy chair with a hot mug of tea and closed her eyes. May Pole erected and covered in ribbons? Check. Firewood chopped and stacked? Check. Cider pressed, boughs gathered, wreaths hung? Check, check, check. Brownies made? Check. She'd finished all her Beltane preparations and could relax.

Darius sprawled on the couch across the end table from her and she sensed his eyes on her, though she kept hers closed. Maybe if she didn't look at him she wouldn't remember she'd made the decision to do the rituals. *All because of Merrilee Fuckstwice.* The name brought back their earlier encounter and the corners of her mouth pulled down.

"Are you well, Sabrina?"

The richness of Darius's voice reminded her she had to tell him about her decision, and she opened her eyes with a sigh. "I'm fine."

He tilted his head, his expression thoughtful. "You said you'd had a rude surprise today. What happened?"

She chuckled ruefully. "Leave it to you to remember my worse moments." She shook her head. "Merrilee Fucks—sorry, Lookstwice—came by Mazie's today, ostensibly to see if I'd survived Marty's attack."

Darius raised an eyebrow. "Merrilee Lookstwice is…"

"The slut who Tommy decided is better for him since she has no children and bigger breasts." She heard the bitterness in her own voice. "Sorry. I'm still a little mad he ran out on his children."

"I can imagine." Darius's face revealed nothing. "What did Ms. Lookstwice want from you?"

Sabrina barked a derisive laugh. "She wanted to make sure I was okay so she wouldn't have to take up being a mother to Tansy and Holly. Tommy is their father, so he'd probably get them if I should die." She grimaced as anger surged. "Although knowing how lazy the bastard is, I suspect he'd let them go to the State first."

Darius wisely changed the subject. "Fortunately, you are unhurt and there's no danger of losing your children."

"Thank the Goddess." She sipped her tea and screwed up her courage to admit she'd changed her mind about the rituals. "She also asked about you and invited us to the big Beltane celebration happening in Durango tomorrow."

"What did she wish to know about me?" The amusement returned to his expression.

"She wanted to know who you were. I didn't think she needed the information." Sabrina shrugged and sipped her tea to bolster her courage. "But I declined her invitation to go to Durango."

"Oh?" Darius managed to look surprised. "Why? I'd think such a trip would be the perfect opportunity to get out of performing the rituals here in Cloudburst."

"It would, you're right." Sabrina nodded. "But the idea of spending several days with Merrilee and Tommy, with the added bonus of watching them screw, made me want to walk barefoot across broken glass."

Darius laughed. "Vivid image, *acushla*."

"*Accurate* image." *Deep breath now.* "The point is I said I already had plans for celebrating Beltane and couldn't attend with them."

"Oh? And what plans do you have, Sabrina Foxglove?"

She met his gaze, hoping her thundering heart wouldn't give away her trepidation. "I'll do the rituals—the full rituals—for the Fae on Beltane."

****

Darius didn't know if he felt relief or sorrow at her admission. He'd expected triumph. Her agreement had been his goal. But knowing she'd probably get with child and he'd return to the Fae Court curdled his stomach. *And I haven't even told her the best part yet.* She didn't know he'd be her partner. *Goddess, can I betray her trust more?*

"Darius? You don't have anything to say?"

Sabrina's voice intruded into his thoughts and he pasted a smile on his face.

"I'm sorry. This is great news. The Court will be pleased to hear of your decision."

"The Court will." She cocked her head. "But not you?"

"No, no, I'm pleased you've made your decision."

"It's certainly easier for you." She sighed and her shoulders slumped. "But I said it out loud to Merrilee, and while she's not important, the Goddess is, and I'm sure She heard it."

"If it really bothers you so badly, no one would force you to it, Sabrina." Where were these words coming from? Had he changed so drastically he'd throw away his future, and his family's standing at Court, for this little witch?

Sabrina raised her eyebrows. "Are you feeling okay, Darius? I thought you'd be gloating."

He shook his head. "I've seen how you are with your family and you have enough going on. I don't wish to add to your responsibilities. Your family is beautiful as it is."

She searched his face, as if trying to determine his honesty, and frowned. "What happened today after I left the police station, really?"

Relieved at the change in subject, Darius gave her a real smile. "Good news, actually. I inquired about the homestead you'd mentioned. The one with the waterwheel and the mill?"

"Yeah. What about it?"

"It has been vacant for quite some time, so the land reverted back to the town's ownership." He reached into his breast pocket and withdrew the title papers he'd received. "Today I purchased it in your name." He spread the papers out on the end table and pushed them toward her. "The homestead and all its environs, is yours."

"What?" Her gaze dropped to the parchment then back to him. "Why?"

"Why what?"

"Why is it mine?"

"I bought it for you and your family."

"Why?"

Darius stopped before he uttered anything else and tried to formulate a coherent answer. Her response to his gift left him scrambling.

"Is it not what you wanted?"

"No. I mean, yes, it's what I wanted, but why did you buy it for me?"

Her question hung in the air between them and he didn't know how to answer it. Why *had* he bought the land? His mind said he'd bought it for her continued prosperity and protection when he'd gone. But his heart said something different.

Love.

And guilt. Even though he'd made the decision to purchase the homestead for her before the Queen had assigned him the position of the May Lord, it rankled. Not only had she agreed to perform the rituals, but he'd enjoy the pleasures of her body in addition to saving his family's standing at Court.

"I want you to be safe and prosperous once I've returned to the Court." The words tasted false in his mouth despite the truth in them. He did want her safe, but he wanted so much more. "I want you to have the opportunity to live your dream and find joy in it. Nothing is worse than working for others because you must, rather than for yourself because you want to." His own life could be summed up by the same notion.

He flattened the papers on the table between them. "This is for you to find your dreams and follow them. It's not because you've decided to perform the rituals. I made this purchase this morning after you left for work."

"I don't know what to say, Darius."

"I believe 'thank you' is customary."

She snorted and grimaced. "Thank you. I didn't expect this. I…" She shook her head. "Just thank you." She ran her hands over the papers, her expression thoughtful.

"Shall we go look at your new homestead tomorrow when Tansy is at school?" He wanted to show it to her more than anything. He wanted to prove he'd offered her this gift out of altruism rather than for reward.

"Yes, I think so. We also need to see the sacred site I'll be protecting and practice some of the warding rituals, at least in motion if not in energy." She rubbed her eyes and he wanted to gather her into his arms to comfort her. "In the meantime, I think I'm going to bed. It's been a long week, and it just started."

"Sabrina, wait." He rose with her and caught her arm, swinging her toward him gently. "Thank you." When she frowned, he added, "For agreeing to perform the rituals."

"Darius—"

"And for accepting my gift so graciously." He pulled her against his chest. "It means more to me than you could ever know." He dipped his head and brushed her lips with his.

Sweet woman and tea flooded his senses and ran straight to his cock. Goddess, he'd never grow tired of her taste. He would have stopped there had she not opened her mouth and licked his lips. Desire for more roared through him and a low growl rose from his chest.

He opened his mouth and stroked her tongue with his, drinking down her sweet moan. She wrapped her arms around his neck and pressed her breasts to his chest. His cock hardened to granite as he grabbed her ass and held her mound against his aching flesh.

"Sweet Goddess, I want you, Sabrina." He kissed the skin of her neck below her ear. "Please let me make love to you. Tonight."

She pushed back a little to stare at him with glazed eyes. "Do you want me, Darius, or just any woman and I happen to be available?"

He stroked the hair away from her eyes and gave her a rueful smile. "Just you, *acushla*. I only want you." The truth burned through him. *Dear Goddess, how will I make it without her at Court?*

"It's been so long, Darius." She swallowed against the whimper in her own voice. "Please, make love to me like you mean it. Tomorrow will take care of itself."

Hot desire and warm love swelled in his chest, and he gathered her into his arms. "I do mean it, Sabrina. With all my heart. Let me show you how much it means to me that you've given me this gift."

She gasped as he lifted her off her feet and carried her into her bedroom, kicking the door shut behind them. Her scent filled her room and his cock flexed with appreciation. This was his woman and he'd mark her with his own scent before long. But he'd take his time doing it. She deserved sweet, swelling pleasure, and he meant to give her every ounce he could.

He set her down on the bed and dropped to his knees before her, sliding his hands up her skirt to the tops of her boots. Her eyes flared with surprised pleasure as he slowly dragged the zipper closures down to her ankles and lifted off each boot.

"You have no idea how lovely you looked this morning in your flared skirt and long boots. I've been thinking of how your skirt swirled about your legs all day." He closed his eyes and savored the memories of watching her walk. "Goddess, it almost required manual labor on my part." He glanced up at her with a wry smile. "Know of anyone who needs their fields plowed?"

She smirked. "Is that some sort of double entendre?"

"What? Oh." He laughed. "No, but if you're offering, it could be." He sighed in pleasure. "No stockings."

"It was warm enough to go without."

He trailed his fingers up the insides of her thighs and she squirmed, but she never looked away from him. Darius delighted in the silkiness of her skin against his palms, but her brazen attention set his blood on fire. When he reached the soft satin covering her mound, he stroked the backs of his fingers over it and watched her wriggle.

The heat behind the satin warmed him from the inside out and he flattened the heel of his palm on her core.

"You're so warm here." She shifted again and he caught the scent of her arousal. "And you look flushed. Perhaps we should relieve you of some of your clothes."

"I don't think it's heat making me flushed."

"No? Then I shall have to work harder."

Darius lifted her skirt and laid a soft kiss on the inside of one knee. Sabrina gasped and gave a short whimper as he licked her silky skin. The sweetness of her flavor stretched his cock until the discomfort made him straighten and stand.

"Come, let's get you out of your sweater." Darius tugged Sabrina upright and pulled the hem of her top up to expose her breasts. Plum purple satin with black lace covered her glorious curves and Darius's mouth watered with the need to taste them. He pulled the rest of the sweater off and cupped her breasts. "Ah, you tease me with this luscious color."

Sabrina laughed a little breathlessly. "I never thought you'd see this bra and panty set."

"It's a set?" He licked his lips and knelt again. "Perhaps I need to inspect them more thoroughly." He pushed her skirt up to her hips and moaned softly as the plum satin met his gaze. He'd never seen anything so beautiful as her skin against the black lace. "Oh, *acushla*, you honor me with your unintentional adornment."

"Are you just going to look at it or do something about it?"

Darius raised his gaze to meet her eyes and found a challenge written there. He gave her his best predatory smirk.

"I intend to look my fill…very closely." Leaning forward, he pressed his nose to the small swath of cloth and inhaled. The intoxicating scent of aroused woman shot straight to his balls and he hooked his fingers over the edges of the waistband before skimming them along the swell of her belly.

Sabrina moaned and writhed, her legs spreading until he could see the outline of her lips against the fabric. Goddess, he wanted to kiss those lips. He slid his hands to her back and slowly dragged the panties off her hips and down her legs, trailing kisses in their wake. Once he'd freed her legs, he pushed his shoulders between them and settled down to inspect his sexy prize.

As in his dream, Sabrina's thatch of brown curls was trimmed and short, and the hairs glistened with her juices in the light. The hot, spicy scent of her pussy dragged a moan from his chest and he leaned in to brush his lips against her weeping slit.

"Oh, Goddess, Darius!"

He chuckled as he pulled back a little. "I've done nothing yet."

"Correction: you haven't done enough."

"Very well, my little witch. I haven't done nearly enough. I shall remedy it immediately."

He sealed his mouth on her pussy, sliding his tongue through her luscious folds, and fell into her sultry taste. Sabrina gasped and burrowed her fingers in his hair, rocking her hips forward to press him closer. The muscles of her pussy clenched beneath his ministrations and his mouth filled with her delicious cream.

Sweet ambrosia hit his tongue and the energy around them surged in an erotic flood. Like all the times he'd helped her heal her injuries, his mind settled into alignment with hers and suddenly the pleasure increased in potency. Darius moaned against Sabrina's sweet, silky flesh as his balls tightened against the base of his rigid cock.

"Oh, Goddess! Please, more, Darius, more."

Her demand flashed through him from his dream with a surge of lust and he pulled back just long enough to rip his shirt over his head. He returned and settled his shoulders against the satin skin of her thighs, burying a finger deep into her clenching pussy. Her wet heat engulfed his hand as he suckled her hard little clit, and Sabrina keened a wail.

Her building lust banged through his mind and she

rocked her hips in time with her desperate moans. Darius reveled in the surging pleasure. *Come for me,* acushla. He inserted a second finger and caressed her g-spot, sucking hard on her clit.

Sabrina's pussy clamped down on his fingers and her orgasm exploded like a fireworks against the night sky, brilliant flares of color splashing through his mind. He'd never experienced his lover's orgasm before and he almost forgot to keep suckling as the release washed through him, taking him with it.

Hot nectar filled his mouth and he drank her down in great gulps, unable to get enough. Sabrina trembled beneath his softening caresses and he reveled in her pleasure. The connection between them remained strong, not fading like it had before, and he had no desire to break it.

Holy Goddess, is this the way it will be during Beltane?

"Oh, Darius, thank you." Sabrina sighed as she slowly came down from her euphoric rise. "It hasn't been so good…ever."

He chuckled as his cock flexed with impatience. "You flatter me, my lady, but I intend to top myself. First, let's free you from your bra and skirt. I believe they've served their purpose."

Darius tugged her upright and reached behind her, deftly unhooking the bra.

"Damn, you're good." Sabrina grinned.

"I try, my lady."

He dropped his hands to her hips and curled his fingers around the waistband of the skirt. He tugged it off her hips and slid it down her still-trembling legs, enjoying her tremors. The light caressed her elegant muscles and glistening mound, and he could barely focus for the lust raging through him. His cock demanded relief and her weeping pussy promised pleasure beyond his imagining.

"You're worthy of the Goddess, Sabrina."

"What? This?" His wanton witch rubbed her hand over her mound, sliding her fingers through her folds. "It's just the same pussy every woman has."

"Ah, there you're wrong." Darius yanked off his boots and pants as fast as possible before climbing onto the bed to sit against the headboard. "While every woman has elements of the divine, your sweet quim is like no other woman out there. And I'm the privileged man to enjoy its magnificence."

Sabrina crawled toward him, her full breasts hanging below her body and begging him to fondle their luscious curves. He refused to resist and his cock flexed in happy agreement.

She paused, her gaze fixed on his groin, and licked her lips. Hot lust surged through him, escaping in a groan as he reached for her. But Sabrina pulled back and a mischievous smile curled her lips.

"May I?" Her hand skimmed along his thigh and his cock jerked.

"May you what?" His brain had short-circuited from her touch.

"Suck your cock." Those lithe fingers stroked the sides of his sac. Between the sensation and her question, his eyes damn near rolled back in his head.

"Oh, Goddess, yes, please."

Sabrina settled her soft breasts against his thighs, grasped his cock, and licked the head. Darius moaned, lost in the exquisite sensations flooding his brain. No other woman had ever offered to go down on him. He thought it a pipe dream unless visiting a whore. But Sabrina willingly fitted her hot lips over his tip and surrounded him with her blistering mouth.

"Sweet mercies."

She pressed her tongue to the soft spot below the head and squeezed his shaft, tightening her lips on the rim. Darius fisted the bedclothes to keep from thrusting into her throat, but his sanity held on only by a thread. The soft sounds of wet suckling built his arousal faster than he expected. Combined with the pleasure from merging their magics, he didn't believe he could hold out much longer.

Swirls of erotic bliss shot straight through his cock to his balls, tightening them until he swore he carried sensitive rocks between his legs. Sabrina showed him no mercy as she caressed the hairs along the sac, tickling and tantalizing him until he bit his tongue to keep from coming.

He tried to think of sharpening his blade with a whetstone, but the very image of sword and wet turned his mind back to the sopping heat Sabrina lavished on his cock. He turned his gaze from her lips stretched around his girth to her sweet body in hopes of slowing his release. But each time her head dropped, her ass elevated and more blood pumped into his groin.

"*Acushla*, stop. Please, stop."

His cock popped out of her mouth and she sat up, her expression concerned. "Did I hurt you?"

"No, not at all."

"You don't like it?"

"Far from it. I just can't hold back much longer with your glorious mouth on me."

"Oh." The mischievous smile returned. "I'll just have to work a little extra harder, then." She lowered her head again, but he grasped her shoulders.

"Not tonight, *acushla*. Tonight, I want to be inside you." He drew her forward to straddle his lap. "I want to feel your tight pussy clasping my cock until we are one and the same."

"Wait."

What had she said? He frowned as she reached past him into the drawer beside her bed, her breasts dragging across his belly. *This part is good.* When she sat back up, she held up a curious square foil package.

"Put this on first."

"What is that?" His cock demanded more of her and he wanted to embrace the urge to slam into her beckoning heat, but Sabrina tore the package open and held up a pale disk.

"This is a condom to keep me from getting pregnant."

He watched helplessly as she slid the odd material over him. He shivered with the touch, but did nothing to stop it. His lust demanded he make love to her and he saw no need to ignore it. He'd allow such a contraption this time, but he'd be damned before he wore anything to stop his seed during Beltane.

"I do this for you tonight, Sabrina, but it will not be so on Beltane."

"I know." She reached between them and held his cock stiffly up, gazing into his eyes as she slowly stabbed her pussy with it. They both moaned as her blistering heat settled around his hard shaft. "Oh, Goddess, you feel so good."

I'd feel better if we were skin to skin, like we'll be on Beltane.

Darius kept his thoughts to himself. He hadn't told her he would be her partner for the rituals and he wanted nothing to spoil this moment. He gazed up at her glorious eyes and lost himself in the arousal there. Of all the women he'd known, none came close to equaling the loveliness perched on his aching shaft.

Emotion swelled, a combination of need, desire, desperation, and love, filling him with the urge to mark her in some way. He wanted no one else ever again. This woman, this little Beltane witch, had stolen his heart, and rendered it impenetrable to anyone but her. Even the Summer Queen's magic no longer held sway.

"Sabrina, *acushla*, ride me now. Take your pleasure from me." He thrust upward, impaling her deeply, and she whimpered as she arched her back.

Her stiff nipples, so hard and delectable, tempted him

to wrap his lips around one straining tip. The sweet scent of her pussy's cream mixed with the spicy taste of her skin, and Darius couldn't get enough. He suckled her nipple hard and Sabrina's sheath clenched on his shaft, shooting pleasure straight to his brain.

She rose off him, only slide slowly down, electrifying all the nerves in his glans. Arousal erupted from his chest in a groan and he switched to the other nipple, his hand plucking the first.

"Yes, suck my nipples." Sabrina rocked her hips methodically to keep her breasts at his face, and squeezed hard with her cunt. Darius almost forgot his task as the lust swelled and he grasped her hips to push her down harder.

"Am I going too slow for you, Darius?"

Her taunting words sparked amazement. How had this little human witch driven him to the edge of his control? He grinned at her and licked her aureole, eliciting a gasp as she threw her head back. His mind sought out hers in the maelstrom of sexual energy pouring off them and merged with a snap, blinding him with the intensity of her arousal and desire.

The surge of emotional connection jerked a growl from him and he thrust up hard, his hands clamped to her hips to hold her steady. He couldn't slow as her pussy caressed his shaft, shots of friction spiking as her clit dragged over his cock-head.

"Come for me, sweet little witch." He growled as he pumped into her, the pleasure building beyond coherence. "Come for me so we might find ecstasy together."

He thrust hard and fast, his lust destroying any hope of slow and steady. Sabrina met him thrust for thrust, her breasts bouncing before him in an erotic dance. Her face glowed as she came, her pussy clamping down hard on his cock, and he dove headfirst into his release. Pleasure surged, connecting them intimately, far stronger than when he'd helped her heal, and Darius lost his heart.

His cock pulsed, sending his seed shooting out, and he gave a silent scream in his mind.

I'm yours, Sabrina, body, heart, and soul. I'll forever be yours!

Stars exploded behind his eyes and her spirit enveloped him, merging together like rain into the ocean. Darius felt as if he'd returned to the source of everything, and he never wished to leave. He stared up into Sabrina's joyous face and one truth became evident. He never wanted to return to the Summer Court.

****

Sabrina returned to her body and wondered how she'd ever lived without sex for so long. *Well, sex like this.* Darius took her body and mind to places she'd never been able to reach. The only sound in her room came from their combined panting. She hadn't meant to fuck Darius hard, but her body had needed the release, and her pussy remained tightly clenched around his softening cock.

She tipped her head forward and met his gaze, reading satiation and something else in his eyes. She smiled her own satisfaction at him and slowly bent down to kiss his upturned face.

"Thank you."

He chuckled. "I assure you, *acushla*, it was my pleasure."

Sabrina shifted and grimaced as her hips cramped.

"Are you well?" He scanned her face, his expression concerned.

"My hips aren't used to this kind of activity." She leaned against his chest to relieve some of the pressure then laughed. "But my body doesn't want to let you go."

Nor does my heart. He muttered something like he didn't want to let go either, but before she could ask, he rolled over on top of her. Darius took his time straightening her legs before pulling out of her body's grip. They both sighed with disappointment at his departure then grinned at each other.

"Believe me, I didn't wish to leave any more than you wished to give me up." He rose and peeled the condom off with a look of distaste. "These things are hideous and it muffled the pleasure."

Her heart sank. "It did?"

Darius held the latex between his thumb and index finger. "Yes."

"I'm sorry."

"Oh, bollocks, *I'm* sorry, Sabrina." He knelt before her. "I'm not saying this right. You gave me great pleasure, even muted as it was. This contraption takes away the myriad of wondrous sensations and blends them into one constant pleasure." A slow smile curled his lips. "I much prefer it without."

Sabrina sighed and nodded. "I'm sure, but it's necessary. I'm only willing to chance pregnancy at Beltane."

She watched his sexy ass stride away and wished with all her heart Darius would be her partner for the rituals. Their bodies had fit together better than any other partner she'd ever had, and her heart had already made its choice. *I'm so in trouble.*

Darius returned from her bathroom with a warm cloth and gently cleaned her pussy and thighs. He took his time, stroking with firm but sensual motions, and she enjoyed the play of the muscles across his broad chest. A fine line of hair stretched from his pectorals own his belly to flare around his cock and balls, and she resisted the urge to trace it with her tongue.

She'd enjoyed surrounding his hard flesh with her mouth and wished she could have another opportunity to suck his cock again. The thought made her shiver and her pussy clenched with lusty memories.

"Are you cold, *acushla*?" Darius stood, heedless of his nakedness, and pulled the covers aside so she could climb under.

"A little." He drew the bedclothes over her body and reached for his pants, but she grasped his arm, stopping him. "Please stay and warm me up."

Darius paused. "Are you certain, Sabrina? I don't wish to overstep."

"Yes, Darius. I want to feel your arms around me tonight."

The idea of sleeping alone after his wonderful loving turned her stomach. She wanted more of his touch, even the simple act of sleeping beside his body. He hesitated and she feared he'd walk away.

"Please. I know it's only for tonight, but...I need you." She rolled onto her knees, aware the blankets had dropped to expose her breasts. She'd use every weapon in her arsenal to get him to stay. "Keep me warm tonight?"

Darius swallowed hard. To his credit, his gaze never dipped to her chest, but his cock gave him away by twitching. She would've smiled if she didn't think he'd walk away.

"It would be my pleasure and honor to sleep wrapped around you, Sabrina."

"But?"

"But nothing. I just want to be sure you won't regret your decision come daylight."

"Regret is for decisions I've questioned. I'm sure about this one." *Even if I know it's just for tonight.* She wanted as many memories of Darius as she could have. Better to have loved and lost...

"Then I'm happy to wrap you in my arms tonight."

The man certainly knew what to say at the right moment, but Sabrina detected none of his usual charm this time. He retreated to the front room, still naked, and she watched his glorious body strut around in the light. *I might not be able to keep him, but I'm definitely going to enjoy him.* Her heart contracted with sorrow. She knew he'd leave on Thursday, but she shoved the emotion aside. He'd stay with her tonight and hold her as if promising forever. And for tonight, she'd pretend everything he gave her meant just that.

When he returned, Darius wrapped himself around her as promised, the heat of his body seeping into every place he touched. Sabrina sighed and settled her back against his chest, inhaling the scents of sex, satisfaction, and warm, spicy man. She wanted to imprint them on her brain so she'd never forget, even after she had to let him go.

CHAPTER ELEVEN

Sabrina woke to an odd sensation. Heat pervaded her body, from the tips of her toes all the way to her neck, and the world seemed right for the first time in years. The oddness didn't come from the heat, but from the man providing it.

He stayed all night. Darius breathed evenly behind her, his face nestled in her hair beside her ear, and her heart squeezed with gratitude. He'd promised to stay, but she hadn't really expected him to be there in the morning. *More fool I.*

Sabrina wished he could stay every night. *Let it go right now. I'm not beating a dead horse again.* She mentally slapped herself even as her heart screamed at her to press her case with him.

"Good morning, *acushla*," he whispered, sliding one hand to cup her nearest breast. "Did you sleep well?"

"Yes, better than I have in years." She hoped the admission didn't hurt her.

"As did I." Why did his words make her heart flutter like a teenager? "Happy Beltane."

"Thank you. Same to you." She nestled back against him. "So far, so good."

She heard him take a breath to respond when Holly's voice carried through the door from the hallway.

"Mommy, where's Darius? He's not on the couch."

Sabrina groaned and Darius chuckled. "Well, at least they'll notice if I'm present or not."

"Of course they will." Sabrina rolled over to face him. "You've made quite an impression on them. On all of us." She grimaced. "We'll all miss you when you go."

"Sabrina—"

"Don't worry. I don't regret any of it. And I'm used to being alone."

"That's not what I wanted to say." Darius stroked her cheek with one hand. "You shouldn't have to be alone. If I could—"

"But you can't. I know." She shook her head. "I still don't regret last night."

"Sabrina—"

"There you are, Darius!" Holly cried from the doorway. "Tansy, I found hiiiimmm."

Pattering feet signaled Tansy's arrival. "Mom! What is he doing in your bed? Were you cold last night?"

Despite the ache in her heart, Sabrina laughed. "Yes, a little. But Darius kindly warmed me back up. Have you gotten ready for school? It's the May Day party today."

"I know. Are you gonna help out for it?"

"Yes, but I can't stay all day. I have some things to do with Darius." He squeezed her hip beneath the blanket. "Holly, you know you can wear your party dress all day today, right?"

"Yeah, I know." Sabrina's youngest looked at her for a long moment, her eyes dancing with secret wisdom. Sabrina wondered what coursed behind those eyes. "Do we get to go with you tonight, Mommy?"

"Not tonight. But you'll get to celebrate with either Matilda or Moira Callahan."

"Awww." But Holly didn't look too disappointed.

"Go get dressed."

"Okay." Holly disappeared from the doorway and Sabrina sighed.

"I guess that's our cue to get up." She squeezed Darius's arm, smiling. "Thank you for last night."

"My pleasure, Sabrina. I will treasure the memory of it forever."

Yeah, he sure knows what to say at all the right moments. She didn't laugh at him, but she didn't say anything in response as she rolled out of bed. She'd cherish her memories of him when she had nothing else to hold. She started the shower, trying to ignore the hollowness in her chest.

****

The party for May Day in Tansy's class seemed like an exercise in physics. How to keep twenty five small objects all going more or less the same direction at the same time. Between singing songs, dancing around a makeshift pole, and eating goodies brought by the parents, the class appeared more like flying ping pong balls than children. Sabrina thanked the Goddess when the lunch bell rang and she could kiss her daughter goodbye. She gave kudos to Mrs. Lincoln for the ability to face the troupe day after day.

Darius had declined to be there and Sabrina didn't blame him. Not only were none of the children his, but she doubted even the Summer Court reveled in such shenanigans. Sabrina savored the quiet of her van as she drove through the sunny streets of Cloudburst. The Goddess had blessed Beltane with mild weather and only shadows held remnants of snow. It would be a good night to celebrate renewal.

Maybe even my own.

She could move on from Tommy and Merrilee's betrayal. Oh, Tommy would always be a jackass, but he wouldn't be *her* jackass problem. Maybe she could finally find her own way. Darius had handed her the Miller homestead title. She could easily start her herb shop and change her life from drudgery to prospects if she had the courage to move forward.

Darius waited for her on the porch of her house, his head tipped back to enjoy the sunshine on his face. Sabrina took a moment to enjoy the strong lines of beauty standing in the sun. The light glinted off the golden highlights in his brown hair and graced his cheeks with shadows from his lashes. Even in this moment of quiet, he looked strong, powerful, and ready to move. A warrior, and yet not without tenderness, he made her pussy clench in a primal feminine need just standing there.

Her tires crunched on the gravel and he turned toward her, the moment lost. But the image of him standing in the sun remained etched on her mind as something to savor. His long strides carried him to her van and he climbed in with a welcoming smile.

"How did your morning go in Tansy's class?"

"It was great, but I have no idea how Mrs. Lincoln keeps all those little kids focused, more or less." Sabrina laughed as she backed out to the road again. "I was exhausted after half a day."

He chuckled. "Then let us take this slowly today. Do you know how to get to your new estate?"

"My estate?" She shook her head. "I'll have to get used to thinking of it in those terms. But yes, I do remember how to get there."

The drive didn't take long, but Sabrina enjoyed each moment as a new start. The date on the calendar read May 1 and the world seemed to open up to her. She had a new path to take, a new world to explore, and a new man to share it with. *Except he's not staying.*

She shoved the sorrow aside as they pulled in to the open space at the end of the gravel road. The old mill still held its shape although the roof looked more likely to let in rain than keep it out. The waterwheel still turned with the force of Oro Creek chuckling along its bed. Tall pines lined the edges of the cleared space, and a granite cliff face guarded the homestead's flank. She knew from earlier explorations a trail led into the hills and the swell of granite held the abandoned mine.

"We're here."

Darius surveyed the open ground before the mill. "This is your dream home?"

She laughed. "It will be. The mill has good bones even if parts are in disrepair."

"I think you mean 'destroyed.'" He shook his head. "Had I known it was this dilapidated, I might have questioned the purchase of it."

"Oh, come on. It's not so bad. I did say it was abandoned." She set the parking brake and turned off the engine. Crickets sang in the aspens and long grasses swaying in the mountain breeze. "It's so peaceful here."

Wild grass and weeds had grown up in the clearing, attempting to reclaim the evidence of centuries of technological advances. Sabrina scanned the old homestead, her mind cataloging everything she'd do to change it to fit her tastes. Despite the silence and peaceful façade, something seemed off. Sabrina closed her eyes and opened her senses. A low, discordant hum filled auditory space beneath the crickets' calls.

"There's something else I need to tell you."

The guarded tone in Darius's voice made her tense and open her eyes. "What?"

"I believe this is the sacred site where you'll be performing the rituals."

"Here? This is a sacred site?" She shoved her keys into her pocket and slid out of her minivan. The scents of warm grass and ponderosa pines filled each breath and she took a moment to savor them, enjoying the silence. The hum faded into the background. They'd driven two miles up a Forest Service road to reach the homestead and only the breeze in the trees broke the quiet.

"Don't be fooled by its commonplace appearance. It's not the outter—"

"Have you been watching cartoon movies with Holly and Tansy?"

"Focus, Sabrina." Darius quelled her humor with a glance. "Let's go around the back. I suspect the ceremony will take place there."

Sabrina bit her bottom lip and Darius took her hand. A tingle ran up her arm from where they touched, and the air seemed to ripple as if from an invisible concussion. Sabrina listened hard for some sort of clue to what occurred, but only the sound of the wind filled her ears.

"It's so quiet, even quieter than where I live."

Darius nodded. "It has been neglected for a long time. The energies are unsteady here."

So that's what I sensed. "Then why are we doing the High Beltane rituals in a place with unsteady energies?"

"Because they must be repaired and Beltane offers the perfect opportunity to restore the conduit. When you perform the High Beltane rituals, it will bring blessings and protection to the land."

His explanation didn't reassure her, but she followed him around the old house, brushing her fingers through the tall heads of the grass. She tried not to watch the way his back flexed as he strode ahead of her, but even in an ordinary t-shirt he had sexy written all over him.

Stop drooling! It's just the energies around Beltane talking. Despite the rebuke, her mind filled with all the times he'd been kind to her children, solicitous to her, and protective of them all over the last few days. *Not. Husband. Material. He's arrogant and he's the Chamberlain of the Summer Court.* Except the arrogance had waned, and he'd made sweet love to her last night. *It doesn't matter. Stop thinking of him as a prospect.*

Darius paused and looked back, his expression curious. "I'm coming. I'm just getting used to this place. Something seems off."

He tilted his head thoughtfully. "I know you don't wish to do this again."

"Stop, Darius. I gave my word I would and I'll stand by it." She looked around the "backyard" of the homestead, noting a lovely ring of aspens rattling softly. "The trees are the sacred circle, aren't they?"

"I believe so. The energies are strongest there."

"Is it safe to build a fire in there?"

"There should be a stone lined pit in the center beside a slate altar."

They pushed through the ring of trees and entered an enchanted world. The grass had been cut and the pit cleared of debris. Sunlight slanted down through the branches, painting a latticework pattern on the ground. The silence deepened within the circle and Sabrina's mundane concerns slipped away. A small altar stood beyond the fire pit, looking more like an Olympic three step podium than a traditional table.

"Has this place been used as celebration grounds before?" Sabrina scuffed her foot through the shortened grass. "The Malachite Coven hasn't used it."

Darius looked surprised. "I would assume so. Have you never done the rituals here?"

"No. Not for Beltane or Samhain or Yule. Seems well-tended for no one using it."

"Hmm." Darius scanned the space. "Perhaps the energies have been strong enough to keep it this well-tended until the renewal."

Despite the sacredness of the rituals, Sabrina's mind easily supplied an image of her bent over the stone altar, Darius pumping into her from behind. *Glory, I've become a wanton woman after one night of sex.* Her pussy clenched at the prospect and she had to blink several times to clear her sight. *It won't necessarily be him. Goddess, I wish it could be.*

Sabrina took a deep breath. "All right. Who will be my partner for the fertility ritual? Has the Queen chosen someone?" She didn't really want to know the answer. The idea of screwing another man in the sacred ritual, even for the honor of the Summer Court, killed her warm, lustful thoughts. She didn't want any other man touching her.

"Yes."

Something in Darius's voice made her glance at him. He met her scrutiny with an impassive mask.

"I will."

She damn near swallowed her tongue as her heart leapt with excitement and hope. "What?"

"I will be your partner."

"But...you're the Chamberlain...and..." She couldn't quite find the words to explain her excitement. But reality intruded as she recalled his duty to the Court. She bit down on her tongue. "What if I get pregnant?"

****

Darius sighed at the look of horror on Sabrina's face. As a fertility celebration, Beltane promoted a renewal of life, and with the attendance of the Summer Queen, he suspected the potency to be increased. Sabrina's expression chilled his blood straight down to his bones. She'd told him point blank she didn't want another child, and he doubted she'd want one from him. But this gave him the perfect opportunity to find a way to leave the Court for good.

He wanted a family of his own, one uncorrupted by intrigues of the Fae. His soul cried out for change, but recoiled at the dismay painted across her face. He'd fought against his attraction for the little human witch, but she'd enticed him with nothing more than her fierce protection of her children and her enduring courage in the face of her attacker's enmity. She'd breached the defenses around his heart as she took up the challenge she had no interest in pursuing.

And then she'd offered her sweet body for him to taste last night.

Her lack of interest in sharing the ritual with him hurt more than he cared to admit.

"If you get pregnant, I will take care of you."

She made a rude sound, grimacing. "Baloney. You have your position at the Summer Court, and I live here. I won't take my children into the wolf's den for anything, and you can't just tell the Summer Queen you're taking a sabbatical."

Sabrina looked away, anger tightening her shoulders. "This is exactly why I said I wouldn't do the rituals again." She swung back to him, pointing at his chest. "Men say they'll take care of everything, but they only want the sexual part of the ritual. When there is responsibility and work afterward, they run or find someone else and give some other excuse why they can't pick up their end of the deal. You'll be no different, except you have a legitimate excuse. You're not even from my world!"

"Sabrina," —he strode to her side and grasped her shoulders—"look at me, please."

Slowly she raised her gaze to meet his.

"If we are blessed with a child from this ritual, I would move heaven and earth to stay with him."

Sabrina shook her head.

"Peace, little witch. I speak the truth." Desperation and hope leaked through his voice. "I would wish for no other to be the mother of my child. I could only hope I'd be a worthy father. I'd be delighted to be your husband." Where were these words coming from? "And the father to your daughters."

Her eyes opened wide and scanned his, her disbelief

clear. "Have you been listening to Marty and his buddies? I don't *need* a husband."

Darius gritted his teeth. "This isn't about need, Sabrina. This is about want. I *want* to be your husband."

"Why?" She frowned. "You don't even live here. You live in the Fae world with the Summer Court."

"But I could live here. With you, and Tansy, and Holly. And…" He caressed her soft cheek with one hand. "Our child."

"Why?"

She searched his face for an answer, her eyes flicking back and forth. Darius tried to put all his sincerity into his gaze, hoping she'd see his heart as well. He had to convince her because to walk away from her would gut him.

"I know how hard it was for you to raise your daughters alone. I don't want you to have to do it again."

Her lip curled. "That's it? *That's* why you want to stay here? To protect me?" She jerked out of his hands. "No thanks."

"What?"

"I've done it before, I can do it again, Darius. I don't need a man to make it better for me."

Despite the hurt in his chest, he bit back his angry retort. "I said this isn't about need, my lady. What do you want?"

Sabrina bit her lip as she turned away from him and he ached to pull her back into his arms. She wrapped her own arms around herself, her shoulders hunching as if to stave off some heavy burden.

He stepped closer with caution. She looked so vulnerable and everything screamed at him to make it better. But he knew she had greater strength than she showed.

"Tell me what you'd choose if you could, Sabrina. What's your heart's desire?"

"Oh, please. I don't live in a fairytale."

He chuckled. "I beg to differ. The Fae will be here tonight. I can't think of any way you could be closer to a fairytale."

As he'd hoped, he drew a laugh from her. "Tell me what you want, Sabrina."

She took a deep breath and bowed her head, exposing her neck and tempting him to kiss it. He laid his hands against her silky arms and breathed in her feminine scent. It ricocheted through him, flooding his mind with illicit thoughts and visions of more of her skin exposed to his sight. His cock hardened and he resisted the urge to rub it against her firm buttocks.

"I want…"

"What do you want?" He brushed his lips against her neck and her breath hitched.

"I want a partner…a friend I can always depend on." She let loose a low moan as he kissed her hair. "I want someone to love me for me, not because I'm a witch or a chess piece on the world board. I want a lover for more than just sex."

He could be such a man. He could easily take the role and more if she'd just accept him for himself. *And who are you, Darius?* The question came out of nowhere and he wanted to thrust it aside, but it hovered in his mind until he had to acknowledge it.

Who was he really? Could he be her partner, her friend? Could he love her for the woman she'd become, the mother she was, and the witch she'd abandoned?

Yes.

"If you'll let me, I can be all those things, Sabrina." The words surprised them both, but he met her gaze steadily as she twisted to face him in the circle of his arms.

"Why do you want to?"

"Because I love you." Darius leaned forward and pressed his lips to hers, begging her to believe him.

"What?"

"I love you, Sabrina Foxglove. Let me be your partner, your friend, and your lover." He ached to slide his hand down her back and grasp her ass, but he suspected she'd expect it of the lothario she thought him. He couldn't deny her claim, but being a man who'd had many lovers, he knew when to hold back to coax his lady.

"How can I believe what you say, Darius?" She pulled far enough back to search his eyes again. "You have probably said it to hundreds of women over your lifetime. And you're still single." She grimaced. "Plus, I've only known you a few days."

She spoke the truth, except he'd never said his words with such sincerity and conviction before. For the first time in the decades of his life, he meant them with all his heart. Sabrina had made him care, made him want, made him feel something other than lust. Her stubborn determination to take care of herself and her children without help had impressed him. It made him want to help her, if only to ease the worry lines on her face and the tightening of her shoulders.

You're safe now, I've got you. The words he'd spoken on the bridge to Tír na nÓg rang in his head, and he wanted them to be true. He wanted to have her back, support her in the difficulties she faced. He could conceive of no greater service.

"I cannot change the past, Sabrina, I can only go forward from here." He offered her his honesty. "I want to take the path with you."

"What about the Summer Court?"

The Queen's command echoed through his head: *Convince the witch to do the rituals or you shall lose your longevity, your sword, your honor, and the Winterbourne name shall be stricken from our records.* He smiled. The threat no longer worried him. Not only had Sabrina decided to do the rituals on her own, but he didn't care to return to the Fae. If he stayed with Sabrina, he'd be content for his remaining years.

"Let me worry about the Summer Court. If our coupling during the ritual results in a child, I would rather stay here and raise our son or daughter with you." He ran the backs of his fingers over her cheek. "Nothing would bring me greater joy than to see you holding our child."

"Darius, I don't want another—"

"Shh, peace, Sabrina. Please." He didn't quite know what he asked for, but he had to stop her from destroying his dream. Whether she chose to complete the rituals or not, he wanted to stay with her when the sun rose after Beltane. "Please say you'll perform the rituals with me, and if I should get you with child, you'll at least give me a chance to stay with you. I beg of you."

She stared at him a long time, each moment measured in heartbeats as she studied him. Emotions moved through her eyes as the breeze ruffled the trees of the sacred grove around them. She seemed to gather herself, squaring her shoulders as she raised her chin, her eyes sad.

"I said I'd do the rituals. I'll even do them with you. But if I get pregnant, you don't have to stay. I don't expect it of you."

He growled and thrust his fingers into her hair. "Expect me to stay! I *want* to, Sabrina. I want you in my life after Beltane."

"But the Queen—"

"Let me deal with the Queen. It may take me some days to resign and prepare my replacement, but I will not be staying in the Summer Court." Darius met her gaze, his heart pounding with excitement. "Please say you'll wait for me and trust I will return to you. Tell me you'll allow me to be part of your life as your partner, your friend, and your lover. Please, Sabrina."

Darius's blood thundered as she took her time deciding. He'd never felt so desperate in his life, but he forced himself to be patient. The importance of her answer meant too much to him to push. *Oh, Goddess, let her see the truth in my words.*

"All right, Darius." Sabrina gave him a tentative smile. "I'll trust you. Do you really want to stay here, in this dilapidated homestead with more rodents in residency than most granaries, with me and my children?"

"*Our* children. And yes, I want to stay."

She shook her head. "They're mine, and you might have to work hard to convince them otherwise, especially when they become teenagers. Goddess help us both, then." She shuddered, but smiled. "But I think we're getting a little ahead of ourselves. We still have to perform the rituals."

Darius wanted to wrap her in his arms, lift her up, and swing her around in jubilation. She'd said she'd wait, and he wouldn't betray her trust. Tamping down his enthusiasm, he contented himself with a grin and nodded.

"Let's start by practicing the energy merge between us. We must be in tune to allow the wards to be strengthened."

"What do we need to do first?" She eyed the windswept ritual circle. "We don't have to get naked yet, do we?"

His cock hardened with the thought of her lithe body shrouded in nothing but sunlight, but he shook his head. "No, first we dance."

"Dance?"

"I'm sure you've heard of it. Two people moving together in a synchronicity of motion?"

Sabrina gave him a dry look. "I know what dancing is. Why do we need to do it?"

"During the ceremony tonight, we'll be dancing to the chants before commencing the rituals. We need to practice connecting to the energy and each other while in motion."

"Oh. Right."

Darius held out his hands and waited for her to step

into the circle of his arms. Sabrina took his hands in a classic waltz pose and time stopped. She fit him perfectly as if they'd been built for one another. *It took me two hundred years to find the one woman who fits?* He didn't have time to wonder at the Goddess's plan before Sabrina crooked an eyebrow.

"Are we going to move or are you just going to stand there, staring at me?"

Darius laughed off his hesitation. "I could spend all day staring at you, but we should really get moving." He sidestepped, pulling her along gently. She moved with him in a gentle waltz step, her movements in sync with his. Each brush of her thighs against his tightened his groin and he prayed his cock would behave itself long enough to complete the rehearsal.

Too bad it's not a dress rehearsal. Or rather, undressed rehearsal.

"You're a pretty good dancer, Darius."

"I've had a little practice."

"Oh, I'm sure." Sabrina grimaced and he tried to find something to say to take her mind off the multitudes of women he'd danced with over the decades. "Now what?"

"Can you sense the energy of the circle while we dance?"

He'd been feeling the rise in power as soon as they started to move. The sacred site responded to their presence as if recognizing those who could secure it. Power flowed like air currents, brushing against his mind with gentle tendrils of energy.

"Yes, I definitely feel it. I felt it when we arrived."

"Good." He led them in a clockwise circle around the fire pit, their motion easy and slow. "Can you see the energy?"

"See it?"

"Yes, in your mind's eye. The magic of this place should look like beams of concentrated light. Each person is different. Some see colors, others see metals. One witch once told me the energies looked like different kinds of wood."

Sabrina closed her eyes as they danced. He loved her serene expression as she sought out the magics surrounding the homestead. Because he held her, he experienced her stretching out her own senses, searching for the power coursing through the grounds. When she touched them, everything snapped into place and Darius jolted right along with her.

"Sweet Goddess."

He couldn't have said it better himself. Everything felt aligned with them as they slowly waltzed around the circle. He had to clear his throat to find his voice.

"What do you see, Sabrina?"

"Beams of light, each slightly different, coming from each tree in the circle." She still hadn't opened her eyes. "They're like spokes in a wheel and the circle is the rim."

"Excellent." The energy between them surged and pleasure bloomed throughout his body. Damn, this witch held power. "These spokes are ley lines of magic, the life sustaining energy of the world. When they are in balance, they appear in proper order, like a color spectrum or repeating pattern of sizes. Each tree is a nexus point, directing the power to the altar of the Goddess."

"The lines are supposed to be connected to the altar?" A frown appeared on Sabrina's face.

"Yes. Why?"

"Because none of them connect to the altar." She gasped in surprise. "All of them are connected to us. They're following us around the circle."

Unease bloomed in Darius's chest. If the ley lines connected to them, it meant the energies within this sacred site had been neglected too long. He'd miscalculated their instability. He suspected even the Fae hadn't foreseen the dereliction of the magics here. *Bloody hell.*

He'd heard of places so unstable, they'd attached to the most powerful being in the vicinity and snapped the unfortunate source in half. But the owner of such power had to be stronger than the average human to attract the ley lines, and Sabrina's announcement meant what he'd suspected since he'd met her. She rivaled the Summer Queen in magical strength.

"What do the lines look like, Sabrina?" He spoke more harshly than he intended and she opened her eyes in surprise. "Are the lines solid and clear? Or do they roil like boiling water or a murky stream?"

She huffed a sigh and closed her eyes again. They kept dancing, but Darius's heart raced with his sinking stomach. *Dear Goddess, let the magics be easily healed. Don't let them kill her.* What had he done? By bringing her to this place without checking first, he may have signed her death warrant.

"They're smoky and rolling, but not violently."

"Thanks be to the Goddess." Their strength wouldn't take her down, yet, but if they didn't do something to anchor the lines to the altar, the rituals would be too dangerous to perform. "Can you tug on them with your mind?"

"Tug on the ley lines?"

"Yes."

"Why?"

"We need to secure them to the altar, even temporarily, or we won't be able to ward this site tonight. It'll be too dangerous. Now, can you move them?"

"I don't know." She frowned harder, squeezing his hand as they moved around the pit. The wind picked up a little and dust particles sparkled in the sunny air. "How do I even attempt to move energy?"

Darius gritted his teeth and tried to think of his earliest magic lessons. "Think of them as ropes, solid enough to gather together in your mental 'hands'. When you have them fixed in your grip, see if you can move them toward the altar, like tying ribbons to the May Pole."

"I...can't. It's like they're sticky."

"Bollocks!" He swirled her closer to the altar in an abrupt turn. "Are they still following you?"

"Me? They're only following me?"

"Are they still?"

"Yes."

"Very well." He danced them up to the stone steps and stopped, leaning her over the top tier. Pressing his chest to hers, he kissed her.

The explosion of pleasure shot out in every direction and damn near made him come in his pants. Sabrina moaned and clutched at his arms, grinding her pussy against the rigid bulge at his groin. Power swirled around them, urging him to tear her clothes off and sheath himself in her hot, silken depths.

Darius's vision filled with spokes of rainbow light radiating from the woman he kissed. His eyes remained closed, but the contours of the sacred circle flashed in brilliant negative around them. Each strand of light pulsed power into Sabrina and she glowed with its particular color as the pulse passed. Vibrant flashes centered on her crotch and heat spread over his aching cock.

"I need you, Darius." Sabrina's husky voice gripped him by the balls. "I need you, now."

Her kisses blistered his mouth with their lusty heat and he fell into them, his mind drunk on power and erotic desire. Darius unbuttoned her jeans and jerked them off before he came back to himself.

What am I doing?

The morning sunlight glistened on her trimmed mound and the scent of her arousal knocked him to his knees. His own arousal ramped up and he buried his nose in her succulent flesh, digging his fingers into her hips. He opened his mouth and tasted sweet heaven as Sabrina rocked her pussy against his lips.

"Oh, Goddess, yes, Darius. Yes!" Her fingers speared into his hair and she pulled him closer to her slick pussy.

Darius couldn't answer with his mouth full of quaking feminine flesh, and he dove in, licking and sucking her ambrosia. The pulses of sexual energy increased in frequency, swamping his mind until only bringing his woman pleasure mattered to him. His woman, his Goddess. He'd serve her until his dying breath, and nothing would divert him from his path.

Sabrina whimpered and rocked her hips harder, striving for release, and Darius suckled her clit with delighted abandon. Sweet cream flowed into his mouth and he reveled in it. He'd never tasted anything better than his lady's divine pussy, and he thrust his tongue into her weeping slit, seeking more.

The energy pulses increased again and the wind in the circle picked up, swirling around them like a dust devil. Sabrina gyrated to each burst, moaning in time with her motions, and Darius suckled harder.

Sabrina slammed her mound against his chin. Darius bit his tongue and the pain jerked him back into the present, his awareness taking in the swelling energies swirling around the sacred circle.

Bloody fucking hell! Sabrina writhed before him, her wet pussy clenching against his still tongue, and she wailed her frustration. Sexual demand beat against his mind, but he realized they had to anchor the magics to the altar, or they'd blow everything wide open, and no one would be safe.

"Sabrina!"

"Darius, I need you. Come to me. Now!"

"No, you have to focus." He laid a teasing kiss against one thigh.

"No, no, don't want to. You have to fuck me. Please!"

"I will, *acushla*, but you must do something for me."

Sabrina shook her head and grimaced, her hand sliding down to rub her clit. "Oh, Goddess. Don't stop, Darius. Please."

"Sabrina, I need you to push the ley lines into the altar." He removed her hand and massaged her mound with gentle strokes, hoping to bring some of the sexual energy to heel. "Take all the energy and wrap it around the altar like the ribbons on the May Pole. Remember? Envision a ring inside the stone and tie the lines there."

"I can't." She tossed her head. "I need you."

"And I need you, *acushla*, but you have to do this, or all is lost." Darius pulled back from her glorious body and gritted his teeth. It was up to her now. If she gave into the seductive pull of the magic, the energy would destroy the sacred site, and Sabrina as well. "Please, Sabrina."

****

What did he ask? To focus on something other than his fucking tongue? *What the hell is wrong with him?* Sabrina struggled to hold on to the lovely arousal he'd been building within her, but it faded into a dull throb as he pulled away from her.

"Please, Sabrina."

Something in his voice brought her back to herself. She opened her eyes and looked around. From her prone position on the altar, everything seemed off kilter, and the world swayed before her eyes. It took her a few moments to realize the world didn't move, but the trees bent and strained under the force of the wind.

"What's happening?"

"The magics are unanchored and they will tear this site apart unless you tie them to the altar." Darius gripped her thighs as the wind whipped his hair around his head.

"How do I do this? I've never done anything like this before!" Panic welled up inside her, burning away any sexual desire.

"No, focus, Sabrina!" Darius held her still. "This is the Goddess's energy. You have it within you, and you're strong enough to manipulate it. Reach down inside yourself and take hold of it."

"I can't, Darius."

"You can! Focus."

Sabrina closed her eyes and tried to picture the energies swirling around them. A vision appeared of a whirling maelstrom of color, like a rainbow tornado, spinning around her. She rested within the calm eye, but tendrils of magic shot out of the swirl with blinding speed, crackling against the tree ring.

Dear Goddess, help me. Sabrina tried to catch the lines of color with her hands, gathering them like reins of carriage horses trying to escape. At first, the "reins" flowed through her fingers without substance, but Sabrina kept after them, raking her fingers through the air.

The first line she caught burned her hand, but she gritted her teeth and held on, reaching for another. Each new line thrummed with untapped power in her grip, but as she added more, the rampant winds calmed around her. At last she held a thick cable of swirling color cords in her hands and the world outside settled into breathless anticipation.

"Very good, *acushla*." Darius's voice bolstered her confidence, but she shook her head.

"What do I do now?"

"You must anchor the lines to the altar of the Goddess." She felt him settle between her spread legs again, and realized she lay half naked on the stone.

"What the—"

"Easy, little witch, there is more yet to do." He patted her mound and some of the energy in the strands surged, filling her with unrelenting lust. "I can smell your desire, but you will need it to help you secure the ley lines."

"How? Oh, Goddess, Darius. I need you so bad."
Desire burned a path straight to her pussy and cream
soaked her nether lips.

"Do you remember how we merged our minds when
healing your head?"

Sabrina groaned as another blast of power shot lust
through her. "Yes."

"We will do it again. I will guide you and you will
provide the strength."

"Are you telling me you're the brains and I'm the
brawn of this operation?" Humor kept some of the
overwhelming sexual need at bay.

He chuckled, his breath fanning over her slick clit. "In
this case, yes. Now, let me in, *acushla.*" And he licked a
warm swath from her clit to her weeping cunt.

Sabrina wailed as she sank into the roiling flood of
passion swamping her mind. She almost lost her grip on the
seething bundle of ley lines, but Darius's hand reached out
and steadied hers.

"Darius."

"I'm here with you, Sabrina. Let's tie these off and go
home." She felt more than saw him smile at her as his
tongue danced on her pussy lips, pushing her arousal
higher.

"Okay. Show me what to do."

In her mind's eyes, a great iron ring appeared sunk in a
thick slab of granite, and Darius helped guide the bundle of
magic lines to the thick loop. He showed her how to wrap
the lines around the ring, twisting them over the iron curve
until they tangled upon themselves in a tight knot. Then he
pulled slowly back and allowed her to survey their work.

"That's it? That's all I had to do?"

"Not quite. Now you must solder them to the ring,
fusing them there long enough for the Fae to arrive tonight
and help secure them permanently." Darius sprinkled light
touches down her thighs and Sabrina remembered her body

lay on the slab in the sacred circle.

"How do I fuse them to the ring?"

"Like this."

Hot arousal surged through her as his mouth sealed to her pussy, and his tongue flicked her clit. He licked her long and slowly, each stroke setting her body afire, and her buried lust flared to life. Sabrina gasped as the ley lines shook on their moorings and Darius inserted a hard finger into her quaking pussy.

"Oh, Goddess!"

"Come for me, Sabrina. Fuse the lines and come for me."

He thrust his fingers into her, setting a hard rhythm to push her into the stars as he sucked on her clit. A burning surge exploded from the base of her spine and shot straight through her, spilling from her hands and searing the ley lines to the iron ring. The flood of bliss took her with it and threw her tumbling and spinning into the sky, wrapping her in warm clouds of joy.

At last, Sabrina settled back to earth and opened her eyes. The sacred circle lay quiet and serene, a gentle breeze teasing the grass around the altar. She lay with her legs spread wide and draping over the edge of the top stone. Darius tenderly cleaned her release from her nether lips with his tongue, each stroke offering a soft reminder of the pleasure they'd shared.

She watched as he withdrew his fingers from her pussy and licked them, his eyes closing as he savored her taste. His evident pleasure warmed her heart and sent a flash of arousal to her groin. She couldn't be ready for him again so soon, could she?

"Thank you, Darius."

He slanted her a satisfied smile. "It was my pleasure, *acushla*. Truly."

She glanced down at his straining pants and quirked an eyebrow. "Are you sure?"

"Watching you come is equally as satisfying as coming myself." He reached down to adjust his bulge. "Besides, I know you will give me release this evening at the rituals."

Sabrina sat up and scanned the circle again. "Did we do it? Is it safe now?"

"You did, little witch. You secured the lines to make them safe."

"Thank the Goddess."

"Indeed." Darius offered her a hand and she slipped off the altar. He helped her get dressed, peppering her skin with little caresses before taking her mouth with a deep kiss. "You were magnificent, *acushla*. It will be a great honor to perform the rituals with you tonight."

He kissed her again and ground his rigid cock against her belly, sending new jolts of arousal through her. Sabrina moaned and fell into his kiss, enjoying the taste of herself on him. Arousal stirred, but it highlighted another emotion wrapping around her heart. She'd fallen deeply in love with Darius. He'd left a little piece of himself in her when they'd merged, but he'd stolen her heart when he retreated. And she doubted she'd ever get it back.

CHAPTER TWELVE

They didn't speak much on the way back from the homestead. Sabrina tried not to dwell too much on her revelation or Darius's declaration of love, but the endorphins from her orgasm and the hope they could be together after Beltane fluttered through her mind. She allowed herself to be cautiously optimistic. Darius had proved to be different than any other man she'd met, but she'd seen enough Prince Charmings turn back into frogs. She'd wait to see how he acted after Beltane, when he no longer needed her.

The proof is in the pudding.

Last minute preparations needed to be finished before the celebration and Sabrina threw herself into them to keep her mind distracted. She called Moira to confirm her taking the girls for the night. Moira promised she'd help them celebrate with dancing around the little May Pole and offering May Boughs made of mountain ash and ponderosa pine to the fire.

"Are you going to extinguish the hearth fire and restart it from the bonfire?"

"Yes." Moira laughed. "I'm not sure Aiden is thrilled with the idea of leaving the woodstove cold until after we celebrate, but I promised I'd make it up to him."

"Aiden will be there tonight?" Moira had mentioned a guy named Aiden from her past, but Sabrina thought he'd left long ago.

Moira cleared her throat. "Yeah, he just returned to town a few days ago and has no one to stay with. Is that okay?"

"Well, I don't really know him."

"He's really good with children. He always has been. He says their minds are the least cluttered with junk and judgment." Moira paused. "And I'll be there all night. I can vouch for him."

"All right. I trust you, Moira. Thank you for taking the girls. I really appreciate it."

"It's no problem. Thanks for trusting me and Aiden. You're one of the only ones."

"Your folks giving you grief over him?"

"They always have." Moira sighed. "Comes with the territory. I promise your kids will be safe with us."

As the oldest family in Cloudburst, the Callahans had been blessed with some sort of magical talent when they founded the town. They'd used those talents to benefit of their town, but it made the members a bit elitist when it came to selecting partners for their children. Especially their only girl. Moira had had to fight to start her coffee shop on her own. Sabrina could only imagine what she went through for Aiden.

"Not a problem. Have fun tonight."

"I will. You, too, Sabrina. It'll be great. I can feel it."

Sabrina tried to ignore the surge of hopeful excitement. "Thanks. I'll drop the kids by the Cloudburst around four today, okay?"

"Sounds good. See you then."

Sabrina hung up the phone and glanced around for Darius. She couldn't find him in the living room or bedrooms, so she searched the backyard from her glass door. Empty. *Where has he gone?*

"Mommy, can I wear my white sparkle dress tonight?" Holly held up a white velvet dress with gold glitter pattern on the skirt.

"Sure. Let's get you and your sister packed." Sabrina guided her daughter back into her room. "Tonight, Moira is going to have a friend over. His name is Aiden. He'll be there to help you celebrate with the May Pole and the feast."

"Is he nice?" Holly grabbed her favorite doll and hugged it, her expression curious.

"I'm sure he is. Moira thinks highly of him."

"Okay. As long as he's nice."

Sabrina smiled to herself. "Yes, I think he is. Come on, help me finish packing so we can have a snack before we go get Tansy."

Holly helped her pack and bind up the May Boughs for their little celebration with Moira and Aiden. They'd made extra so she could cover her own blessings for her home and land before she danced for the Summer Court. Each bough had been cut from the trees around their house to tie the blessings to this land, and fastened with a golden ribbon. Sabrina loved the scent of ponderosa pine burning and prayed the blessing would translate to her new homestead.

I can't believe Darius bought it for me. Where is he, anyway?

Holly helped Sabrina pack everything into the back of her van, including Tansy's favorite stuffed dragon and blankie, and Sabrina glanced at her cell phone. The time had arrived to pick up Tansy from school, but Darius hadn't returned. She wished she could call him, but she'd never seen him with a cell phone.

"Where's Darius, Mommy?"

"I don't know, honey, but we have to go get your sister. Get clipped in now."

Sabrina half-expected to see the garage door to the house open and Darius stride through, but the door remained stubbornly closed. She tightened her hands on the wheel as she backed out and her stomach clenched. *Where is he?* Had something happened to him? *He didn't leave, did he?*

She scanned the roads for Darius as she drove, her shoulders tensing with each empty street. Once she caught sight of a man in a long trench coat and her foot stuttered on the gas pedal, but he looked her way to cross the street and a tie showed at his collar. Her shoulders slumped as her gut churned. The Queen wouldn't recall him this late in the game, would she?

"Mommy, where's Darius?"

"I don't know!" Sabrina took a deep breath. "I'm sorry, Holly. I didn't mean to snap at you."

"Do you think he's okay?"

"I'm sure he is, honey."

But her certainty faded as they pulled in to the school for Tansy. Her eldest daughter waved at her teacher and scampered for the van, only to pause as someone called to her. Sabrina followed her daughter's gaze and all the tension washed out of her as Darius appeared beside her girl. He smiled and waved then escorted her to the van and opened the passenger door.

"Where have you been?" Sabrina grimaced. "I'm sorry. When I didn't see you at home, I got worried."

He smiled and patted her arm. "I'm sorry to have caused you alarm. I made the last little arrangements with the Court. They shall be at the sacred site at the gloaming." He settled himself as they drove toward town.

"At twilight? Why do they need to be there so early?"

"They will set the bonfire and make preparations for the rituals. The Queen won't arrive until the dancing and chanting begins."

"Is everything okay?" When he raised an eyebrow, she

waved her hand. "I mean, everything ready to go and no snags for us to do this tonight. The site is secure?"

"Everything is fine, Sabrina." He gave her a warm smile. "Are you looking forward to it?"

Sabrina let her gaze unfocus on the road. "A little. It's been a long time since I've done the High Beltane rituals, but I remember liking the pageantry of it all." She slanted him a glance. "I think it helps that you'll be there with me."

She expected him to flash an arrogant smile, but the expression on his face held more tenderness and joy than arrogance, and her heart swelled. She wanted him to love her as much as she'd fallen for him, but experience warned her to protect herself.

"This will be my first time in the role of May Lord, but I couldn't have chosen a better partner for May Lady."

"You get to be May Lady this time, Mommy?" Holly chirped from the back.

"Yes, honey."

"I wanna be May Lady." Tansy met her gaze in the rear-view mirror. "Can I do that tonight?"

Sabrina smothered a laugh. "You'll have to ask Moira. But I'm sure you and Holly can both be May lassies this year."

Darius asked about the party and her overall day, and Tansy bloomed with his attention. Sabrina's heart clenched with joy at his care of her children and she dared to hope he'd meant his words of love from the morning.

They arrived at the Cloudburst and dropped the kids off with Moira, Tansy and Holly chattering away as fast as they could. Sabrina kissed and hugged each girl, then had to swallow back tears as her daughters gave a special goodbye to Darius. He appeared as delighted by their actions as she. Moira waved them off and Sabrina couldn't help the surge of excitement as she drove away.

Tonight would be momentous no matter what happened.

"How are you feeling, Sabrina?" Darius unclipped himself as she pulled into her garage.

"I'm…excited and nervous and happy and scared." She laughed. "Does that answer your question?"

He chuckled. "Completely. Would it help you to know I feel the same?"

"You, the great Darius Winterbourne, Chamberlain of the Summer Court, nervous?"

"Well, when you put it like that…" He squeezed her hand before they opened the door to the house. "I have something for you."

Sabrina followed him into the kitchen and he led her to the table. A large, elegantly carved wooden box rested on the surface with maple leaves etched on the lid. Sprigs of lavender ringed the sides, and plumes of ponderosa pine needles showed between the maple leaves. The wood glowed a rich red between the hand painted foliage, and the scent of cedar filled the room.

"What's this?"

"Open it." Darius gestured to the box. "It's for you."

She touched the satiny wood and lifted the lid. It rose silently on hidden hinges and revealed a lavender confection inside. Surprise and delight mixed within her as she lifted out a gossamer gown with long trailing sleeves. The v-necked bodice sported embroidered lavender sprigs along the collar, and the skirt flared in an empress waist, open at the front.

Easy to walk in and easy to get into.

The humor flashing through her did nothing to diffuse the delight of the dress. Beneath the dress lay a pair of loose-fitting lavender satin pants with a draw string to hold them to her hips. Sabrina raised her eyebrows at Darius.

"Won't those make it difficult to get to me?"

He chuckled darkly. "Not for me, *acushla*."

She laughed with him as arousal rose. "Thank you for these."

"They're not from me. They're from the Queen in thanks for your willingness to perform the rituals." He looked at her with approval. "But they'll look lovely on you and display your feminine assets to the fullest."

Sabrina shook her head. "Just what every woman wants to hear." She glanced around her kitchen. "Did you get some finery to wear tonight?"

"I did."

"Can I see it?"

"In due time. First, let's make a meal and sate our stomachs before we satisfy our bodies."

His evasiveness surprised her, but she nodded and tucked the lovely clothing back into the ornate box. Together, they prepared an elegant meal of chicken and wild rice, snow peas, and rosemary rolls. While cooking wasn't her favorite activity, with Darius it became an event of sensual interaction. He stood shoulder to shoulder with her, offering little touches and kisses when she didn't hold a knife. Each caress flooded liquid to her pussy and electrified her skin, preparing her for the evening.

Darius produced candles from somewhere and a bottle of sweet white wine she'd never heard of. He guided her to her chair and pushed her gently into it, caressing her shoulders. When he joined her, he set a small box on the table, this one a more traditional white cardboard.

"What's this?"

His teal eyes glittered in the candlelight. "It's my gift to you for your agreement. But first, let us toast to a fruitful and prosperous Beltane."

Darius poured the wine and rich scents of grape, blackberry, and a hint of honey filled the air.

"To Beltane." They clinked glasses and Sabrina sipped, swirling the wine around in her mouth. Warmth, joy, excitement, and arousal trickled through her as she swallowed. Heady stuff, but so tasty and complimentary to the meal.

"What is this wine?" She twirled her glass carefully, enjoying the pale gold color of the liquid inside.

"It is a special vintage from the Fae, made especially for Beltane participants."

Unease deflated some of the warmth from the wine. "This is a Fae wine? Are you insane? Talk about causing trouble before we've started. What's it supposed to do, make us so wanton we fuck like rabbits before we even make it to the sacred circle?"

Darius's mouth quirked into a grin. "I believe that's the idea, yes. Notice I did not pour more than half a glass and I left the bottle in the kitchen."

"Probably wise." Although she mourned the loss of more wine, she didn't want to act like a drunken party girl at the ceremony. "Besides, I have to have some sort of focus to be able to do this."

"Indeed. I will help you as much as I can, Sabrina. You're not alone in this." He held up his own glass. "It's a great honor."

"I know it is."

"No, it's a great honor *for me* to perform the rituals with you." He set his glass down and grasped her hand. "In all my years of arranging the Beltane rituals, I've never been asked to perform them, nor have I yearned to do so. Until now. To be the May Lord to your May Lady is a greater gift than any I've ever hoped to receive."

"You *want* to do the rituals with me?"

"I'd never do them with anyone else." He squeezed her hand.

Heat and pleasure bloomed through her and her arousal built a little more. His words filled her heart with excitement and joy, and she wanted to throw her arms around his neck and rub her breasts against his chest. The light painted sensual shadows on his face and her mind flooded with erotic images of his lips on her pussy.

Holy Goddess, what's in that wine?

"Are you well, Sabrina?" Darius tipped his head and gave her a languid smile.

"Yes, I think so. I never did thank you for this morning, and your help with the ley lines." Her face heated as she recalled just how he helped her. "I couldn't have done it without you."

"You're most welcome, *acushla.*" His hot gaze roamed over her body and she felt its scorch everywhere it touched. "Now I have something for you."

He slid the white box across to her and sat back, his expression expectant.

Sabrina resisted asking the inane question and lifted the lid. Inside, nestled on a delicate red gold chain, rested a pendant of gold filigree around a strange mineral cluster. It looked like several shafts of sorrel crystal had been tied together at the center, then wrapped in gold wire.

"Glory, Darius, it's beautiful." She lifted out the necklace and he rose to help her settle it around her neck. "What is it?"

"It's gold wire, for your beloved Oro Creek, and aragonite, for renewal, protection, and connection with the divine." His warm fingers clasped the chain around her neck and rested on her shoulders. "This particular crystal has come from the cliffs behind my ancestral home. It's to symbolize the connection between my line and yours."

He crouched beside her and took her hands. "I love you, Sabrina, and wish to be with you always. You're my heart, my family, and my soul." He drew her face down to his lips and kissed her.

An explosion of arousal and desire hit her along with the flavors of rosemary, chicken, and wine. Sabrina moaned and threw her arms around his neck, diving into the kiss with abandon. She wanted to push him to the floor, free his cock, and ride it hard until they both found release. Darius answered her moan with a growl and his arms wrapped tight around her, his hands squeezing her ass.

"Oh, Goddess, Darius. I need you."

"I know, *acushla,* I need you, too. But we must wait."
He bowed his head and pressed his forehead against
hers, taking great gulping breaths.

"Holy crap, what's in the wine?"

"I suspect it's to get us in the mood."

"Yeah, well, we don't seem to have a problem with
mood." Sabrina forced herself to release him, but couldn't
help checking his groin where his cock pressed in a hard,
long ridge at the front of his pants. Her pussy clenched in
desperate anticipation and she squirmed on her chair.
"Let's finish dinner and clean up. It might give us a
measure of control."

He laughed, but it sounded strained as he pushed away
from her and resumed his seat on the opposite side of the
table.

"Did you mean what you said?"

For a moment, Darious looked confused. "What I
said?"

"Yes, that I'm your heart, family, and soul."

His expression smoothed out into a tender smile. "Yes.
You're everything to me. I want you and no other."

Humor beat back some of the rising lust. "Pretty bold
coming from a man of your experience. Are you sure
you're feeling all right?"

He grimaced ruefully, but amusement glinted in his
eyes. "I'm feeling a little off kilter from the wine, but my
heart knows what it wants. And we both want you,
Sabrina." Fire flared in his gaze and tingles shot to her
pussy from the heat. She wanted to leap at him, but she
forced herself to sit back and pick up her fork, praying she
wouldn't bend it in her fist.

She focused on her food and tried to swallow it down
with the last of the wine, but her skin tingled with
awareness of the man across the table. He seemed to be
faring no better. They spoke little and soon returned to the

kitchen to clean up.

Even the simple task of cleaning dishes and putting away food took on an erotic flavor. Sabrina's awareness of Darius rose to a new level and he responded to her hot looks with small torturous caresses. The sight of his cock stretching the front of his pants shot more fluid to her pussy and her inner muscles tingled and clenched with need. Each time he brushed against her, whether accidental or with purpose, Sabrina wanted to rub her stiff, aching nipples over his chest, or hands, or back, or anything.

The scents of aroused male only heightened her need and she could barely keep her hands off him as she moved around the kitchen.

What is wrong with me? Sabrina glanced at the clock. The little green numbers above the stove read 6:47. Two hours until the Fae arrived, another three until the rituals started at midnight. *Holy Goddess, how I am going to make it for another five hours without fucking him?*

Her body ached for his touches and she squeezed her legs together to relieve some of the building pressure in her clit. But the friction of her clothing only added to her torment and she had to lean against the counter to relax.

Darius moved up behind her and rubbed his hard bulge against her ass, sending her arousal into a tailspin. She gritted her teeth and her knuckles whitened where she gripped the counter as she resisted the urge to tackle him.

"You appear tense, Sabrina. Shall I help you relax?" Darius trailed his hands down her back and slid them around to cup her breasts. She moaned and pressed her chest forward into his palms.

He dropped soft kisses on her neck. Sabrina wanted to fall into the passion rising between them, but a voice of warning shouted at the back of her mind. There was something they weren't supposed to do. Darius gently pinched her nipples through her shirt and nuzzled her ear.

Goddess, she'd happily jump into bed and fuck him

until blind.

Wait! Wait. Beltane. No fucking until midnight at the rituals. They had to save their energy to ensure the potency in strengthening the magical wards surrounding the sacred site.

Logic finally broke through some of the arousal and she twisted out of his grip. He gave her a puzzled look as she backed away from with him a loony grin.

"I think I'm going to my room for a while." She met his smoldering gaze and her pussy clenched with longing as she grabbed the decorative wooden box. "Yes, going to my room until it's time to go." He licked his lips and she moaned, almost giving in. "Thank you for the necklace and the help. But I have to go…" Darius's expression turned predatory. "Right now!"

She bolted out of the room and he charged after her with a growl. Joyful excitement surged through her just as she reached her door and slammed it in his face. *Just five more hours. Dear Goddess, give me the strength to wait.*

CHAPTER THIRTEEN

Darius breathed deeply, but his cockstand refused to abate. Damn the Fae and their enhanced wine. He'd never been a recipient of the wine, but he suspected it had been used for centuries to relax the participants of the High Beltane rituals. Unfortunately, it also fired his blood and destroyed any control he had over his libido.

When Sabrina had run from him, he'd lost all of his sanity and chased after her like a rutting bull. But she'd found the wisdom he'd lost and gave them both the opportunity to calm down enough before they fell to fucking hard and fast. While he'd like to blame the wine— and it was mostly to blame—he suspected they would've given into their mutual attraction anyway.

Darius sighed and closed his eyes as he smoothed the hunter green tunic over his chest. He wished the hands belonged to Sabrina. Every moment apart from her grated on his calm. He'd paced the living room, trying to think of anything other than his sexy, wanton witch with her lavender eyes and rich mahogany hair.

Bollocks! He rearranged his cock and balls for the thousandth time and glanced at the clock above the mantle. The hands showed five minutes to eleven and the time hadn't come soon enough. He'd tried meditating, but he'd only seen Sabrina's succulent rosy nipples behind his eyes. He'd tried shadow fighting to burn off some of the lust tearing through him, but the exertion only made the arousal flare. He then tried pushups, but the excercise only reminded him of his chest brushing Sabrina's breasts and he gave up with a whimper.

The click of Sabrina's bedroom door had him spinning around and wishing the soft pants he wore could stretch a bit more in the groin. His glorious witch glided down the hallway in the lavender dress from the Queen and he stopped breathing.

The split skirt parted around her hips covered by her own loose pants, baring her gently rounded belly, and Darius's half-mast cock rose to salute. The aragonite necklace hung between the perfect mounds of her breasts and matched the copper colored embroidery on the long trailing sleeves. She'd gathered her hair into a plaited chignon and copper drops hung from her ears.

"By the Goddess, you're beautiful."

He'd never seen a woman so magnificent. Even the Summer Queen paled beside the beauty of Sabrina Foxglove in her Beltane finery. His heart swelled and he wanted to gather her against his body, make sweet love to her, and never leave her side. His inner barbarian roared *my woman* and he pushed out his chest.

"Thank you. You're pretty handsome yourself." Sabrina let her gaze slide down his body and he felt it like a smooth caress. His cock jerked in appreciation. "Are you ready for this ride?"

You have no idea. He suspected she'd used another one of her curious idioms, but he pictured her sitting astride him and rocking hard, and almost groaned.

"I am. How was your time alone?"

"Miserable." She smiled brightly. "But necessary or we wouldn't have made it to the ceremony." She licked her lips as she scanned him again and he tightened his hands into fists to keep from grabbing her.

He cleared his throat and gestured toward the garage. "Do you have a shawl to wear? It's not summer yet and we should get going." *Before I bend you over the divan and take you hard.*

Sabrina's eyes flared as if she heard his thought, but she retrieved a deep purple shawl from the closet beside the door and wrapped it about her. It blocked his view of her luscious breasts held in lavender silk, but it did nothing to calm his cockstand.

Two hundred years old and I can't control myself better than a boy of sixteen. Bloody Fae wine.

He felt a bit odd allowing Sabrina to drive them to the sacred circle. A gentleman always conveyed his lady to their destination, but she knew the roads best in the darkness and how to handle her vehicle. She deftly guided it to the old homestead and parked it before the mill.

A soft flickering glow suffused the trees behind the structure. The brush of Fae magic flowed over them as they exited the van. Musical voices intoned the sacred chants and the air filled with power. Darius's heart swelled with the energy from the chants and he fought against the urge to take his lady against the trunk of the nearest tree.

His thoughts shattered as another set of headlights cut through the darkness. Sabrina spun toward them, her shoulders tense. Darius grasped her arm and pulled her close to his side as a large SUV skidded to a dusty halt beside her van.

Three men exited the vehicle, leaving the doors open and the headlights on. Though back-lit, Sabrina gasped as she they came into view.

"Oh holy Goddess, what is he doing here?"

"Thought you got rid of me for good, tramp?" Marty Robinson sneered and tapped a large iron bar against the palm of one hand. "Not even your asshole boy toy can stop me this time. We'll even the odds a little, won't we?"

Anger swelled in Darius's chest, but he lifted his chin with a mild smirk. "Think your friends and your meager weapon will save you this time, churl?" He chuckled. "You'd be wise to get back into your vehicle and retreat while still whole. You've intruded where you're not welcome."

"Shut up, wise guy." Marty pointed the bar at Darius's chest. "This time you don't got that sword of yours and this woman needs a real man to set her straight."

"I thought you said he wouldn't come back." Sabrina's voice held anger and frustration surged inside Darius.

"I thought he'd be wise enough to heed my warning. I believe I misjudged his intelligence."

"Are you calling me stupid, asshole?" Marty took two steps forward as his friends muttered darkly.

Darius bared his teeth in a mean grin. "If the boot fits…"

Marty growled and Darius braced himself, his attention centered on the bar. If he caught it on the swing, he could use Marty's momentum to wrest it from his grasp and put him down. Marty launched himself at Darius, but before Darius could move, a tall, slender warrior darted between them and caught the bar with a sword. Metal screeched and sparks flew as Sabrina yelped in surprise. Darius swung toward her, his heart in his throat as another Fae warrior took on Marty's ill prepared friends.

"I have you, my lady." Darius wrapped Sabrina in his arms and backed them toward the millhouse, watching the battle.

It ended within moments, Marty once again whimpering and whining beneath the weight of his attacker. His friends lay at the feet of the second warrior, unconscious.

"Oh my glory, are they dead?" Sabrina turned her head to look at the combatants.

"No, my lady. We merely subdued them. You may attend to the ceremony without any interruptions." The slight warrior over Marty turned and Darius realized the little prick had been bested by a woman.

"Come, Sabrina. We must go. The time draws near." Darius tugged at her, but she resisted.

"What will you do with them?"

The female Elf tipped her head to eye Marty's fetal form. "We will take their memories of this night from them and send them home."

"One request, if I may." Darius caught the woman's eye and she nodded. "Take their memories of Sabrina Foxglove as well. Let them never recognize her again."

Amusement flashed across the warrior's lips for a moment then disappeared. "As you wish, Lord Chamberlain." She bowed her helmed head and turned to Marty once more.

"Come, Sabrina. It's time to go."

"They won't hurt them, will they?"

"Not any more than they already have. And you'll be safe now. They won't remember you or this night ever again." He kissed her forehead. "Come. The Fae are awaiting us."

He guided her back toward the millhouse where two more Fae stood. Sabrina gave one last look toward the downed men then resolutely faced the man and woman waiting for them. She bit her bottom lip, squaring her shoulders, and took a deep breath.

"Why are they waiting?" Apprehension filled Sabrina's voice as she tightened her hands on her shawl.

"Peace, little witch. They will escort us into the sacred circle. I must leave you for a time."

"Leave me? What are you talking about?" She turned wide eyes to him and he read the fear in her expression.

He almost reached out for her, but thought better of it when the energy between them crackled with unspent passion. He stepped back a pace and tightened this hands into fists.

"The May Lord and May Lady enter the rituals at different times. Worry not, Lady Foxglove. You're in good hands." Not as good as his, but good enough for now.

A frown marred her brow when he used her title, but he'd be damned before the Fae Court knew where his heart lay. *Let them believe it's the wine spurring my desire.*

"Lady Foxglove?" the Fae woman called. Sabrina glanced in her direction, but she still hesitated.

"Blessed be," she whispered before retreating to join the Fae lady.

"Blessed be." He enjoyed the sway of her hips beneath the sheer material and his cock flexed against his trousers. *Sweet mercies, she's magnificent.* He watched until they'd disappeared behind the millhouse. The ladies couldn't be more opposite, but only the human witch held his attention. The tall Fae looked like an emaciated child beside her. Why did he ever believe the Fae attractive?

"Let us begin, Chamberlain Winterbourne." The Fae man gestured toward the same path the women had taken, but when they rounded the structure, the women were gone.

"Are you aware of your duties, Chamberlain?"

"I am." Though he'd never performed the rituals himself, he'd attended enough High Beltane events to know what should occur.

"Very well. When you arrive at the circle, please don your mask and join the dance, sun-wise, around the fire."

Despite his knowledge of Fae Beltane, he still stopped in his tracks when they arrived at the sacred circle. Between the pulse of the magic wafting through the trees and the wine spurring his arousal, Darius stood dumbfounded at the spectacle before him.

Light suffused the circle of trees from floating "mage fyre" balls, and the crackling bonfire in the great pit at the center. Crystals and ribbons hung from every branch, flickering and glittering in the shifting light. Dancers swirled around the fire's bed in rich colors similar to his own jewel-toned costume, each wearing a horned mask to disguise their features. The current dancers were all male. Though he'd been chosen as the one to be the May Lord, tradition dictated his arrival to be camouflaged by the other males in the group.

His Fae escort handed Darius a mask, an elegant, leafy eye covering with spreading antlers reaching nearly two feet above his head. He feared it would be ungainly for the dance, and certainly for later activities. However, when he tied it to his head, it rested with no more weight than the hood of his cloak.

"Be ready, Chamberlain."

Darius dipped his chin and watched the pattern of the dancers as his heartbeat sped up. The chorus of the pipes, fiddles, lutes, and drums fired his blood, and made him want to throw his body into the dance. Performed by the men only, this portion of the rituals built the foundation of the magic with strength and power, punctuated by heavy beats of the drums. Darius shook with the need to join the ancient rhythms.

"Now."

Darius leapt into the pattern, his heart soaring and his feet flying in the steps. He'd seen this performed countless times, but he'd never danced it himself. Despite his lack of knowledge, his body seemed to know the moves, and he flowed into the crowd of male dancers without a ripple.

Power surged through his veins and Darius lost himself to it. The music and pounding beat throbbed within him, sending his feet flying and his body twisting in the moves with the others. Darius grinned, primal joy and exhilaration surging from his gut. He wanted to shout with the sheer glory of the dance, but focused his energy on moving faster and with more dexterity.

Time became elastic and when the trumpets blew to

announce the arrival of the Summer Queen, Darius only
noticed because the pattern in the dance shifted. Each male
performed an elegant pirouette before Her Majesty and
Darius followed suit, as if he had no connection to the
Queen at all.

When he rose from his bow to look upon the her, he
realized the dancers were not the only ones affected by the
pounding beats of the music. For all her stillness, the Fae
Queen appeared wilder and more primal, as if she wore a
mask of serenity to disguise her true feral nature. Her eyes
glittered with untamed desire and she watched the dancers
avidly, her hands gripping the arms of her gilded chair with
white knuckles.

Darius recognized the lust and desire for sex in the
lovely woman's face, but despite his roaring libido, he
found nothing to attract him. He swirled away with the
other dancers, content to twist and writhe to the drugging
beat.

Then the women joined the men. They came in a great
flood of pale pastel colors, a soothing and gentle rainbow to
mix among the richly-tinted males. They, too, wore horned
masks covering their eyes, but the horns were shorter and
elegantly shaped, gracile to the men's robust mantles.
Darius inhaled the scent of the newcomers, the hot musk of
aroused females called to him. But still he found none to
sway him from the dance, even as the music softened with
feminine gentleness.

He spun and twirled, delighting in his body's strength
and agility as he dodged the out-flung hands of the female
dancers, and their trolling eyes. He'd never be caught. He
wore wildness like a cloak and reveled in his ability to
remain separate as the other dancers paired.

A flash of lavender, burnished in a copper glow,
disrupted his motion and he stumbled, stopping dead as *she*
stood before him. The May Lady.

She wore an elegant horned mask of auburn leaves

gilded in gold. The horns rose only a few inches above her head, the tines glittering in the light, but they matched the pattern of his own antlers. Her body undulated, the lavender dress hugging her breasts flowed around her hips with distracting flutters, deteriorating his restraint. Lavender eyes met his briefly and a seductive smile curled her full lips before she turned away, her body swaying to the music.

Darius's cock rose with his temper. How dare she turn away from him? He wanted her and he'd have her before the night had ended. When she twirled around to face him again, she met his gaze and raised her chin in mute challenge. *Want me?* she seemed to ask. *Come take me.* Darius growled and stalked her through the dance, weaving in and out of the other revelers as he pursued his prey. *Mine.*

Around and around the fire they danced, she dodging and swaying before him, always close but just out of reach. Darius gritted his teeth and sped up his moves, gaining ground on her. Her laugh carried over the music, tempting and taunting him. He'd have her. She was his. She'd slake his thirst for sex and pleasure.

At last he caught her, his hand closing about her arm and swinging her body against his chest. They stopped dead in the midst of the dance and the other dancers eddied around them, flowing past without pause. Darius panted with his exertion and his heart pounded with the chase, but he had her, the woman he'd mate with tonight.

His mate looked up at him and her eyes burned with her own lust and need. Her strength rivaled his, yet without the hard, warrior edges he carried. He wanted to bury himself in her softness until it soothed the belligerent fury of his masculinity.

"You're mine, woman." His growl widened her grin, but she said nothing, only raised her chin in mute challenge once more.

Her response to his declaration spurred his lust and he pushed her up against the nearest obstacle, a stacked pile of stones much like large steps. As soon as they touched them, electricity tingled through him and he grabbed her face below the mask, staring at her full lips.

"Mine," he snarled and gave into the driving need to taste his mate.

CHAPTER FOURTEEN

Sabrina's world blazed white at the moment her mate crushed his mouth to hers. The flavors of sweet wine, hot sex, and male arousal flooded her senses and her pussy responded with enthusiastic clenching. Liquid lust coated her nether lips and slid down the insides of her thighs. She'd never been so turned on in her life and she only wanted more.

When her masked partner thrust his tongue into her mouth, she caressed it with her own in a slow tease. He moaned and thrust harder, grinding his hard cock against her belly as his hands gripped the braid at the back of her head. Each time the stiff ridge of his sex rubbed across her mound, stars burst against the back of her eyes.

More. The primal voice came from deep in her soul and she agreed. Snaking a hand between them, she mewled a whimper as she grasped his straining cock, and squeezed.

The great horned male pulled back from the kiss and hissed, his eyes slitting as she tugged on his hard flesh. She reveled in her power over him and stroked him harder. He rocked his hips in time with her caresses, his hands digging into her shoulders. She wanted him hard, hard enough to bring her to release with his rigid cock. An image of his hot flesh penetrating her weeping cunt swept her away and she faltered in her command of him.

A primal growl brought her back to the moment and the horned man pulled her hands away from his cock. He slammed his hips against hers, his rigid shaft sustaining constant pressure on her clit as he bent his head and kissed her throat. Electric pleasure surged and her pussy contracted. She squirmed under him, but the pressure of his cock against her clit only increased with her motions.

Mind reeling from lust, Sabrina wailed in surprise as her mate's hand found her breast and caressed the nipple under her bodice. His eyes flashed to her face as he fondled her with firm strokes until the nipple stood in a tight peak. He freed it from her dress and sucked it into the hot cavern of his mouth.

Glorious heat slammed into her and she arched her back to get closer to his teasing tongue. He flicked the tight bud, then sucked hard, sending stars shooting through her vision. She rocked her hips to feel more, and he met her thrusts with his own, pushing her over into a sudden orgasm. A breathy wail escaped as she cascaded over the edge of bliss, her pussy clenching and weeping with each pulse of joy.

Her horned mate kept suckling and thrusting, his blazing eyes fixed on her face as she returned to the hot throb of music and drums. Sabrina stared at him with drugged satisfaction and he pulled back from her breast, primal triumph stretching his mouth in to a wicked grin. Without warning, he shoved his hand beneath the waistband of her pants and slid his fingers into her slick folds.

Sabrina keened at the caress and rocked her hips, her arousal building again. He met her thrusts with a hard rub before removing his hand from her pussy. She whimpered and clutched at his hand, but he growled and spun her around, pushing her down on the stone step beneath her.

Altar. The voice came from far away. Sabrina had a hard time focusing on it as her mate pulled the drawstring of her pants and jerked them down her legs, exposing her ass to the cool air. The scent of her own release wafted between them and he rumbled his approval. The sharp cold on her inner thighs revealed her juices and the horned male held her against the step, spreading her legs wider.

"Oh, fuck yeah."

Sabrina didn't recognize the voice, but she understood his desire and she wiggled her hips, enticing him with her weeping pussy. The cool rock bit into her chest and the scents of burning ponderosa pine, tangy arousal, and spicy male filled her nose. Then her world went white.

A hot, wet tongue slid between her folds and flicked her clit. Sabrina shrieked her pleasure as the tongue stabbed into her wet slit, setting off more fireworks behind her eyes. Her inner muscles clenched on the slick intrusion, but before she could rub herself on it, it retreated. She mewled her disappointment and wriggled.

The mouth returned to her clit, suckling and pulling on it as a thick finger plunged into her grasping cunt. She thrust back against the finger as the tongue and mouth seared her clit, dragging her closer and closer to her release. But not close enough.

Again he pulled back and she squealed her indignation, reaching for him to return. He rumbled a lusty laugh at her when her hand grasped nothing, and she looked over her shoulder at him.

His lips and beard glistened with her juices as he shoved his pants down his legs and drew out his hardened cock. The tip shimmered in the firelight, already wet with precum. She licked her lips and wished he'd push his straining flesh into her mouth. His burning gaze met hers and his nostrils flared with arousal as he watched her tongue slide over her lip.

"You're mine." He grasped her hip with one hand and

pushed down on his straining cock with the other just before he slowly, inexorably thrust his hard shaft into her hot core.

Oh, Goddess, he's so big! Sabrina moaned at each steady inch impaled her and her pussy clenched around the solid intrusion. She wriggled her hips to coax more sensation, but a second big hand caught her other hip and held her still as he growled. She whimpered and squeezed her inner muscles, begging for more.

Slowly, he withdrew, the slick slide of his cock against her nether lips dragged another wail from her chest. Then he pushed back in with deliberate motion, slow and relentless. Sexual fire burned up her spine, building her lust and arousal. But it wasn't enough. She needed it harder, faster...*more.*

"Please." She whimpered and squirmed, needing his strength, his power, his cock. "Please, fuck me harder." And she clenched her pussy tight on his shaft.

Her mate growled and pulled out so fast she didn't have time to complain before he slammed his rigid flesh back into her quaking cunt. Sabrina screamed as the simmering fire of her arousal exploded into a blazing conflagration, consuming everything in its path. The horned man drove into her, each successive thrust coming harder and faster. The scrape of his cockhead against her inner walls set off the beginning of her orgasm as his hips slammed into her ass and his balls slapped her nether lips.

Then he snaked a hand around her hip and stroked her clit with rough fingers.

"Come for me." The erotic growl in her ear set her off and she shot out into the night sky on a searing comet trail of sensation. Pleasure crashed over her in relentless waves as he stiffened behind her. Hot jets of cum filled her core and elicited more pleasure, sending her streaking across the universe. Power surged with the pleasure and she felt a series of clicks, as if loose mooring lines had fallen back into place.

She ignored it as she settled back down to earth. Her mate dragged his cock slowly out of her clutching pussy and rubbed the tip along her buttocks. Delight and arousal returned as she realized he remained hard. Lust surged and she wanted more. More cock, more pleasure, more power.

Sabrina pushed back from the altar and turned around to stare at her big lover. He towered over her, his eyes blazing with arousal and hunger, as if he hadn't been satisfied with only one release, either. She cocked a hip and offered him her best sultry smile, enjoying the slide of his cum down her thighs.

"Think you can take me again, stud?" She slid a hand down her belly and lightly strummed her own clit. He watched her hand with hunger, licking his lips as he wrapped a fist around his flexing cock. He growled and took a step closer.

Sabrina pulled her hand away from her pussy and licked it, enjoying both the tangy flavor of her release and the way the lust flared in his eyes. She stepped toward him and grasped his shirt in her fists, turning him until his ass faced the altar. He shifted without comment, his curiosity as heady as his hand stroking his rigid flesh.

She watched the leisurely motions of his hand and licked her lips again. She wanted his hot shaft in her mouth, but she didn't want to lose the opportunity to fuck him again. *I'll suck him later.* Why she thought there'd be a later, she didn't know, but she wanted to ride him too much to pause now.

Sabrina met his smoldering gaze and pushed gently on his chest. He released his cock long enough to slide onto the altar, his thick legs dangling off the stones. His straining flesh rose against his belly and she moaned with the thought of riding his sweet pillar. She held out her hands to him and he grasped her waist, lifting her until she straddled him.

Sabrina paused and studied him, recognizing the teal eyes staring out from behind the emerald mask. *Darius.* For just a moment, Sabrina found herself in the center of a Faerie ring, drums pounding, surrounded by couples dirty dancing and the Summer Queen watching with avid intensity. Lust and arousal surged through her, sucking her back into the pull of her lover, and she reached between them. Her hand closed around his solid shaft, and she positioned the tip at her dripping pussy. His cock flexed in her hand and she met his gaze once more.

"Make us one, Darius. Come to me in the name of the Goddess."

She lowered herself onto his hot shaft and they both moaned as he came to rest balls-deep inside her. They didn't move for several heartbeats, and Sabrina lowered her head to brush his lips.

Darius opened his mouth and swept his tongue across hers with unexpected tenderness, and she fell into his kiss. His hands slid up her sides to cup her breasts and he thumbed her nipples into taut peaks as his tongue teased her. Sizzling magic and energy built between them like static electricity and her pussy clamped down on his cock with anticipation.

"As you wish, my lady. I'm yours to command."

Hearing his deep voice deferring to her turned her on and fresh liquid coated her cunt and his cock. She rocked her hips to brush her clit against his shaft and he groaned, dropping his hands to her waist once more. Darius helped lift her off his cock then let her slide slowly down onto him again.

Sabrina gripped his shoulders to steady herself as they moved in an easy rhythm and arched her back, brushing her aching nipples against his chest. He dipped his chin and nuzzled her breasts, kissing the skin above her bodice. Electricity shot straight from her chest to her pussy and she clenched again, making Darius growl.

Arousal smoldered at the back of her mind as they moved together. She met and held his gaze, falling into the teal depths. The gilded mask glittered and flashed in the light of the sacred circle, and Sabrina realized she fucked the ancient god of fertility and virility. Lust surged, burning at path straight to her pussy as the magic between them grew and strengthened.

She rose off his cock faster, slamming down harder as she angled her head to kiss him. The rich taste of wine combined with the throbbing beat of the drums pushed her arousal higher. She tightened her fingers in the shoulders of his tunic, wishing she could touch the flesh of his hard chest. He seemed to have the same idea because he palmed one breast and squeezed gently, rocking his hips as he thrust into her.

The pressure built and she whimpered as she threw back her head, riding the pulse of desire. Darius growled and thrust, then dropped his hand between them where her mound ground against the base of his cock. His thumb found her clit, swirling over it with determined motion, and her orgasm broke free from her control.

"Come for me, sweet Goddess. Take my seed and become one with me."

The sexy words spoken in his husky voice sent her straight into the stars, carried on wings of passion, and something else. Something more.

Love.

Her release burst through her like fireworks, but instead of flashes of light, the world blazed white. Pleasure exploded through her and filled her with delight of renewal and strength. Scents of new grass, wet mountain air, and fresh pine hit her nose, and a warm, summer breeze caressed her cheeks, both of her face and of her ass.

Sabrina gasped and opened her eyes.

The world around her solidified into soft mists and glorious new growth. The breeze cleared some of the mists and the ends of a suspension bridge appeared, leading off into the fog. Darius stood before her, holding one of her hands. He still wore the horned mask and the long hunter green tunic, but his eyes glowed with teal fire as if lit from within.

Sabrina wanted to ask where they were when someone ambled toward them from the direction of the bridge. *Sweet glory, who is this?* The figure clarified into a tall, statuesque woman with eyes full of stars and rich, nut-brown hair. Sabrina recognized the Matron form of the Goddess. Amazement stole her breath and Sabrina bowed her head in reverence as She stopped beside them, a gentle smile on Her lips.

"Be welcome, May Lord and Lady." The feminine voice rolled over them like a velvet balm. "You have come here to seal your sacred site against negligence and misuse, and to finalize the paths you both have taken to get here. It is with great love and respect I offer you my blessing on this endeavor, and accept the gift of your communion this Beltane."

The Goddess's gaze fell on Sabrina and she wondered if any of this could be real.

"Yes, dear little witch. More real than you might later realize. You've been offered a great many gifts by those who love you. Have faith and take them to heart."

She turned her gaze to Darius. Sabrina heard nothing but the breeze through the ropes of the bridge and her own throbbing heartbeat, which seemed to be growing louder. The Goddess rested Her hand on theirs where they joined and power flared, turning the world white once more. But before everything faded away, Sabrina caught the pale smudge of a great spreading tree emerging from the mists. *Tír na nÓg.*

White hot bliss seared all conscious thought away and the throbbing music and drums returned full force. Sabrina panted with the aftereffects of her release, the bliss slowly draining away. She came back to herself seated on Darius's lap and her pussy tightly gripping his cock. He seemed just as winded and surprised to return to the bonfire in the sacred circle. He met her gaze and she read wonder and awe in his eyes.

"Did you see Her?"

"Yes. She blessed our offering." His cock flexed within her and she moaned, her pussy squeezing in appreciation.

"What else did She say to you?"

Darius took a breath to answer, but a fanfare broke out, and they turned their heads to watch the Summer Queen depart. Courtiers gathered to follow after, taking their mage fyre globes with them. The music had dwindled to the whistle of the wind through the trees and the thunder of their own heartbeats. The Queen disappeared into the trees, taking the light and excitement with her. Sabrina and Darius sat alone on the altar to the Goddess with a few pairs of dancers reclining together at the edges of the sacred circle.

The bonfire had settled down to crackle happily in its bed, its heat retreating as its fuel dwindled to charcoal. A breeze snaked across the open space and caressed Sabrina's bare buttocks. She shivered and cuddled closer to Darius's chest. He smelled of wood smoke, hot sex, and...*home.*

"Are you cold, Sabrina?" He wrapped her in his arms, surrounding her with his heat.

"Yes, a little. My ass is hanging in the wind." He chuckled at her words and slid his hands down to grip her butt. "Oh, glory, that feels good." The heat of his hands seeped into her.

"Perhaps we should get dressed." He moved his hands to her waist under her skirt, caressing as he went. "It looks as though the party's over."

Sabrina nodded, but didn't move to get up. She held his gaze in the fading light of the fire, trying to decide if she should say anything. She didn't have much time and it could all be for naught, but she screwed up her courage and took a deep breath.

"I love you, Darius."

****

Darius couldn't have been more surprised if someone had cracked him over the head with a club. *Did she just say she loved me?* He sat with a sexy, wanton woman on his cock and lost all coherent thought to his overwhelming joy and excitement.

"Darius?"

"Yes, sorry. Can you repeat that?"

She gave him a shy smile. "I love you."

The joy bubbled up and spread across his face in a wide grin. "That is most excellent news."

He reached up and tilted her head to his lips. She sighed and opened for him. Her acceptance warmed his heart as he slipped his tongue into her mouth and kissed her with all the joy pouring out of him. The slide of her tongue against his stirred his cock, and she moaned, breaking the kiss.

"I think I should get down. My knees are starting to hurt."

Nothing like reality to kill an erotic moment. He murmured an apology and helped lift her off his half-hard shaft. She hissed as she straightened her legs and stood to the side of the altar, rubbing the backs of her knees. His own hiss lit the air as the cool wind touched his wet cock, wrapping fingers of cold around him. He rose and searched for his discarded pants, belatedly recalling she wore less than he.

Darius searched the grounds beside the altar, spotting her clothes first.

"Here, *acushla*, let's get you dressed and wrapped up.

The wind has turned chill." He offered her the trousers and watched as she slipped them over her legs. Shivering as the breeze nipped his balls, he found his pants in a pool of shadow. He jerked them on and tied the drawstring, sighing with relief as the cold cut off.

"Feel better?" Sabrina's voice held amusement. Her lavender eyes glittered through the mask in the dying light of the fire and the aragonite necklace flashed as she turned. "Come on. Let's head home. I think the Fae want to clean up and we're just in their way."

She held out her hand to him and chagrin slid through him. Where had his manners gone? He grasped her hand and tucked it into the crook of his elbow, gathering her against his side. She sighed and snuggled closer, a sweet smile curling her lips. The smile fueled his joy and pride. His mind ran around in happy little circles like a puppy when its mistress returns. *She loves me. She loves me.*

The magic energy floated around them in swirls of sparkles like pixie dust, but the tingling flurries cut off as soon as they stepped out of the trees. Darius took a deep breath with the sense of a new life unfolding before him

Sabrina retrieved her shawl just outside the sacred circle and he helped wrap it around her, stealing a kiss when she stood encircled in his arms. The noses of their masks clacked together and she giggled.

"Maybe we should take these off." She trailed her fingers over her auburn mask, lifting it off her face. She'd looked exotic in the mask, but the beauty of her face stirred his cock, even after all the sex.

Darius pulled his own mask off and tucked her close to his side again. "Come. Let's get out of the wind. Shall I drive us home?"

"Do you want to? I can do it."

"I'd be happy to drive us back."

"Okay." She handed him the keys and he escorted her to her door. She pulled it open and he handed her up into the seat. She gave him a tired and grateful smile as he closed her in.

A warm and companionable silence enveloped them as they drove back toward her house. Darius glanced over at the woman he loved seated beside him and his heart swelled. She was perfect. Strong, intelligent, and beautiful, he thanked his lucky stars she'd returned his love. His admiration for her had grown over the time he'd spent with her, and he drove on with the determination to stay in her world.

The headlights of her van swung across the front of her house as they turned up the gravel drive and unease slid across his gut. A subtle golden glow illuminated the front porch and he swallowed hard when he caught sight of what waited for them.

The Summer Queen and a few privileged members of her Court stood in the trees beside the house. The Queen looked lovely in her pale green and gold finery, elegant and regal, but cold. When she offered a sweetly malicious smile, Darius's heart sank. *What is she up to?*

****

Darius pulled the van to a stop and sat for a few moments with the motor running. Sabrina followed his gaze to the Summer Queen and wondered why her smile gave Sabrina the willies. Something had gone wrong, but she couldn't think what. They'd performed the rituals. The Goddess had blessed them and accepted the offering. What else needed to be done?

"Darius?"

He gave her a wan smile and handed her the keys. "Come. Let's find out what Her Majesty needs."

Sabrina slid out of her seat and tossed the door closed as she wrapped her shawl around her shoulders. While the Fae Court looked beautiful, her instincts wailed in warning.

She didn't think the Fae Queen usually made house calls to the witches who performed the rituals, and Darius's reaction supported her belief.

"Welcome, Chamberlain Winterbourne and Lady Foxglove." The Queen's musical voice floated over them along with her magic, but it didn't ease Sabrina's worry. "We wish to offer our thanks for your efforts in the rituals, Lady Foxglove."

The Queen inclined her head and Sabrina resisted the urge to curtsey.

"You've chosen an excellent guardian for the sacred site, Chamberlain Winterbourne. We are pleased someone of such strength shall preside over it."

Benign gratitude suffused Her Majesty's words, but despite the magic cajoling them to believe, Sabrina waited for the other shoe to drop. She glanced at Darius as he bowed graciously, but tension mantled his shoulders. *He knows something's up, too.*

"We are honored by your approval, Your Majesty." Darius gave his own false smile.

"In honor of your faithful and excellent service, Chamberlain, We shall grant you two boons. Because you've upheld your end of our agreement, you've been reinstated as Chamberlain at Court, you shall retain your longevity, your family sword, and your honor, and the Winterbourne name shall be held forever sacred, with respect and honor. Your position is assured."

Darius dipped his head in acknowledgement, but Sabrina's gut clenched. "*Agreement?* What agreement?"

"The agreement to keep his position in exchange for your performance of the High rituals." The Queen offered her sweetly malicious smile again. "And you performed admirably, Lady Foxglove."

Sabrina heard the compliment, but anger seethed in her gut. *Darius did this to keep his job?* It didn't matter she'd decided to attend the ceremony on her own. He'd betrayed her for a position at Court. For family honor and name. For a *sword.*

"Thank you, Your Majesty." She curtsied to hide her expression.

"And now for your second boon, Chamberlain."

"Perhaps Your Majesty would grant me the opportunity to ask for this boon at a later date." Darius shot a wary look in Sabrina's direction, but she ignored him. "Your generosity is beyond my expectations."

The Queen smiled at the flattery. "Very well, Chamberlain. We shall grant your request as We are feeling quite generous tonight. But We expect your report on tonight's events as soon as you return to Court."

"Thank you, Your Majesty." Darius bowed again.

"You're returning to Court?" Sabrina couldn't stop the incredulous question bursting out.

"Please excuse us a moment, Your Majesty."

The Queen inclined her head as Darius took Sabrina's hand and dragged her away from the Fae, their curious eyes gleaming with renewed interest. Nothing like a good intrigue to send the gossip flying.

"What's going on, Darius? Did you really make a deal with the Summer Queen?"

"Yes. At the time it was the only way to protect my family and my honor."

"And your job and your sword, according to her. What happened to 'I love you and want to stay with you forever?' Was it all part of your plan to save *your job?*"

"Not just my position, Sabrina. At the time she threatened me, you hadn't made your decision yet. I never hid my intentions from you. I needed you to do the rituals."

"And aren't you lucky I made the decision for myself. Made it so easy for you." Her stomach curdled. "Fucking for employment. You're the perfect man-whore, Darius. You even got paid with position, honor, name, and sword. Nicely done."

"Sabrina—"

"No." She pulled away from his reaching hands. If he cradled her against him, she'd capitulate. "Get away from me. Don't touch me. You've made your choice and secured your job. Go back to your Fae Court and live with your 'honor' for your long life with your sword. As far as I'm concerned, you have no *honor*."

"Sabrina, please." He reached for her again, but she stepped back. "She threatened to ban my family from Court and strike our name from the records. I couldn't destroy their hopes."

"No, of course not. I see where I stand in terms of what's important to you. Family name, honor, sword, then lover. Or am I even in that category? The way it looks, I'm just another pussy in a long line of them."

"No, *acushla*, you're so much more to me."

"Don't call me that." She snarled straight into his face. "Nice job stringing me along. I applaud you on your skills of manipulation. I fell for all of it."

"Dammit, woman, listen to me!" He grabbed her arms and glared, nose to nose with her. "I want you and I'd sacrifice everything to stay." He softened his grasp and gave her a pleading look. "You promised you'd give me the time to take my leave. You said you'd wait for me to return to you."

"I said it when I thought you meant your lies. But now you're free. You don't have to return. Ever. Your position and family honor are evidently more important to you." She gritted her teeth and met his gaze, barely holding back her urge to spit at him. "Go back to your life and leave me alone."

"Sabrina."

"Get away from me, Chamberlain Winterbourne. I don't need a man to save me, and I certainly don't need you."

The rage festering in her gut only made her voice

harder and he released her, stepping back. Hurt and bewilderment shot through his expression before he resumed his Courtly mask.

"Very well, Lady Foxglove." He bowed to her and turned, retracing his steps toward the Summer Court. They welcomed him with their tinkling musical voices and he accepted their greetings.

Sabrina stood back and watched them as they gathered to go, her heart folding in on itself. *I don't need a man, I never did. I knew he was a player. It's my own fault if I fell for him.* Her pep talk did nothing to stem the pain as the Fae faded into the new summer forest. But before they disappeared, Darius turned to face her, his expression solemn. He watched her as they vanished from view and Sabrina held it together until they'd gone.

Roiling emotions coursed through her as she unlocked her front door and stepped inside. The silence of her home gripped her heart and she crumpled into a heap on the welcome mat, the tears flooding down her cheeks. He'd said he loved her. He said he wanted to be with her forever. But he'd chosen his job and his sword over her. The knife of despair twisted deeper. *Oh, Goddess, how will I get over this?*

CHAPTER FIFTEEN

Darius paced the great hall with a measured stride commensurate for the Chamberlain of the Summer Court. He nodded and smiled graciously at the passing courtiers, even taking the time to hear some of their petitions to put before the Queen. He exchanged pleasantries, shook forearms, and agreed to hear their words. He performed his duties and dressed with the utmost care.

Since returning to the Court, he'd been more popular than ever. The Queen had honored him and his family, making a public proclamation of the service he'd rendered and the sanctity of his family's name in the records. Invitations to all members had been issued for Court attendance and they came, even his brother Phinnius, who'd joined the military.

Darius swung his gaze over the teaming ballroom and met many a lady's eye as he passed. Several twittered behind their fans while dipping their heads in coy invitation for more than just a passing look. His popularity among the Fae ladies had reached epic proportions, but his own interest had waned. He found none of them measured up to his ideal of beauty despite their elegant clothes and fanciful chignons. They appeared unfinished and ethereal to him, without the earthy feminine charms he wanted.

Men sought his company and advice. Lords, once disdainful, approached him for discourse on issues of sovereignty. Women touched his arm or added an extra smile when he passed, all because he'd gained favor with the Queen. Darius played the part of the dutiful and powerful Chamberlain, offering smiles and encouragement to those who approached him.

Everything to hide the emptiness inside.

Darius's heart ached and each gesture felt like a counterfeit affectation barely hidden. None of the words spoken or promises made held any truth. The courtiers merely observed the game, went through the motions, and postured for the best possible appearance.

It was all artificial.

Bollocks. His heart sat empty. The music, elegance, and beauty of the Court showed its age. Cracks appeared in the glorious façade and the magic of the Queen no longer thrilled him. The same games, the same meaningless posturing he'd experienced for the last century played in an endless reel. He didn't want to remain among them anymore, but he had nowhere else to go.

All I have is my job, my honor, and my sword.

Sabrina's mocking words echoed in his head and pain stabbed his heart so sharply, he paused to take a deep breath.

"Are you well, brother?"

Darius looked over his shoulder and met the gaze of his elder brother Tiberius. The current Lord Winterbourne stood just a few inches shorter than Darius, but his shoulders had greater breadth and his eyes shimmered emerald green. Silver showed at his temples though only a decade older, and a slight paunch had developed over his belt.

"Yes, quite well, Lord Winterbourne." Darius grasped his brother's forearm and gave another false smile.

"Welcome. I trust your journey here was pleasant?"

"Quite." Tiberius looked smug. "It has been a momentous time for our family. The Queen has bestowed great honor on us."

On me, you pompous ass. And it all means shite. "Indeed."

Two Fae ladies strolled by and inclined their heads to Darius. He nodded back and smiled, to which they twittered and fluttered their fans.

"I see your reputation hasn't diminished with the honor heaped on our name." Tiberius eyed the ladies with lascivious interest. "Perhaps some of that goodwill shall spread throughout the family."

Tiberius's allusions to trysts with females other than his wife sickened Darius. He'd often taken advantage of such infidelity, but his beliefs toward the practice had changed. He refused to cuckold a man just to scratch an itch best relieved by his hand.

"I'm sure you'll find many a willing partner, brother." Darius tried to disguise the sour edge to his voice, but Tiberius eyed him with surprise.

"What are you moping about, Darius? I'd have thought you'd received everything you wanted." Tiberius gestured to the Court as they strolled, nodding graciously to the other courtiers of the Summer Queen. His brother reveled in his element, his elegant clothing matched only with his faux serene expression.

"Of course. And I'm not moping." Darious's disgust at what the Court found valuable festered within him, but he covered it with bland cordiality. "The family's honor is intact, I still hold my position at Court, and Kainon remains in my keeping." He shrugged under the sword's weight. "I'm not moping."

"Yes, you are. Ever since you returned, you've drifted through your duties and barely remembered to invite your family to Court." Tiberius sniffed. "If the Queen hadn't issued the invitation, I doubt we would have heard from you." His brother eyed him narrowly. "What is eating you, brother?"

"It's nothing." Darius had no intention of revealing his aching heart to anyone, least of all his position-coveting elder brother.

"Does nothing have a name?"

"What?"

Tiberius snorted and raised an eyebrow. "I've never seen you this way. Hell, you've rarely visited us throughout your career with the Queen so I've barely seen you at all." His expression morphed into a mild sulk. "Do we hold no value in your life since you've become the Chamberlain?"

Darius growled. "Don't be absurd, Tiberius." His brother had no idea all he'd lost in favor of his family's good standing. Flashing lavender eyes and mahogany hair materialized in his mind, but he shoved the lovely image away. "I daresay you've never made me feel welcome after I assumed my duties to the Queen."

"Certainly not my fault." Tiberius drew himself up with an arrogant sniff. "The position is suited to someone who has had organizational experience, not someone who did no more than clerk for a lord."

Darius barked a laugh. "Such as you, I suppose? With all your years minding the estates?"

"Exactly right."

"As I recall, brother, when I became Chamberlain, you'd only just begun to learn how to run our ancestral home. And I seem to remember a few times when you had to mortgage a few lands to make ends meet."

Tiberius flushed and his lips tightened. "It's not my fault the foremen are lazy, thieving bastards."

Aye, it's never your fault, brother. Darius wanted to needle Tiberius until the older man felt the same frustrated helplessness consuming him. *I gave so much up for you. At least you could be grateful.* But he'd never told his family what he'd left, much less what he'd loved. And he'd never tell Tiberius. The ambitious man would use it against him to gain favor from the Queen.

Bloody hell, he can have it.

"Of course not, brother. It's so hard to find those who will work for the pittance you pay them. I can't imagine why anyone would attempt to get ahead in life."

Darius had delivered his statements in an even voice, but his brother's face turned white. When Tiberius had executed the family's trusted steward for the alleged crime of embezzlement, scandal had broken through the Court. No one knew the truth, but Tiberius had mortgaged much and chose not to pay the servants during the time.

"Forgive me." He gave Darius a stiff bow. "I see my lady beckoning me."

Darius watched his elder brother stride over to Lady Winterbourne with his anger mantling his shoulders. *He'll have to learn to better disguise it or the Court will eat him alive.*

Darius sighed and turned his attention to the Queen. She laughed at something and all the courtiers around her twittered with careful amusement. They jockeyed for position to be the Queen's favorite, but the mercurial Fae woman rarely kept them long. He'd been in her favor the longest, and now it had lost its attraction. Empty gestures, empty smiles, intrigue around every corner. Once he'd seen it as a challenge, now it appeared a waste of effort.

"Pardon, Chamberlain, might I have a word?"

Darius sighed inwardly and turned, a carefully constructed smile forming on his lips until he saw the speaker. A grin stretched his tired muscles. "Phinnius, by the Goddess! I'm glad to see you. What brings you to Court?"

He embraced his youngest brother and his heart melted a little. He and Phinnius shared a closeness he'd never experienced with anyone beyond his mother. And Sabrina.

But he ruthlessly squelched the thought.

"Other than the official invitation of the Queen? Nothing." He chuckled and thumped Darius on the back. "It seemed like the perfect time to come see you, brother. I've heard much about your exploits." Phinnius grimaced as they glanced over to Lord and Lady Winterbourne. "I see our older brother has taken full advantage of your accomplishments, and attributed them to the family. He always was a pompous ass. How do you put up with him?"

Darius laughed. "I don't. I left him safely ensconced on the estates in the country. But one of the boons granted me when I returned included a visit to Court for the rest of the family."

"I'm grateful." Phinnius gripped Darius's forearm with real affection. "I got to see you. Tell me, how goes the role of Chamberlain?"

"Well enough. I have position, power, the ear of the Queen, such as it is." Phinnius's sapphire blue eyes narrowed at his sarcasm. "Everything a man could desire."

They walked together through the crowd and some of the hopelessness unwound from Darius's heart. His brother's company brightened the dismal sentence of being at Court.

"So why are you so miserable?"

"Why do you say I'm miserable?"

"Darius." The tone of reproach in Phinnius's voice made him look over at his brother with surprise. "You couldn't sound more bleak if you stood on the front lines at Waterloo." Phinnius crossed his arms over his chest. "What's wrong, brother? Surely your life is as you want it?"

"Of course, it's perfect."

"Then why do you look so forsaken?"

Because I'm tired of this game and I miss the woman who holds my heart. The woman who told him to go and never return. He thrust the thoughts away and shook his head.

"Perhaps I've become too cynical and jaded for Court."

Phinnius sucked in a surprised breath. "You? The most adept at political intrigue and posturing? Jaded?" He laughed. "About time."

"What?"

"Darius, I knew this life would only suit you for a while, and I'm glad it's at an end. But I'm curious what has changed your view." Phinnius slapped him on the shoulder. "It can't be Tiberius's need to be at Court. What has captured your heart, brother?"

Darius let the silence between them expand as he sauntered through the courtiers mobbing the room. If he could trust anyone with the secrets of his heart, Phinnius held the honor, but the rest of the crowd acted as the Queen's ears. He tugged his brother over to an alcove off the main ballroom and scanned the space around them. The Court learning of his personal life, particularly his elder brother, remained on the list of things he'd like to avoid.

"You know I've returned from arranging the High Beltane rituals in the human realm."

Phinnius nodded. "The news seethed all over the Court. Even the soldiers heard about it. What of it?"

"The Queen asked me to secure the talents of a witch to conduct the rituals, and for all my hard work, the she gave me the "gift" of being the May Lord."

"Congratulations." Phinnius grinned. "It must have been some night to leave you in such a state."

"It wasn't just the ceremony, Phinn. I stayed with Lady Foxglove and her family for a sennight. I learned about her, experienced a small measure of her life." He'd experienced a whole world, greater than he'd ever imagined. And with its loss, the greatest sorrow. Darius's heart still ached. "I miss her."

"By the Goddess!" Phinnius laughed. "Have you

actually gone and fallen in love, Darius?"

"Not so loud." But he couldn't find the anger to truly reprimand his brother. "She told me to go, Phinn, when she discovered the deal I'd struck with the Queen. She told me to go and never return."

"What deal?"

Darius surveyed the room again as if lost in thought, searching for listeners. When he found none, he gave a bitter smile to his brother. "The Queen threatened to release me from my duties, ban our family at Court, strike our name from the records, and take Kainon from our keeping if I didn't convince the witch to perform the rituals."

"Did she need to be convinced?"

"Yes. She feared pregnancy."

Phinnius frowned. "Strange. Children are blessings. Why wouldn't she want one?"

"Because she already has two, and no partner or husband to help her raise them."

"Mother had no one to help her and we turned out well enough." Phinnius thumped Darius in the shoulder with his fist.

"Mother no more deserved the role than Sabrina does. Father was a prick."

"Sabrina, is it now?" Phinnius winked.

"Hush." Darius wanted to take his dagger and dig out his aching heart. Why did this hurt so badly? He'd only known her for a week. One glorious week. "Her world is not like ours. She is alone, and often ridiculed for her solitude."

"Darius, do you think Sabrina is pregnant with your child?"

"I can only surmise the magic created a new life within her, what with the strength of it and the Queen's presence for the rituals." Goddess, he hated the idea of leaving Sabrina without his company. "And with the Goddess's blessing at the end."

"Sorry?" Phinnius looked startled.

"The Goddess appeared to us at the end of the rituals. To Sabrina and I."

"Bloody hell. Which form did She take?"

"What?" Darius shook his head.

"Which form? The Goddess holds four forms, the Maiden, the Matron, the Warrior, and the Crone. Which did She take?"

Darius thought back to the star-eyed woman who had approached them at the bridge to Tír na nÓg. "The Matron, I'd guess. Too old to be a maid and too young to be a crone. Why?"

Phinnius sighed. "If She wore the Matron, She represented home, family, and children. I'd say you've gotten your witch with child."

Darius's heart sank and his gut churned. Sweet mercy, he'd become the basest pond scum alive. No better than his prick father.

"And I left her."

Phinnius shook his head. "So why are you here?"

"I have my duties to the Queen." Phinnius made a rude sound. "And Sabrina told me to go and never return. Her anger rose incandescent."

The pain in his chest almost doubled him over. Disgust at leaving Sabrina with child ate at him, along with the sorrow of betraying her, and the loss of her companionship. He glanced over at the Queen, luminescent in her golden dress and glittering jewels, and found her gaudy and ridiculous. All the courtiers appeared the same, fawning over the Queen, jockeying for position, all of it meaningless. Even his elder brother Tiberius and Lady Winterbourne fluttered around Her Majesty, begging for scraps.

"Anger can be assuaged with honesty, Darius." Phinnius gripped his shoulder. "Don't wait, brother. Make her yours now." He paused and gave him a piercing look.

"Help her raise your child, be a better father than ours, and soothe your heart."

Darius gaped at his younger brother. When had Phinn learned such wisdom? He spoke with the certainty of the Goddess.

"What about the Queen?"

"Take your leave of her. Resign. Return to your Lady Foxglove." Phinnius winked. "The Court will take care of itself."

Darius narrowed his eyes. "Do you covet my position as well?"

"Me?" Phinnius scoffed. "No, not at all." He shuddered theatrically. "But I can see your misery as if you're wearing a feather headdress. I suspect others can as well. You don't want this life anymore, Darius. It's quite obvious."

"What about the family? If I resign, we'll lose our position of honor at Court."

"We could have lost it at any time, brother. The Queen didn't need you working for her to secure it. She'd like you to think it's all dependent on you, but she could have ripped it away without regard for any of us. You're not held here because of our honor." Phinnius shoved at Darius's shoulder. "Go, take your leave, and return to your witch. She needs you more than we do."

Could he walk away from the life he'd carved for himself? Darius scanned the room around him with all its counterfeit beauty and glitter. The magic no longer attracted him or held his heart. He found little joy in his duties and in time, it would bring dishonor to his family.

The Goddess always meant for me to leave the Court after Beltane. He had no idea where the certainty came from, but it resonated so strongly through him, he trembled.

Overwhelming relief and joy surged through Darius and he wrapped his brother in a bear hug in gratitude. "Come find me some time, when you can, Phinn. You'll always be welcome, even if I'm alone."

"If you're alone?"

"Sabrina was terribly angry."

Phinnius gripped his forearm in farewell. "Never give up, Darius. I daresay she's worth it."

His brother had the truth. Darius descended the stairs to ask for his second boon and take his leave of the Queen.

CHAPTER SIXTEEN

Sabrina stared at the little strip of plastic and felt the inevitable crash over her. Pregnant. Again. She'd have another February baby. *Bloody hell, I'm running out of dates for birthdays.* The attempt at levity spurred her sorrow and tears spilled down her cheeks.

"Dammit!" Pregnancy hormones sucked. So did morning sickness, but she hadn't experienced that little gift yet.

She wiped her eyes with her sleeve, tossed the plastic tab in the trash bin, and returned to the kitchen to clean up dinner dishes. The house seemed too quiet, too empty since she'd told Darius to go. He'd become a welcome fixture there.

You need to get over it. You knew he wouldn't stay. He only proved you right.

It still rankled. She didn't want to be right about him. She'd wanted him to be different, to mean all the things he'd said about loving her and wanting to be the father to her children. Especially the new baby.

The Goddess's words came back to taunt her. *You've been offered a great many gifts by those who love you. Have faith and take them to heart.*

Oh, she'd taken them to heart. Especially the new life growing within her. She *wanted* the baby, Darius's child. She wanted the memories she'd made with him and the embodiment of the love she'd felt for the man. Even if he broke her heart.

It didn't help to hear about Merrilee Fuckstwice everywhere she went, either. The woman paraded around town with a massive superiority complex because of being selected to perform the High Beltane rituals in Durango. Sabrina couldn't get away from the news at Mazie's, and the few times she'd seen Merrilee in town had been torture. *Not only did she take Tommy, but now she thinks she's the Goddess's emissary to Cloudburst. My great honor? To be pregnant and alone. Again.*

Grief hit her with new waves until she had to retreat from the sink full of dishes before she rubbed her eyes full of soap. She sat down in the living room and tried to swallow her sobs, but they rattled in her chest until she started to hiccough.

At least Marty Robinson no longer presented a threat. Sabrina had almost run into him at the grocery store. He'd apologized and helped her pick up the apples she dropped before walking away as if they'd never met. It appeared the Fae had followed through with Darius's request.

Oh, Goddess. Darius. She shook her head fiercely. *Dammit. Think of something happy...*

Her gaze rose to the set of horned masks she'd placed on the mantle. She'd found Darius's mask in her van the morning after Beltane and she couldn't bring herself to throw it away. The tall antlers reminded her of the spectacular night she'd spent with the May Lord. The virile, handsome, sexy, strong man who made her feel like a goddess, and brought her more pleasure than any lover before him.

Her throat closed and tears overflowed her eyes. It didn't matter. He'd picked honor and duty over her. She wished it could be different. She wished he hadn't been a lying sack of shit. She wished...

Someone knocked on the door before she could finish the last thought and she stilled. Who the heck would stop by at this hour? Sabrina wiped her eyes with her shirt hem and stood, taking deep breaths. Maybe she could blame the puffiness of her face on the pregnancy. A pregnancy she'd told no one about.

Ah hell.

Sabrina squared her shoulders and strode to the door. *I'm fine. I'm good. See?* She opened the door and her breath left her. A groan of fury burst from her chest as she tried to slam it shut on the backswing.

"Sabrina! Please, wait, hear me out." Darius braced his foot in the doorjamb and his hands against the panel.

"No, I don't want to hear it, Darius."

"Please. I need to explain. If I haven't convinced you of my honesty when I'm done, then I will go. Please, Sabrina."

The sound of his voice made her heart ache and she leaned her forehead against the door. She didn't want to want him. He'd tricked her into believing he loved her and traded her help for his career. *But he asked me to trust him. He said it might take him some time, but he'd quit the Court and come back.*

Sabrina gritted her teeth and looked around the door at Darius. The earnestness on his face and in his eyes made her pause. He looked gaunt and haunted as if he'd pushed himself beyond his limits.

I'm just imagining things.

But her traitorous heart agreed to hear his petition, and she stepped back, allowing him to enter. "Fine. Come in."

"Thank you." He stepped inside and set a large duffle bag on the floor.

"You have ten minutes. Then you will go."

"If I can't convince you otherwise."

Ah, the old Darius she knew and loved. Always so sure he'd get what he wanted. Never mind that she wanted the same.

"Clock's ticking, Darius."

"Please, Sabrina." He gestured to her living room. "Sit with me and let me explain."

She sat in her favorite chair as he removed his long jacket and she noted he no longer wore the sword scabbard with the oak leaf embroidery. *At least he didn't bring the nasty thing into my house.* He sat down on her couch and leaned forward, his elbows on his knees as he gathered his defense.

"When I first arrived here in Cloudburst, I thought I knew what I could expect." He spread his hands. "Another place for strengthening the wards, another witch upon whom to bestow the honor of the Beltane rituals, another task to perform for the Queen. It seemed simple enough.

"But you weren't anything like I expected, Sabrina." He raised his gaze from the floor and met her own. "You didn't want the honor or the recognition. You didn't even want me in your home, and you forced me to learn your way of life. You never backed down from your duties or responsibilities, yet you refused to take on more." He chuckled. "You alternately frustrated and impressed me over it."

Sabrina sat back and crossed her arms over her chest.

He cleared his throat. "My task was to get you to do the rituals and I thought it would be easy. But you refused and each time I spoke with the Queen, she insisted on your participation. As it turned out, your abilities justified her faith."

Sabrina snorted and unfolded her hands to lay one on her belly. *Too bad I misjudged you.* "You made a deal with her, Darius."

"Originally, yes." He nodded. "The Queen threatened me with a loss I wasn't prepared to make. She threatened to dismiss me from my duties, banish my family from Court, strike our names from the records, and take the sword held in my family since my grandfather's grandfather. I couldn't take such a legacy away from my family." Darius sighed. "But as I got to know you and your family, I couldn't force you into performing the rituals."

"Fortunately for you, you didn't have to, did you?"

"Sabrina, you made the decision all on your own, but I would have given it all away even so." He reached for her hand and wrapped his around it. "Court life is about appearances and position. Everyone wishes favoritism from the Queen, and I had it, as long as I fulfilled my task. But I wanted to tell her to go to hell to be with you. I'd grown tired of the posturing, and the last time I spoke with the Queen, I no longer felt compelled to do her bidding. Her magic had no effect on me."

Sabrina raised her eyebrow. "Come on, the Summer Queen, one of the strongest Fae out there, and her magic couldn't suck you in? You must think I'm really back-woods."

"It's true, *acushla*, and you're not back-woods, as you call it. Your power surpasses hers."

"Don't call me that." Anger burned brighter as she shook his hands off. "I'm not your 'dear heart.' You don't trick or hide the truth from those you care about."

"You didn't give me a chance to explain!" Darius clenched his jaw. "You called me a deceitful man-whore and sent me away before I could tell you I'd made a different decision. The Queen's deal no longer applied to me. But you believed her, a woman who has made a career of manipulation and division for her own entertainment."

"And you went, didn't you? You must have really felt strongly about me if you left and didn't fight for your choice to stay." Tears threatened to slide down Sabrina's cheeks again, fueling her anger. "Goddess, Darius! I believed you when you said you loved me and wanted me in your life forever. I believed you and I could be together as a family. And I wanted it. I wanted it so much."

"Oh, Sabrina." He rose and gathered her into his arms. "I want it, too."

She struggled against his hold as the tears fell harder and harder. "Don't touch me. Leave me alone." She tried to ignore how good he smelled.

"I have left you alone for far too long, *acushla*. And I'm sorry." He only held on tighter, cradling her against his warm, wide chest. "But I'm fighting for what I want now. And I want to stay here with you, be your lover, your husband, whichever you desire, as long as I'm with you."

"But the Queen—"

"No longer has any control over my whereabouts or actions."

Sabrina stopped struggling. "What are you talking about?"

"I've resigned my position as Chamberlain in her Court."

"Why?"

"Because I want to be with you."

"But what about your honor and your family?" Goddess, she wanted to believe him and just snuggle in his warm embrace, but this seemed too good to be true.

He laughed softly. "My younger brother Phinnius reminded me the family could take care of itself and I only lost honor if I didn't take care of my own needs and responsibilities. As for the sword, I bestowed it upon the male heir who became a soldier. Surely he needs a well balanced blade more than I."

Darius tipped her head up to look in her eyes. "But you, Sabrina, are what I want and need. You, and Tansy, and Holly." He dropped a hand to her belly. "And the new little one growing here."

Sabrina gasped and pulled back to look at him. "How do you know I'm pregnant?"

234

He studied her face for a few heartbeats before he smiled ruefully. "Come sit with me on the div—couch." He returned to his seat and pulled her down beside him, taking one hand in his. "I suspected we would make a child given all the renewal and fertility magic of the High Beltane rituals, but the Goddess's words at the gateway to Tír na nÓg only make sense now with your confirmation."

Sabrina frowned. "What did She say?"

"She told me I'd have to face some obstacles to my dreams, but they wouldn't be insurmountable. She said to fight for what I wanted and follow my heart because my children would need my strength and guidance."

"Do you have any other children?"

"No." Darius squeezed her hand. "Only Tansy and Holly."

"But they're not yours."

"They could be. If you'll let me be your partner, lover…husband."

Sabrina's heart leapt with hope, but she studied his face, searching for truth in all the pretty details. She needed him to give her honesty this time.

"I'm trying to figure out what you want, Darius. What's your motivation for coming back here? Is it only the child? Because I can take care of a child without a man's help. I've been doing it for years."

Darius's jaw bunched as frustration flashed across his face, but it dissipated after a moment and he laughed ruefully. "I came back because I said I would. I came back because you've stolen my heart and tucked it away safely among your deviled eggs and bedtime stories, wrapped in the beauty of your smile and strength of your determination. My heart is here with you, and I can't live without it."

He laid his hand over her belly and warmth seeped in through her clothes. "I know you can take care of a child without my help. But I want to be here to help raise our children. I want to read stories to Holly and help Tansy learn to dance, and teach our new child how to tie his shoes."

"His?" Sabrina quirked an eyebrow.

"Ah, well, the Goddess is all about balance and I strive to follow Her example." He winked and she chuckled. "Please, Sabrina. Give me this chance to fulfill my promises to you, and to help you with our family."

Sabrina tilted her head. "What promises are you talking about, Darius?"

"The promises to take care of you should I get you pregnant. To move heaven and earth to stay with you and our child, and to stay in your life after Beltane as your husband." He kissed the side of her head. "They weren't just promises to you, *acushla*. They were also promises to me."

"Why?"

"Do you recall when I asked you what you wanted if you could have anything?"

"Yes, at the sacred circle when we visited the homestead."

"Correct. You told me you wanted a partner, a lover, a friend. Someone who loved you for you." He shifted on the couch to face her. "I realized I wanted to be that person more than I wanted honor, a memorable name, or the Summer Queen's regard. Because I loved you. I still love you."

"Then why did you make the deal with the Queen? And why did you leave?" Her questions held no logic, but the pain of his departure still burned.

"The deal had been made before you told me you'd perform the rituals, but I'd already decided I wouldn't push you into them." Darius drew her hand up to his lips and kissed her knuckles. "I meant to leave the Court, consequences be damned. But then you agreed on your own and I knew I had the freedom to choose. So I asked you to wait so I could resign my position."

He had asked her to wait, but she'd been furious when she'd thought he'd seduced her to keep his job.

"As for why I left…" Darius grimaced and shook his head. "I'd never faced such anger from a woman I cared for and I didn't know how to counteract it. But I do now."

Sabrina raised her eyebrows. "Oh, yeah? How?"

He took her face in his hands and pressed an achingly soft kiss to her lips. "With love, truth, and honesty. I will never hide anything from you again, Sabrina. You are my heart, my soul, and the source of the joy in my life. I've come to you to beg your forgiveness for my mistakes, and allow me to cherish you and our children by letting me stay. Please."

He dipped his head and kissed her again, swiping his tongue across her bottom lip as he sought entrance. Sabrina wanted to resist him and her mind shouted, *Can I really trust him?* But her heart already knew the answer and she moaned as she opened her mouth to receive his delicious caress.

"Please tell me I'm yours, *acushla*." She'd never expected the proud and arrogant Chamberlain of the Summer Court to beg. "The past weeks have been torture without you."

She wanted to laugh but his kisses stole her breath and soaked her panties. Her pussy clenched with sense memories of his hot, silken flesh buried there, and she squirmed closer to him on the couch. Goddess, she wanted him. Had always wanted him, and he could be hers, if she accepted his words as truth.

Sabrina pulled back from the kiss to look Darius in his teal eyes even as her body screamed not to stop. He stared at her with all his love and honesty shining through his gaze. She recalled his mastery of the artful look, but her gut told her he'd stopped playing. Sabrina inhaled a deep breath and took a chance.

SIOBHAN MUIR

"Tell you what, I'll promise you're mine if you take me to bed. Right now."

It took a few moments for her words to sink in, but his eyes blazed with arousal and he whooped as he jerked her into his embrace. He secured one arm below her knees and the other around her ribs, hauling her off her feet.

"You have yourself a deal, Sabrina Foxglove."

Darius carried her into her bedroom and tossed her on her bed, kicking the door shut behind him. He smirked as he yanked off his coat and unbuckled his leather belt. Sabrina lay where she'd bounced, watching as the sexiest man she'd ever loved revealed his glorious body.

"Tonight I will see you naked and revel in those lovely breasts of yours." He pulled off one boot then the other before shucking his pants to the floor. The scent of hot, spicy, aroused male filled the room, contrasting with her own vanilla and pine scents, and her pussy spasmed. "I will worship you as my own personal embodiment of the Goddess."

His sexy words only drove her arousal higher as he stood naked before her. His cock rose stiffly to his belly and drops of precum slid over the head. Sabrina licked her lips and rolled forward onto her hands and knees, wanting to take his dripping cock in her mouth and taste him.

He grasped his hard shaft with one hand and stroked it in short motions. "Is this what you want, Sabrina?"

Arousal surged and cream leaked between her thighs as she watched his hand. She nodded and reached for him, but he stood back with a smirk.

"Then strip. I want to see your glorious body. Only then will I give you my cock."

Sabrina tore off her shirt and yanked off her sweatpants, dragging her panties with her in her rush to taste him. But then she paused as a delicious idea slid through her mind. Turning her back, she pushed the straps of her bra off her shoulders one at a time until she freed her

238

arms. Then she stopped.

"Will you help me unhook my bra, Darius? I can't quite reach." She glanced over her shoulder at him.

He groaned as he stepped behind her, unhooking the garment. The lycra cups fell off her chest and he slid his hands around to fill his palms with her breasts. They both moaned as he rubbed his straining cock against her ass and bent down to kiss her shoulders.

"Sweet mercy, Sabrina. You're lovelier than I remembered." He plucked her nipples sending pleasure shooting straight to her pussy. "I've dreamed of holding you thus."

His choice of words always made her smile, but accompanied with his tender ministrations, they melted her heart. She arched her back, shoving her breasts harder into his hands and her ass against his cock. The hot, stiff flesh burned across her cheeks and she squirmed, hoping to feel more.

He growled and dropped a hand to her mound, holding her tight against him as he rubbed his cock into her. His fingers dipped between her thighs, sliding through her slick folds and massaging her clit in tight circles. Sabrina gasped as more fluid flooded her pussy, soaking his hand.

"You're so wet for me and I've dreamed of tasting your cream again." Darius rubbed her clit a little harder, spiking her arousal until her breath came in short pants. "Do you want my tongue on you, Sabrina?"

"Oh, yes, Darius. Give me your tongue."

He pulled his hand away from her clit making her mewl in protest, but he pushed her forward until she bent over the bed. Then he knelt behind her, running his hands over her hips and buttocks until he gripped her thighs with gentle fingers.

"Spread for me, *acushla*."

Sabrina shifted her feet apart as her pussy dripped with anticipation. Just the idea of him licking her folds from

SIOBHAN MUIR

behind had her arousal swamping her mind. Her nipples pebbled into aching peaks and she rubbed them on her coverlet, thrusting her ass back at him.

"You smell so sweet." His breath tickled the damp flesh of her pussy and she whimpered. "Let me see if your flavor matches your scent."

Hot slickness seared her nether lips as he licked from her clit to core. She squealed and squirmed, but his hands held her still as he moaned with ecstatic joy. His breath on her sensitive flesh excited her as much as his caresses and she wriggled her ass for more.

"Please, Darius, lick me more."

"As you wish, my lady."

His lips sealed to her pussy and his tongue explored her folds with loving attention. Slick heat seared through her and drove her closer to the edge of orgasm. Sabrina writhed in his grip, but he held her to his mouth and lapped up her juices. Teasing sparks ignited her fire and she squealed again as he suckled her clit, pulling on the hard little nub.

"Oh, Goddess, yes, Darius. Suck my clit!"

He didn't bother to reply, but tightened his mouth around her clit and sucked hard. She rocked her hips to increase the friction as he slid a thick finger into her pussy and rubbed her inner walls. Sabrina wailed as her arousal shot for the precipice of ecstasy and Darius added another finger, pumping in and out of her while he suckled.

"Oh...oh...oh, yes. Yes! Yesyesyesyes!"

Darius thrust his fingers a few more times before pulling out and fastening his mouth to her contracting cunt. He lapped up her release as she shot into the sky, blazing stars and exploding fireworks accompanying her. Love screamed with her as her orgasm kept going, burning an ecstatic path into the universe.

At last, she came down to feel Darius's lips on her inner thighs. Pleasure warmed her while he kissed and licked away all of her cum. She sighed and collapsed on the bed, her breath coming in tired gasps.

"Oh my glory, Darius. I think I could totally get used to this."

His dark, husky chuckle flowed over her as he helped her to her feet and escorted her onto the bed. His rigid shaft bumped her shoulder as he lifted the covers and she grasped his cock, rubbing the precum into the head with her thumb.

Darius hissed and pumped his hips a few times as she tightened her grip on him. Then he closed his hand on her wrist.

"Please, *acushla*, though I love your hands on me, I've waited several weeks to feel your pussy on my cockstand, and I cannot bear to come without it."

She whimpered and licked her lips, wishing he'd let her lick his cock. He groaned and swayed the plump head closer to her face, but pulled back at the last moment and crawled into the bed beside her.

"You are a tempting minx, my little witch." Darius slid his hand over her breasts as he settled his body against her, rubbing his cock on her hip. "I love that about you." He leaned over and captured one tight peak in his mouth, swirling his tongue over her areola.

Sabrina groaned and wrapped one hand around his hot shaft again, stroking the velvety skin for her own pleasure. She loved the sensation of his precum between her palm and his head.

Her nipple popped out of his mouth and he groaned. "Oh, sweet mercy, I love it when you stroke me." He dragged his hand down her belly and dipped a finger between her folds, strumming her clit. Searing pleasure shot straight to her brain and she gripped his cock hard.

"Bloody hell, you'll be the death of me yet, woman."

"I promise to make it good for you." Sabrina rocked her hips and stroked his cock.

Darius exhaled a high-pitched whimper of hopeful delight and pulled his hand away, wiping her juices on her lips. Then he covered her mouth with his, licking and suckling the wetness with his tongue. She opened her mouth and teased his tongue with her own. Darius growled and took control, stroking her with renewed ferocity.

Sabrina stabbed her hands into his hair and held on as he pulled away from her mouth and licked her throat below her ear. Lust built to a shrieking point, but his caresses gentled, turning sensual rather than dominant.

"I want this to last, to take my time and savor your delectable body." He reared up on one arm and looked down on her, love and arousal suffusing his features. "I'd love hard and fast, Sabrina, but tonight I want to go deep and slow with you. Please grant me this one wish."

"Is that all you wish?" She arched a brow.

"For now." His smirk scorched her with its deviousness.

She turned on her side and arched her leg over his thigh, rubbing her knee against his balls. "Are there any other things I should know about you?"

He chuckled as he ground the base of his cock against her knee. "I cannot stand haggis or horror cinema, and I'm rather partial to the Foxtrot."

Sabrina laughed. "I wondered about your dancing skills. I loved dancing with you at Beltane, and I adore making love to you."

"As long as you don't mind making love to an old man." He smirked at her as he fondled her nipple.

"Old? Heh, I'm not exactly a spring chicken at thirty two. How old are we talking, here?"

"I turned two hundred and twenty eight on May first, Beltane."

Sabrina studied his face, waiting for him to tell her the punch line. "Wait, you're serious? I missed your birthday?"

He blinked at her as if caught off guard. "Well, no, not

exactly." He winked. "I believe you helped me celebrate in fine style." He rocked his hips against her thigh, the head of his cock painting a wet stripe on her skin. "Best birthday celebration I've ever had to date."

"I'll have to work on improving on it. Now, about the two century mark…"

"Yes?"

"Are you really so old?"

He tilted his head. "The year I was born, your country had won its revolutionary war and ratified its Constitution in nine of the first thirteen colonies."

"But…how can you live so long? Aren't you human?" He didn't look Fae.

"I am. My people are known as the Kaerians, a race of long lived human warriors who have served the Fae kingdoms for millennia." He shrugged with one shoulder. "I believe they took our people with them because we possessed earth magic, a connection to the Goddess they didn't have and wished to cultivate."

Sabrina bit her lip and Darius groaned. "But I'm just a regular human. You know, who only lives about a hundred years? And I'm thirty-two years into it. Good chance I'll die way before you." It might not be a deal breaker, but certainly something to consider.

"Sabrina, I have seen over two centuries worth of life, and nothing has brought me more joy than being with you for the week I spent here at Beltane." He rolled his body over hers, bracing himself on his elbows as he held her face in his hands. "If we *only* have fifty more years together, I'll value them more than the previous two hundred." He brushed her lips with his own. "Besides, I suspect the Goddess's blessing to us on Beltane extended further than we will ever know, and gives me hope for our union."

"You think She made our lifespans equal?"

"I wouldn't put it past Her." Darius dipped his head and kissed Sabrina's lips with seductive tenderness. "So let us celebrate Her gift in the best way." And he slid his cock into her slick pussy, balls deep.

"Oh, Goddess, I've missed you, Darius."

"And I've missed you. You're so sweet and tight." He slowly withdrew until only his head teased her clenching slit, then pushed back in at a measured pace.

Sabrina didn't think she could get more turned on, but the drag of his head against her contracting inner walls set her afire. She grabbed his hips and held on, arching her pelvis until each motion dragged him against her clit. The scents of sex and hot cum perfumed the air between them, and built her arousal higher.

"Oh glory, Darius, it's so sweet." She moaned and arched, needing more tightness, more friction, more hard cock.

"Do you like slow and deep, my little minx?" He sounded out of breath, but his teal eyes blazed with feral fire as he stroked his cock in her pussy achingly slow.

"Yes…" She threw her head against the pillow and arched her back. "And no. I need you, Darius. I need more…"

"More of…this?" He increased his pace, rocking with shorter, harder strokes.

"Yes, please, Darius."

The fire of her arousal caught and expanded as her pussy spasmed with need. Darius groaned as she clamped down on him and he thrust a little harder, ramming his cock deep into her pussy. She grabbed his ass, digging her fingers into the hard, flexing muscles.

"Do you want me, Sabrina?"

She opened her eyes—when had she closed them?—and met his blazing gaze. He looked primal, barbaric, and yet so sexy she couldn't stand the idea of living without him.

"Yes, I want you, Darius."

"Do you love me, Sabrina?"

Her only hesitation came from needing breath. "Oh, Goddess, yes, Darius."

"The come for me, *acushla*, come for your lover!"

Darius thrust harder and Sabrina took flight, her pussy squeezing tight around his shuttling cock as her arousal burst into an inferno and tossed her into the night. She screamed her pleasure to the ceiling, riding his hot shaft with everything she had.

"I love you, Darius!"

He roared and stiffened, searing jets of cum filling her pussy and scorching her with his physical love. She'd never felt so satisfied after sex as she did with Darius and she needed him in her life, for better or for worse, till death parted them.

Darius collapsed on top of her then carefully rolled to the side to remain sheathed in her rippling pussy. He gathered her into his arms and kissed her cheeks, her eyes, her chin, everywhere he could reach.

"I love you, Sabrina," he gasped, peppering her skin with more kisses. "Dear Goddess, I love you. Please be my wife, my lover, my minx for all time. Marry me, Sabrina Foxglove."

She didn't even have to think. "Yes." She giggled for the first time in years. "Yes, I'll marry you."

He whooped and crushed her to his chest. "Thank the Goddess. I couldn't be more happy, *acushla*. I'll always be here for you."

Settling down in the arms of the man she loved, Sabrina chuckled. "Even when we have to move and completely clean out the mill on the Rainshadow homestead?"

"Rainshadow? Intriguing name."

"Yes, I thought it ironic in a town called Cloudburst."

Darius chuckled. "Very true. How many rooms will it have when it's finished?"

"Uh, I don't know. Why?"

Darius rocked his hips and her pussy clenched on his hardening flesh. "Because I think we should christen each one with the Goddess's blessing. Don't you?" He thrust again.

Sabrina gasped. "Oh, Goddess, yes. Can we start right now?"

He chuckled and strummed her clit with this thumb. "Definitely."

THE END

A WALK IN THE SAND
THE IVORY ROAD, BOOK 1
SNEEK PEEK

The adventure of Ivory's lifetime might just be the death of her...

When it comes to make believe, A-list actress Ivory is a professional. But when a desert hike takes her across a dimensional rift, her real-life self, Iliana Rory, must separate fantasy from reality. The man she swears is the costar in her next movie might share the same surname and appearance, but there are no sets in this Mr. Crowe's world, no props, and no director to yell "cut" before blood is spilled.

With a fortune in stolen treasure and the forces of the Knalish army hot on their trail, Brandon Crowe and his partner, Ahmad, must cross a desert neither of them knows well. Mistaken for their guide, Iliana seizes any chance to stay ahead of the army and survive in this new world.

Adventure straight out of a Hollywood blockbuster might be on Iliana's bucket-list, but she never dreamed there'd be the real possibility of death when the end credits roll. A Walk in the Sand is the first story in the four part serial recounting Iliana's journey along the Ivory Road.

THE NAVY'S GHOST
BAD BOYS OF BETA SQUAD, BOOK 1
SNEEK PEEK

A SEAL is strongest with her Team…

Ensign Christiana "Ghost" Brickman is the only female SEAL to survive BUD/S training, a real Navy Jane. But when an ambush ends her career as an active SEAL, she's free to pursue other interests. Like her two best friends Lt. Jim "Retro" Waters and Chief Warrant Officer Todd "Magic" Hunter. She's wanted them for over a year, but never dared to approach them while in the squad.

Retro has fought his dark desires since high school, certain the need to share a woman unnatural. Magic had never considered sharing before Ghost mentions it, but it solves his dilemma of choosing between his best friend and his woman. But Retro balks at Ghost's offer to share and retreats from both when she marries Magic.

Everyone feels Retro's loss, but he ignores the ache of their broken connection in favor of living 'normal.' When Ghost and the other wives of Beta Squad are kidnapped, Retro must reevaluate how much both Ghost and Magic mean to him. And he must decide how far he's willing to go to save the woman he loves, before she becomes the Navy's ghost.

OTHER BOOKS BY SIOBHAN MUIR

Her Devoted Vampire (from Evernight Publishing)
Queen Bitch of the Callowwood Pack (from Siren Publishing)
Not a Dragon's Standard Virgin (from Siren Publishing)

Cloudburst Colorado Series
A Hell Hound's Fire (from Three Lakes Books)
The Beltane Witch (from Three Lakes Books)

Christmas I.C.E. Magic (Happy Holidays from the Crescent Moon Lodge Anthology)
Cloudburst Ice Magic (from Three Lakes Books)

Rifts Series
Take the Reins (from Three Lakes Books)
A Centaur's Solstice Wish (from Three Lakes Books)

Bad Boys of Beta Squad Series
Bronco's Rough Ride (from Three Lakes Books)
The Navy's Ghost (from Three Lakes Books)

The Ivory Road
A Walk in the Sand (from Three Lakes Books)
Outback Dreams (from Three Lakes Books)

Coming Soon
A Dance Between Worlds (The Ivory Road #3)
Order of the Dragon (Warbler Peninsula #1)
Second Chance Succubus

ABOUT THE AUTHOR

Siobhan Muir lives in Cheyenne, Wyoming, with her husband, two daughters, and a vegetarian cat she swears is a shape-shifter, though he's never shifted when she can see him. When not writing, she can be found looking down a microscope at fossil fox teeth, pursuing her other love, paleontology. An avid reader of science fiction/fantasy, her husband gave her a paranormal romance for Christmas one year, and she was hooked for good.

In previous lives, Siobhan has been an actor at the Colorado Renaissance Festival, a field geologist in the Aleutian Islands, and restored inter-planetary imagery at the USGS. She's hiked to the top of Mount St. Helens and to the bottom of Meteor Crater.

Siobhan writes kick-ass adventure with hot sex for men and women to enjoy. She believes in happily ever after, redemption, and communication, all of which you will find in her paranormal romance stories.

Connect with Siobhan online at:
http://siobhanmuir.com
http://www.facebook.com/siobhan.muir.35
http://www.tsu.co/SiobhanMuir
http://twitter.com/SiobhanMuir
http://siobhanmuir.blogspot.com
http://pinterest.com/siobhanmuir.35